BENEATH THE COPPER SKY

THE NIGHTSHINE SERIES
BOOK ONE

EMÉ SAVAGE

Contents

Prologue

In the Beginning, there was the Void. It was all that there was and all that there had ever been since before time began. There was no light. There was no darkness. Only the Void.

An ember sparked in the deep. It came from somewhere and nowhere all at once, a bright pinpoint of light burning into the deep. Like cancer, it festered in the tissues of the Void.

Stardust exploded across the sky, moving at a rapid pace across the Void. The invasion of matter was unprecedented, and the Void was quickly reduced to small clusters between Darkness and Light. Galaxies pinwheeled across the sky, burning, colliding, traversing the universe at breakneck speeds.

The Sadool lived in the spaces between the stars. Mostly they kept to themselves, preferring the quiet certainty of the Darkness. They had always been and had never been. Most of their existence spent in a non-corporeal state, feeding off of the dark energy that flowed in abundance. They were taught to avoid the burning orbs and spinning wheels. And so, an uneasy truce had been maintained for trillions of years between Darkness and Light.

A young Sadool did not understand why Light was avoided. Mesmerized, it wondered what it must be like to live among the dazzling displays of light. When it asked the others, they would tell it this was always how it was and how it would always be.

"We are Darkness. Light is not for us," said one older Sadool.

The young Sadool didn't believe them. It decided it would visit Light, then it would know with certainty.

Millennia passed as it traveled to Light. The spinning wheel was brilliant and bold, holding many stars within its arms. The closer the Sadool came to the galaxy, the more it pushed against it, as if the Light wanted nothing to do with its kind.

The others would say that was confirmation enough to stay away, but the young Sadool was confident that if it searched long enough it would find a way.

It would not have to wait long.

A small unassuming entity flirted with the edge of the bright spinning disc of light. It was not made of Light or Darkness, but of something else entirely. The Sadool exerted its will, determined to reach that small creature at the edge of the galactic plane.

The more it pushed the more the galaxy repelled until something gave. It surrounded the strange being. The repelling force ended and what remained was the sensation of perfect balance. Then it consumed the entity. For the first time, it understood what Light was, what the space surrounding it sounded, felt, and tasted like. It was intoxicating and terrifying all rolled together.

As quickly as the sensations began, they ended, leaving the Sadool bereft in their wake. The creature was gone, destroyed by its contact.

After a period of contemplation, it decided it wanted to experience the sensations again. Perhaps there were more creatures it could consume. That meant moving closer to Light and the magnetic forces generated by those oh so brilliant stars. It tested the space around it and found that the push and pull of the galaxy no longer affected it. It was free to move as close or as far away as it wanted.

Staying where it was, knowing what it knew, was no longer an option. Its senses had been awakened and it needed to find out what else Light provided. Maybe it could take it back to the others and they would experience what it had experienced. Perhaps this could change everything for them. Why stay in Darkness, when Light provides such enticing benefits?

Chapter 1

Amione

"At bottom every man knows well enough that he is a unique being, only once on this earth; and by no extraordinary chance will such a marvelously picturesque piece of diversity in unity as he is, ever be put together a second time."
— *Friedrich Nietzsche*

Copper haze parted as the spacecraft expertly touched down on the landing platform. Saturn hung in the sky, ever watchful, as Titan made its trek around its immense bulk. The sun was a brilliant white pinpoint in the sky, giving off enough light to power their basic power grid.

Amione Dhau looked out of the craft's small window at the city she called home. Her gaze briefly alighted on her drawn features reflected in the cabin's lone window. She hadn't slept well in many days; not since she had gotten the news. She smoothed a trembling hand over her brow and let it drop to her side. Her short light brown curls drooped around her shoulders, having not been washed in several days. Violet eyes looked back in deep sorrow; full lips were drawn down into a grief-stricken frown. Her light brown skin seemed sallow in the unnatural gold glow of the cabin's lighting.

Another face drifted into view behind her. With a furrowed brow, her friend, Curphay, placed a gentle hand on her shoulder and gave it an insistent squeeze. She gave him a shaky smile. His mocha hooded gaze was filled with uncharacteristic worry as his hand rasped against his neatly trimmed beard. Even so, his olive skin seemed to glow with health beneath the same light, making her envious of her exceedingly beautiful friend.

"It will be a few minutes before they are ready for us to disembark," his bass voice rumbled.

Amione wrapped her arms around her middle and turned away from the view. She plopped onto the seat she had occupied for most of their journey from Ta'na,har, an ice planet where the Academy for Genetic and Geophysical Studies was located. She was in her last semester of studies when *it* happened. Her mind skittered away from the reason for her sudden trip home.

"It's been a long time since I've been here. I wonder if it will be as I remember it." She worried her bottom lip as she kept folding and unfolding her hands. She finally settled on placing them beneath her thighs.

Curphay sat next to her. "I'm so sorry you are going through this."

Amione tried to meet his sincere gaze, but she couldn't. It was all too raw. She sprang to her feet and paced, trying her best to get the excess energy out of her system before they stepped off of the ship.

Not only was she anxious about her current situation, she was also distressed with the prospect of being surrounded by people she hadn't seen in four years. She wanted to crawl under the covers and hide from everyone. She wanted to go back to the Academy and the comforts she had grown so fond of.

On Demeter, space was at a premium. At the Academy, she had an entire apartment to spread out in. Food and water were not rationed. There was no monetary system. Everyone had equal access to whatever they wanted.

As much as she wanted to embrace her new life, her old one always found a way to assert itself. She always finished all the food on her plate, and drank every drop of water. She wore clothes long past the point of usefulness, and rarely purchased anything that wasn't absolutely needed.

Growing up on Titan, she learned quickly that the only value you had is what you could do for the Company. Such a system was designed to breed scarcity for those at the bottom and wealth beyond measure for those at the top.

She stopped in front of Curphay, still declining to meet his steady gaze. "I am grateful you are here with me. I don't know if I could get through this without you."

He grasped her hand. "You would have. But I'm glad I could help you. If things get to be too much, just squeeze my hand." He demonstrated by applying firm pressure to her slender fingers. "I will step in and give you a break. Ok?"

Amione gave him a quick glance, returning the pressure, then resumed pacing. She stopped at the window once again, looking unseeingly into the haze. Memories flooded her mind. When was the last time she had seen her Da? Four years ago?

JOHN DHAU'S angular deep brown eyes always seemed to twinkle like there was some cosmic joke only he was in on. She used to watch his brows to see what mood he was in; furrowed meant concentration, right brow lifted meant surprised, or he would waggle them at her when he was in a particularly good mood. Today they were still, a rare state, but appropriate since Amione, his only child, was leaving for Academy.

Amione was simultaneously excited and terrified. She had worked her entire life to go to Academy and to learn about human and other sentient species genetic makeups. She believed the future of human evolution could be found in their past. She absorbed whatever information she could find on Old Earth History. Knowing the stories of the past could help her make leaps in logic that other geneticists might overlook. At least, that is what she hoped.

She had never been to Old Earth. A combination of climate catastrophe, war, and finally a massive asteroid hit, had rendered much of Earth uninhabitable in the late 2250's. 250 years later, it was still recovering from such an enormous blow. Fortunately, they had become an interplanetary species by then, including Titan.

Titan was of strategic and scientific importance early in its formation. First the scientists came and built a small orbiting platform called Edo. It was originally established by a joint venture between the old Korean Aerospace Research Institute (KIRA) and Japanese Aerospace Exploration Agency (JAXA) in the early 22nd century. Later, corporations saw the value of mining Titan for the hydrocarbons, which were plentiful on its surface.

Other orbital platforms were created and mining operations established on the surface. These platforms were used as waystations for ships, pushing themselves to the Kuiper Belt and beyond. However, the colony's biggest achievement were the floating cities of Titan, which brought tourism from within and without the solar system.

The Dhaus were a family of miners who had lived there for 300 plus years. John and Amione were the last of the Dhaus on Demeter. He never made Amione feel she had to continue with the family business. Her father always believed she was destined for greater things.

"I'm afraid, Da." She folded and unfolded her hands.

"Why? You will do great!" His light tenor was full of warmth and pride.

"But I have to leave you." She tucked a wayward curl behind her ear which sprang back to its former position.

Her father looked into her eyes as he held her shoulders. She noticed how calloused his hands were. A lifetime of work had made them rough and stained. "Little Bird, you were meant to fly to greater things."

He had called her Little Bird for as long as she could remember. She had thought it was just something he called her, then she found literature on the Audubon Society from Old Earth. The sheer variety amazed her. Most of them were gone, destroyed in the Great Cataclysm. A few species populated some of the colonies, but none existed on Titan.

They were delicate, and yet surprisingly strong. She didn't see herself that way, but the idea of flying in the air on brightly colored wings was an image that stayed with her.

"You will be alone." She couldn't keep the worry from her voice.

"Nonsense! I have Dino, I have Leto and the others, and I have the work. It will make me so happy to know you are learning great things." He leaned forward, pouring all the reassurance he could muster into his gaze.

"What if I mess up? My teachers told me that Academy wasn't for someone like me. What if they are right? What if my chaos keeps me from graduating? What if—"

"Amione, there is nothing wrong with you. You are exactly who you are supposed to be right here and right now. You will become who you were meant to be in time. Someday you will see what I see right now."

She frowned at him. He was her Da, of course he would say things like that. The rest of the world told her that she was lacking in so many ways. If so many were saying the same thing, wasn't it true?

"Now, the ship is waiting." He hefted two bags onto his shoulders and exited her room.

Amione took one final glance around the only home she had known, and followed him to the ship and to her new life.

THE MEMORY FADED as Amione stepped across the threshold into their home. Piles of plates, cups, and papers were everywhere. A half-finished transistor sat in the middle of the dinner table. Stray conduits, power units, and biomimetic gel packs were strewn across the surface. It looked like an ongoing project, as if he would return to it at any moment. A layer of dust covered most of the unused surfaces. The floors were clean, but Dino, the little robotic unit, had always been good about keeping that clean.

On cue, Dino peered around the corner. "Welcome home," it intoned using one of its few preprogramed greetings.

Her eyes misted. "Thank you, Dino."

Dino returned to his power caddy in the corner of the living room.

She could feel Curphay behind her, and wondered what he thought of her home. This was probably causing him intense anxiety. Until she had gone to Academy, she had not realized just how chaotic their living environment truly was. Perhaps if her mother had been around... She let the thought hang.

She went down the short hallway to her room. An "A" was carved into the cool metal door. A ghost image of her father with an embossing torch appeared carving freehand into the metal. The image faded as she ran her fingertips over the intricately whorled design.

Her hand hesitated over the panel before waving over the controls. The door swished open. Copper light poured through the small horizontal window near the top of the ceiling, providing just enough light to see. If she climbed on top of the bed and scrunched far enough in the corner, she could catch a glimpse of Saturn on the horizon. Otherwise, the view was primarily of copper haze that shifted and flowed around the structure.

She resisted the urge to go to the window. Instead, she looked around at the things she had left behind four years ago. Posters of Old Earth plastered the walls, an astrolabe sat on the table next to her bed. On the ceiling was a full representation of the Milky Way Galaxy.

A low whistle sounded behind her, causing her to jump. She had forgotten Curphay was there.

"So, this is where the Amazing Amione grew up." He chuckled, looking at the posters with interest, and picking up one artifact, then another to examine. "I can see your obsession with old things was not a new thing."

She plucked an Old Earth kitchen utensil out of his hands. "Of course not. These are delicate, do you mind?" She arched her brow in mock annoyance.

He smiled giving her bed an experimental bounce before swinging his legs up and laying back on her pillows.

She sniffed at him and shook her head at his audacious behavior.

She stopped, staring at a carving on her bookshelf with a note in her father's handwriting. She could see that the dust had been disturbed recently.

"What is it?" She heard Curphay roll off the bed, coming to stand beside her. "Mione?"

She didn't answer, instead she reached for the figurine with shaking fingers and cradled it in her hands. It was carved in the same way as the "A" on her door, delicate whorls and swirls with little flowers and leaves mixed in. The overall shape was that of a little bird in flight.

Her vision blurred as she ran her thumbs over the carefully wrought gift. He must have made it in anticipation of her graduation from Academy. A sob escaped as she crumpled to the floor. She felt Curphay's arms wrap around her. She cried big ugly sobs as the immensity of her loss crushed her beneath its weight. Everywhere she looked was a reminder of their life together and all that was lost.

An unbearable ache filled her chest. What she wouldn't give for one last hug from her Da, to hear his voice rumble in his chest, and to bask in the glow of the one person who had been there for her through it all. He was gone, and all that was left was these little moments captured by the exquisitely capable hands of her Da.

The accident—No. She couldn't think of that now. Not right now.

A handkerchief appeared in front of her eyes. She gripped the little bird tightly in her left hand and used her right to wipe her eyes and blow her nose. She gave a watery smile of thanks and Curphay smiled back. He helped her to her feet.

"What is this?" He pointed at the note.

"A note from my Da."

He looked back at her with a raised brow. "How quaint. I wonder why he didn't just use a data crystal."

Tears threatened again. "Because he knew how much I loved handwriting."

"I'm learning so many new things about you. You love *handwriting?* I knew your Old Earth obsessions ran deep, but this is really deep." Curphay leaned against a wall, looking around at the posters.

She gently lifted the note from the shelf. "You can tell a lot from someone's handwriting." She warmed to one her favorite subjects. "How they were feeling. Whether they had a physical ailment. Whether they are right-handed, left-handed, or both. Even something about their personality."

"Where did he learn how to do it?"

"He learned from me." She smiled at the memory. Every bit of paper they could find was relegated to her and her Da learning how to form the flourishing script.

He laughed, shaking his head. "You are so weird."

She frowned at him.

"That is a compliment. Trust me." His smile widened.

The envelope fluttered in her hands. This was the last thing he had written to her. She wasn't sure if she wanted to read it yet.

Curphay sensed her hesitation. "There is no reason you have to read it right now." He placed a hand over her trembling one.

She glanced at him, then nodded. He was right, of course. There was time to read it later. She would read it in the quiet of the night, when she was alone. She folded it carefully and placed it inside her vest pocket.

She headed to the front room, stopping when she saw a solitary figure standing at the window staring out at the copper haze. She immediately sought Curphay's hand and squeezed it tightly.

"I never understood what he saw in this place."

Amione would know her contralto anywhere.

"Hello, Mother."

Chapter 2

Oal

"Some things are too strange to be a coincidence."
Unknown

Oal drifted through space. It was normal to travel in hibernation for millennia, however long it took to get to the next moon, the next planet, the next solid object. He was one of millions of seedlings that traveled this way. The Tromfeld memory was long, but subject to lapses in time, depending on how long it takes to connect to the Continuum of Knowledge. Their entire history was contained in the tiny filaments that made up the majority of their bodies. When they reconnected, all that had happened across the vast network was downloaded into their being.

Oal was the size of a small seed that fit neatly in the palm of a human hand. Eventually, he would grow to the size of a mammoth tree that could live up to a billion years.

Oal remembered when he was born. His parent was Yael on the planet Trom, the Tromfeld home planet. The entire surface was covered with Tromfelds going back trillions of years. He remembered what it looked like from the memories of the others. So many Gaos, the Tromfeld version of the soul, had lived and died there.

No one seemed to know when the decision to go beyond their home occurred, only that it had happened after an extensive discussion that took place over the course of millenia. Their lives were so long that it was natural to take that kind of time, especially for a decision that would change their species forever.

Oal was one of the first to leave their system with a group of thousands. Most settled on other planets within their star system. Oal kept going with a few hundred more seedlings, and most of that group settled in the neighboring system. Oal kept going with a few dozen more seedlings and they settled in the system beyond. Then he was alone.

He could have settled with the others, but he felt pulled another way. He set off toward a distant star. It wasn't a particularly unusual star, quite ordinary actually, but something deep within himself called him forward. He knew the journey would be a long one, but whatever lay on the other side was essential to his existence.

Tromfelds delighted in storytelling. Storytellers were some of the most revered members on their world. Once a Tromfeld took root it was the only way to pass the time. There were many tales told, mostly about the Continuum of Knowledge, at the heart of every Tromfeld was a need to understand the universe from the smallest component to the vast reaches of space, which is why the decision to send seedlings off world came so quickly. They needed new stories to feed the Continuum, both the real and the fantastical.

There was one story that lodged in Oal's mind. Out of all the quadrillions of stories why this particular odd story stuck, he could not say, except for one notable difference. It spoke of a time that had not yet occurred. Prophecy was a theory, a myth, an impossibility. No one could predict the future. If it were possible, they would have already done it. Yet, the story persisted, and Oal decided to pursue it wherever it might take him.

It spoke of a time when Light and Darkness would be joined together by Chaos, and that these three primal forces together would change the universe. Oal understood what Darkness was. It was the opposite of what they were. The galaxy was where Light resided, and Darkness existed beyond the galactic plane, to be avoided at all cost. Chaos was completely unfamiliar, and the Tromfelds had no reference for what that might be, and how it would join Light and Darkness together. Since it was only one story among many, it was dismissed.

And yet, he could not get it out of his mind. He chose a path that no others traveled. An extraordinary story required extraordinary action. It was the only way to see if the prophecy might be true.

Eons passed. He slept. He passed by other systems. He slept some more. He passed by phenomena both bright and bold. He slept on and on. He reached the edges of the galaxy and that is when he woke.

Something curious crept at the edges of the galaxy. Something with intelligence and knowledge of the dark energy beyond the galactic plane. The seedling watched and waited, wondering if this was what he had been looking for.

Chapter 3

Awakening

"You are not IN the universe, you ARE the universe, an intrinsic part of it. Ultimately you are not a person, but a focal point where the universe is becoming conscious of itself. What an amazing miracle."
Eckhart Tolle

Amione had not seen her mother in ten years. It had not been a happy visit then either. Each time her mother came, she hoped the result would be different. It never was.

She quickly learned that her mother was cold, remote, and completely uninterested in her daughter. As Amione got older, she pushed her feelings aside and focused on her work, ignoring that other girls had loving, involved, and kind mothers. After she graduated secondary school, she wondered how her father could have ever loved a woman like Jheslae Dhau.

Jheslae was medium height with iron gray hair cropped close to her head. Dark skin looked burnished by fire in the copper light. Her black eyes were opaque and inscrutable. Full lips pressed into a sharp line with her jaw locked. She wore a gray suit jacket that fit her form in the exact right way, with pants that cinched at the ankles and sturdy gray boots. A small silver pin was the only indication of her status as Head Geophysicist at the ARK Project.

She had always looked severe and imposing. Time had not changed that impression with Amione. In fact, she looked exactly the same, as if time itself wanted to avoid Jheslae's displeasure.

Her mother turned those black eyes on her, assessing, evaluating, and coming to conclusions that Amione knew meant that she found her lacking.

"Daughter," she paused, then added, "You look unwell."

Disappointment blossomed in Amione's chest. In spite of her past experience, she had hoped for a more compassionate response. Amione let out a frustrated grunt and turned away.

"Hi. I'm Curphay." He stepped around Amione and held out his hand in greeting.

Jheslae ignored it and gave him a quick once over before dismissing him.

Curphay dropped his hand and stepped back trying his best to hide his awkwardness. "I could go into the other room." He hooked his thumbs over his shoulder.

"Yes," Jheslae responded.

"No!" Amione panicked at the same time.

Jheslae pinned her with a stare. "We have things to discuss."

Amione looked from her mother to Curphay. Her shoulders bent in resignation. She nodded to Curphay.

"I'll be in your room. Just call me if you need me." He gave her a reassuring smiled before he beat a hasty retreat.

"Thank you." Amione felt sick to her stomach. The last thing she wanted was to be alone with her mother.

She watched as Curphay disappeared around the corner. Then turned her gaze back to her mother. She blinked at her mother's intense examination. Clearing her throat. "What do you want?" She folded her arms across her chest and leaned back against the counter.

Jheslae moved away from the window and took a position directly opposite from Amione. It felt as if her mother was about to square off against her. Probably accurate. Amione was feeling more than a little combative.

"You are nearly finished with Academy." Her tone was matter of fact.

"So?" Amione shrugged.

Jheslae folded her hands behind her back. "I have followed your progress. You are top of your class in your discipline."

Amione raised her left brow. *Why had she bothered to keep track of her?* She nodded, wondering what her mother was getting at. "And?"

"You have been requested to join the ARK Project."

Amione's heart skipped a beat. The ARK Project was the dream of every student at the Academy. It is the center of scientific research and, for her, the only thing she thought about since she was a little girl. She wanted to jump for joy at the revelation. Then suspicion crept in, stealing her initial joy. "Why are *you* telling me this?"

Jheslae shifted her stance and an unidentifiable emotion flickered briefly across her face. "Because you are the most qualified."

"Impossible. There must be thousands of scientists with experience and more intelligence." Something was wrong.

Jheslae went very still. "You will take it."

Amione pressed her lips together before she said something she would regret. She drew in a deep breath, letting it out in a slow measured release. "I will think about it."

Her mother relaxed. It was a small gesture, but Amione noticed. It was important to her mother that she accept the assignment. "I will be here for another twenty hours. Please let me know what you decide."

Without another word, she turned on her heel, only breaking her stride when she waved herself out of the apartment. The last view Amione had of her mother was her rigid posture before the door closed. Amione stared at the closed door for several seconds, wondering what her mother's angle was.

"She really wants you to go."

She jumped at Curphay's sudden presence at her shoulder.

"Yes." She ran an agitated hand through her curls and flopped down on the couch in the living area. She leaned her elbows on her knee and tried to sort through the revelation.

"You should take it. It's what you have always wanted." Curphay took a seat on a low-slung chair. Amione smiled inwardly as Curphay tried to arrange his long legs into a more comfortable position.

"It is what I wanted, but my mother will be there." Frustration made her voice rough.

"The ARK is a big place. As big as a planet. I doubt you will run into each other if you don't want to. She is in an entirely different area of study," Curphay reasoned.

She growled. "You are right, of course. I just didn't want to give her the satisfaction of saying yes right away."

"She seems...intense." Curphay frowned as he idly examined a random conduit laying on the table in front of the couch, then tossed it back on the glass surface with a clatter.

Amione jumped to her feet and paced around the living area, settling at the window where her mother had greeted her not long before. "I haven't seen her since I was eight. She hasn't changed." A feeling of loss invaded her thoughts. How she could mourn something she never had? She wasn't sure, but the feeling persisted every time.

"There is one thing that is bothering me." Curphay's whiskers rasped as he rubbed his chin. She could hear him move from the chair to the couch.

"What?" She looked back at him in alarm.

"Why would she be the one to offer you the position? Wouldn't that come from official channels? Maybe even the Head of Paleogenetics?" His brows furrowed as he tried to work through the puzzle.

She was glad she wasn't the only one who was suspicious. She had wondered the same thing. "Maybe she insisted on bringing the news herself since my Da died."

"Yes, but from what you have told me and what I have observed, she doesn't seem to be the sentimental type. No, A, there is definitely more to this." He leaned against the back of the couch and looked over his shoulder at her as she paused behind him.

Curphay echoed her thoughts, but she decided to mess with him. "What? I don't deserve the position? I'm not good enough to be on the ARK?" She kept her face straight.

"No, I..." His face flushed as he stammered an apology.

She busted out laughing. "I'm kidding. I understand what you are saying. This whole thing reeks of... something. I can't put my finger on it."

"So, what are you going to do?" He twisted around to face her more fully.

"I'm going to accept, of course. But I'm going to put a condition on it." She folded her arms across her chest and looked him in the eye.

"A condition?" Curphay's manicured brows rose.

"That you come with me."

Curphay had the grace to flush. "A, no, you can't do that. I'm not going to jump the line when someone else more deserving should get a position. You know how competitive the Project is."

"Curphay, you are the most gifted geophysicist in the Academy. They would be lucky to have you. Besides, I need you. I don't think I could bear going there alone." She started to shake. "I want this so badly, but I can feel myself getting overwhelmed by the idea."

Curphay studied her carefully, then nodded. "Ok. But you owe me." He pointed at her, a twinkle in his eye betrayed him.

She laughed. "Add it to my tab."

Night had fallen, or what passed for night on Titan. Saturn burned brightly on the horizon, but inside shutters blocked out the light to simulate the circadian rhythm written into their DNA. Clouds of methane swirled beneath the city, unleashing rain onto the surface below. The cities floated tranquilly above the cloud deck; murky pinpoints of light dotted the sky in a copper tinted haze.

Curphay snored blissfully on the couch in the living area. She had offered him her bed, but he declined. She watched him sleep for a moment, marveling at how untroubled he looked.

His bliss only amplified her restlessness. It was strange being back home without her father. She could feel his presence everywhere and, at the same time, a gut-wrenching absence.

She had avoided going into his bedroom, but decided it was the only thing she could do if she was to get any rest tonight. She stood in front of the door to his room for several minutes before she mustered up the courage to wave her hand over the control panel. The door swished open in perfect working order.

The lights came on automatically as she stepped inside. She stood in the center of the room, looking around at her father's sanctuary. Unlike the front room, his bedroom was tidy except for his unmade bed. He never made his bed. "Why make it when I'm just going to unmake it when I go to sleep," he said.

Soft copper lighting illuminated the area around his bed, the area over his desk, and the small workbench in the corner. She went to the bed and lay back against his pillow looking at the numerous pictures of her at various ages: one where she was running through the Arboretum, one where she is gliding over Titan an oversized helmet framing her smiling face, and another with them both laughing.

Several shots of Titan showed what Saturn looked like at ground level at the mines. Large mining equipment was dwarfed by the massive planet in the background. The Hesper Mining Company Logo was painted in bright blue on the sides, a blocky representation of Saturn with the Hesper "H" creating negative space in the center. It was the second oldest mining Corp on Titan and the largest. Her Da had worked for them for decades, starting soon after he finished secondary school and entering their apprentice program.

It was his job to keep the decades old machinery running. The company did whatever they could to keep costs to a minimum even cutting corners. The governing body on Titan was supposed to conduct safety checks, but many times they were paid to look the other way.

Knowing her Da, he would fight the management whenever possible, pointing out when something or someone could be killed or injured. It had happened at other sites, but her Da was determined to keep his site running smoothly.

So, what happened? No one had explained to her how he had died, only that it was on the surface and involved one of the extractors. She had been too distraught to ask any questions. Her father was dead and nothing would change that. Now that she was here, questions surfaced. How could a man who was so careful with safety end up losing his life?

One of the pictures caught her eye. It was a picture of an extractor, but something wasn't quite right with it. She plucked it off the ceiling and examined it more closely. Why would he keep a picture of a piece of equipment over his bed?

She went to the work bench and looked at the electronic components neatly sorted into bins. It was tech that was hundreds of years old; something he enjoyed tinkering with during his off hours. Wires, old style processing chips, and crude crystal tech, were all categorized in a system only her Da understood. Her eye caught an inconsistency. In the middle of the ancient crystal tech was a modern data crystal. It sparkled green in the nest of blue, hardly noticeable unless a person had enhanced visual acuity, like Amione.

She was born with a congenital eye defect, common among children of Titan. About one out of every ten births showed the mutation. Various augmentations had been used over the years, but the current version actually enhanced vision beyond normal human sight. She should have inherited her father's warm brown eyes or Jheslae's hard black ones, but instead, the augmentation gave her eyes a distinctive violet tint. She was so young when the procedure was done, she didn't remember life any other way.

The augmentation allowed her to see the electromagnetic fields around things. Older items had a distinct sepia or a soft worn blue. Newer items were sharp, almost lacerating with the variety of colors and hues.

All things faded which is why the newer data crystal stuck out starkly against the older tech. Perhaps a normal sighted person would have found it, but she suspected her Da wanted her, and her alone, to find it.

With shaking fingers, she plucked the small green crystal out of the bin and held it in her hands. She rubbed a thumb over it, judging its quality. It didn't look corrupted. She glanced at the desk and found the viewer carefully set in the center. She cautiously examined the placement of each item on the desk. If he left the picture and the crystal for her, what other clues did he leave?

A crystal bird hung from a stand seemingly flying to who knows where. She turned on the blue Gaze light, a lighting source that creates the purest white light possible. It's been said that the light is similar to Old Earth and best for human eyes. It made no difference to her sight.

The light revealed nothing out of the ordinary. There was an award for forty years of service given to her Da two years ago. A small box with sheets of paper and a writing utensil graced the right side of the desk. She carefully lifted the viewer and found a bare surface. Nothing.

She sat down in his chair. It seemed a little low so she adjusted it so she could reach the desk at the right height and that's when she saw it.

Her breath caught in her throat. If she had left the chair at the regular height, she would have missed it entirely. There was a silver tear in the wall. She moved at several different angles, making it disappear and reappear.

She leaned forward running her fingers over the irregular seam. She could feel the surface give. She pulled her hand back.

She wanted to know what was in seam, but she had the feeling that whatever it was, would change her life forever. She hesitated a moment longer, then pushed her fingers into the rift.

She felt something tug on her fingers; a force that guided her hand forward until she found an object. As she gently probed, she could feel that it was smooth, round, and cool to the touch, not much larger than the palm of her hand. She scooped the object into her hand and drew it out of the filament.

As soon as her hand cleared the opening it disappeared. She ran her other hand over the spot where the crack had been moments before and it looked as ordinary as the rest of the wall.

She opened her right hand and looked at the object up close. It didn't look like it was made by human hands. Rose colored seams circled the object in an elegant and purposeful way. What that purpose was, she didn't know. When she handled it, she couldn't feel any imperfections. It looked like it was fitted together, but there was no indication, at least through her touch, that it had any seams. It was much older than anything she had ever seen before.

"Where did you come from?" she mused aloud.

She picked up the data crystal. Maybe there would be more answers here. She set the sphere next to the stand with the bird, making the crystal prism across the desk. She lifted the viewer and inserted the crystal in the port on the left. The viewer came to life, bathing her in its soft green glow.

She selected the only file listed. Her Da's face flashed into view. She paused the transmission and stared at his image. Since the last time she had seen him, he was greyer at the temples. Crow's feet were more pronounced, and the lines around his nose and mouth were deeper. The same warm brown eyes gazed at her with the twinkle she remembered so well.

She brushed her fingers over his image. Tears dropped onto the view screen, causing it to lens and blur the image. She hastily pulled her sleeve over her hand and wiped them off, then wiped her eyes.

She took a shuddering breath and resumed the recording.

"Little Bird, by now you have finished your time at the Academy and I am so very proud of you. Your instructors tell me you are the most brilliant student in paleogenetics they have had in three centuries." She could hear the pride in his voice and it made her smile. "Though, you could have told me, you know. Don't be afraid to let other people know how well you have done. You deserve every accolade they put on you."

She squirmed in the chair. She wasn't comfortable with that kind of attention, preferring to do the work without the anxiety of hearing people compliment her.

"I knew you could fly and whatever you choose to do next, I know you will soar to new heights while doing it."

She sat forward when she saw a shift in his expression. His brows were furrowed as he contemplated the next bit as if weighing if he should tell her or not. Though this was the past she felt herself urging him on.

"Things have been happening on the surface, Amione. It's more than the company trying to cut corners and save money." Whatever it was, it was it distressed him. "They found something buried deep in the Titian soil. Something unusual."

"No one is telling us everything, but two workers have been injured in mysterious accidents and another man killed. They blamed it on the machines malfunctioning, but I inspect those machines regularly. There is nothing wrong with them. At least nothing that would explain how these accidents have occurred. I've been ordered to keep out of it. But Amione, you know I can't do that."

Her heart sank. It was true. She could have begged him not to pursue things, but that wouldn't have mattered. People were getting hurt and killed. If there was something he could do to prevent it, then he would do it.

"If something should happen to me, I need you to find the picture of the equipment on the ceiling above my bed. You will notice right away. And there is another thing. Behind my desk is a pocket universe I created. It contains an object I found in one of the caverns. Remove it and the pocket will close behind it. I designed it so that it would only respond to your DNA."

He shifted in his chair rubbing his forehead.

"Keep it safe at all costs. I don't want to put this burden on you, but I feel as if something bigger is going on and that little thing is the key to it all."

A reminder beep went off behind him. He glanced at the time, then grimaced.

"I have to go to the transport. I don't want them to think there is anything wrong. Destroy the data crystal as soon as you view this. Don't let ANYONE see it. It will put your life in danger. I don't know what the object is, but with all your knowledge I think you are the only person who can find out."

He paused; a smile returned to his face.

"I love you so very much, Little Bird. I hope all of this is unnecessary, and I'll be home as always to greet you. You are the best thing I've ever done in this life. The best thing." He stared for a moment longer, then the recording stopped.

Amione sat in stunned silence. She looked at the sphere sitting benignly on the desk. Whatever happened to her father was not an accident and this was the reason. What terrible secret did it hold? Who was killing the workers at the mine? What was she supposed to do now?

Chapter 4

Contact

*"It's best to go into first contact without any assumptions. Doing so is a good
way to get yourself killed."*
Kyles Dhagger, 11th diplomat to the Ingvari

Oal woke him from his slumber. He reached out with his senses
and detected a presence nearby as he drifted to the edge of the
galactic plane. Filaments of dark matter were nearly invisible,
connecting galaxy to galaxy. Noone of his species had ever dared to travel
down one of these paths. Mostly because it was theorized that dark
matter would repel normal matter. He wondered how they were formed,
why they existed, and if anyone had ever used them.

Something caught his attention, an imperceptible movement, a
shadow among shadows. He would have believed that there was nothing
there at all, except that the presence was curious about him.

"Hello?" Oal called out into the darkness.

The darkness did not respond right away, but maneuvered in a
languid ever tightening circle around Oal. Much time passed with Oal
and the entity locked into a strange dance. Neither seemed in a hurry,
but both were curious about the other.

It replied, "What."

It wasn't a question, but a push for knowledge. Maybe it wanted to
know what he was? Maybe it wanted to know what he was doing here?
There were so many possibilities that Oal decided to take his time
responding. It would not do to give the entity information he was not
seeking.

More time passed as the entity continued to draw closer. Oal decided on a response. "I am."

After further study, Oal realized the entity had no form, no mass, no energy signature that he could sense. In other words, the entity was not from normal matter. If Oal was something, then this being was nothing.

The entity considered Oals words and withdrew a short distance before resuming its circle. He imagined that the entity found the idea of matter just as foreign as he thought the lack of matter was. And yet, here it was, existing.

More time passed. For the Tromfelds, the length of time between words was one of the most precious gifts they were given. Mistakes caused many grievous issues, and were to be avoided at all cost.

"What am I," the entity said.

Oal could not tell if the entity was asking a question or had ordered the words in its own way. Did it understand what it was asking, or was it repeating whatever Oal said? This took much longer to assess.

Finally, Oal determined that it was how the entity ordered its thoughts and replied, "I don't know."

That seemed to satisfy the entity. They traveled in an uneasy togetherness until they came upon something new. It was a small creature that drifted without thought or consequence. Instead of the entity repelling the little creature, it absorbed it.

Oal could see the entity become substantial. It was a brief flicker as the matter of the creature mingled with its core self. Oal could sense the entity's surprise.

"What was that?" Clearly, the entity had never experienced corporeal existence.

"Life. It is what we call life," Oal said.

The entity mulled over the experience, then replied, "More."

Oal wasn't sure if this was a good thing or not. What would stop the entity from consuming him?

Chapter 5

Entropy

"Life, this anti-entropy, ceaselessly reloaded with energy, is a climbing force, toward order amidst chaos, toward light, among the darkness of the indefinite, toward the mystic dream of Love, between the fire which devours itself and the silence of the Cold."
Albert Claude

When Amione was small she thought The Arboretum was the grandest, most wondrous place in the universe. Several of Old Earth's plant life and some insect life had been carefully conserved here. Originally, it was a piece of decadence created by wealthy benefactors as a way of flaunting their excessive wealth. Now, it had been relegated to the working class who now occupied Demeter.

Trees filled the space and created a small canopy. Brightly colored flowers and plants filled the spaces between. Some were fruit bearing and these offerings were carefully rationed to the residents. The rest were sold to wealthy clients to maintain the work. Carefully manicured paths wended their way through the space, ending in a small square of stone curated from Titan's surface. Their unusual gold and red hues gave Demeter a distinct look.

Amione sat in a small room connected to the Arboretum. Her leg bounced as tumultuous thoughts ran rampant through her mind. She didn't want to be here, but it was expected. Her Da deserved to have a memorial ceremony surrounded by people he loved and respected and who loved and respected him in return.

She listened to an eight-minute recording designed to trigger her body to calm itself. It took the edge off, but did nothing for the gnawing anxiety in her stomach. She opened her eyes. Curphay watched her with concern. She frowned slightly.

"Are you ready?" He encouraged a smile from her.

She snorted. "No, but I don't think it will get better until I get through this."

"Are they really that bad?" He tilted his head.

"You grew up in a populous colony. How many people lived there? A hundred thousand?"

"Give or take." He leaned back folding his arms across his chest. He wore a ridiculously ornate jacket with a pewter flower pinned to his lapel. The steely gray ensemble made his mocha eyes stand out more than usual.

"I don't know if you have noticed, but Demeter is much smaller. Maybe twenty-five hundred to three thousand residents at any given time."

"So?"

"So?" She jumped to her feet and paced in agitation. "Everyone knows everyone."

"It actually sounds kinda nice." He shrugged, clearly confused by her agitation.

"Nice?" She stopped and placed her hands on her hips. "Nice, he says." She laughed without humor.

"So, what is the problem? Really. I'm asking because I don't know." He stood next to her looking earnest.

She blew out the breath she had been holding, causing the curls on her forehead to jump. "The problem is that people don't forget. They see me the same way no matter how much I have done or where I have been. I will always be that chaotic Amione Dhau." She hated that about Demeter. No one could ever grow beyond the walls of the city. Change was frowned upon, and the order of things should never be upset, ever.

He smiled fondly at her. "I love chaotic Amione Dhau. Where would I be without her?"

She grabbed his hand and squeezed, tears welling up. "Thank you for that."

"It's the least I can do." He squeezed her hand tightly before releasing it. "Now, are you ready?"

She nodded curtly and squared her shoulders.

"Ah, Amione Dhau, who got my Mindy in trouble in primary."

Amione's head dipped as she closed her eyes. Sally Corman was one of those people who knew everyone's business whether they wanted her to or not. It had been over fifteen years and Amione was still known as the troublemaker.

Amione plastered a smile on her face and turned to the offensive woman. "Hi, Mrs. Corman."

"So, what are you doing nowadays?" The stocky woman pursed her lips as she went through the motions of small talk.

Amione screamed inwardly. What was the point of small talk? She wished that Mrs. Corman would just get to the point or better yet, not talk to her at all.

"I'm finishing up Academy, and--"

"Oh, that's nice, dear. I was sure you would have dropped out by now." Mrs. Corman looked off to the side, totally uninterested in what Amione said.

Amione fumed careful not to allow her mask of civility slip.

"When are you coming back to Demeter for good? My Mindy has been married for three years already. She has a little boy now. He's the smartest little thing. Do you have a mate?" Her pale green eyes assessed Curphay.

"No."

Mrs. Corman pursed her lips in disapproval again. "I'm sure you will find *someone*."

Amione murmured something appropriate while imaging what it would be like to throat punch the woman.

"Oh, there is Head Magistrate Dodd. Isn't he wonderful for coming here to support all of us? I need to say hello to him. Nice seeing you, Amione. Oh, and I'm very sorry about your father," she added as an afterthought.

Amione watched Mrs. Corman leave and go to the Magistrate. He was tall and angular. His pure white jacket stood out glaringly against the more subdued attire of the residents of Demeter. His expression was remote only observing the basic niceties. Everything was calculated right down to every strand of hair.

Piercing light-colored eyes, found her gaze. She looked away quickly, but risked another glance. His boredom had turned into intense interest centered on her.

She turned away, unsettled, and walked further into the Arboretum. Small clusters of people smiled politely and returned to their conversations. She was relieved that no one else felt compelled to engage.

"What a delight." Curphay's comment dripped with sarcasm.

That coaxed a laugh out of her. "She is Mrs. Corman."

"What a terribly unhappy person. She must nose in other people's business because her life is so dreadfully boring. Can you imagine?" He leaned down and captured her gaze with his mirthful one.

"I've always been a little envious of her, to be honest," Amione confessed, clasping her hands tightly in front of her. She had always felt conflicted about living in this city. One moment she wanted to rebel and leave them all behind, and the next she wanted their approval.

Curphay's brows raised. "I don't see why you would be. She's a sad sad woman."

"Maybe, but then she has all this family here; a mother, a father, siblings, cousins, kids and grandkids. There must be something lovely about it all."

Curphay grew thoughtful. "Maybe there is something to that." He shrugged. "You know my family history. I don't feel deprived because of it. That is what I got, and I'm making the most of it."

Amione felt sadness for her friend. He had never told her the whole story. She picked up enough to know that Curphay had witnessed whatever trauma had taken his brother from him. "You never wanted a family?"

"Of course. I chose you, didn't I? You are my family." He smiled.

She chuckled. "It helped that you were assigned my lab partner. Hooray for Alphabetical Order which was purloined from the Greeks who stole it from the Etruscans, who took it from the Phoenicians, who then totally plagiarized it from the Sumarians!"

Curphay raised a brow. "Is this Old Earth stuff again?"

"You should really know your history." She clucked her tongue.

"All I need to know is this: Dhager and Dhau forever!" Curphay chortled, causing more than one person to look their way with interest.

"Shush! You are attracting attention!" Amione admonished.

He leaned down again with an unrepentant grin. "I think that ship has sailed."

Amione paused. "What an odd saying. What does it even mean?"

"I don't know. I heard it from an old codger one time and liked how it sounded."

"I'll have to look it up." Amione nodded.

Curphay rolled his eyes. "Great. I'll lose you yet again down another black hole."

"You know I can't resist anything related to Old Earth, especially dead languages."

"English is hardly dead. It's one of the few languages that has evolved over time," Curphay corrected.

"Look at you! All fancy scholar all of a sudden," she teased.

"Ain't nothin fancy about it, sis." Curphay grinned.

An older gentleman approached them from the gazebo in the center of the Arboretum. He was tall, slightly bent and had a well pressed suit on with a pin shaped like Saturn with an "H". Amione immediately recognized as the Hesper Mining Corp logo. She looked more closely at the man's kind face.

"Leto?"

The man smiled broadly. "Mione!"

She gave him a hearty hug, a genuine smile on her face. Leto had worked with her father for many years. Both were master mechanics and both had started at the company at about the same time. They had many enjoyable dinners. Plus, Leto would perform simple magic tricks to the delight of a scrawny awkward eight-year-old. She had figured out most of his tricks by the time she was 10, but still wanted him to perform them anyway.

"I was hoping you would be here." Amione sombered.

"I'm so sorry, sweetheart. Is there anything, anything at all, I can do for you?" His blue eyes were brilliant with tears. Leto was more than a coworker, he was her Da's best friend.

She teared up. "No. But is there anything I can do for you?"

He cleared his throat and blinked back his tears. One escaped and he quickly thumbed it away. "No, but you know where to find me, if you would like to come for a visit. Are you staying long?"

"Not too long. I still have to finish my last semester."

Leto smiled fondly at her. "You know he was incredibly proud of you, right? He talked about you all the time. We are both proud of you."

She could feel her face flush. It was good to hear it, but the feeling of being overexposed was too much for her to handle. "Thank you." The urge to hide grew stronger.

Leto shook his head in bemusement. "Still the same Amione. Can't take a compliment."

She covered her awkwardness by turning to Curphay. "This is my friend, Curphay."

Curphay held out a hand and Leto shook it heartily. They both exchanged pleasantries while Amione looked around.

An unusual figure caught her eye. He was dressed in coveralls used by the miners on the surface, unlike the rest of the community which were dressed in their finest clothes in muted grays and taupe. Everyone looked the same, expected, but this young man did not.

Truthfully, he would have stood out anywhere. He was large with broad shoulders, and a solid build, very different from slimmer builds common among the citizens of Titan. It reminded her of the pictures in her Old Earth Books.

When she moved to intercept him, he turned and left the Arboretum through an access door concealed behind some bushes.

How odd, she thought to herself.

She wanted to follow the young man, but the spiritual guide called for everyone's attention. She and Curphay moved to the box next to the gazebo reserved for the grieving family and took a seat in the center. The box was large enough to fit a family of eight. She felt small and insignificant in all that space.

Curphay gave her hand a squeeze, and her anxiety dropped to a more manageable level. She couldn't hear what the guide was saying. It was something along the lines of energy that cannot be destroyed or created; that it only transforms. Knowing that was little comfort. Her Da was gone, and all that remained was the bits of matter that he left behind, and the memories that resided within her.

Curphay gently nudged her. She realized that the guide had stopped and now it was her turn to speak. She didn't want to stand up in front of the entire town, but it was important to remember her Da.

The podium quickly adjusted to match her height with a series of *clicks* and *whirrs*. She gripped the sides, focusing on the smooth surface beneath her fingers. She was acutely aware of all eyes watching her, some friendly, but most were indifferent. She could walk away right now and never return, but for her own peace of mind she needed to do this.

She took a deep breath and raised her eyes to the crowd. Her heart pounded in her chest as she repeated "breathe" over and over in her head.

"I learned many things from my Da but there are three that really stuck out." Her voice came out tremulous at first, then gained strength. "He was there for me and encouraged me. He worked hard, but somehow always found the time to come to my school events. Every science fair, every school presentation, every conference, he was there smiling and encouraging me. He would tell me that there isn't a force in the universe that could stop me if I was determined to do something." She smiled to herself at the memory. "Sometimes love is encouragement."

She paused. She could hear people shifting in their chairs or on their feet. Some were engaged, some were wiping away tears and still others looked glassy-eyed and bored. She took another deep breath.

"We both loved things from Old Earth. Things that most people would consider junk, we viewed it as a portal through time. He came home really excited one night because he had gotten a new box of stuff from a trader and couldn't wait to open it with me.

"We went through each piece wondering what it was, where it came from and how it was used. Then we found this can of pressurized stuff. It literally said 'Great Stuff' on it. The label was badly degraded, but we figured there couldn't be any harm to try it out. So, he pressed the nozzle and it popped off. White stuff started going everywhere!" Chuckles rippled through the crowd. She smiled and relaxed a little before continuing.

"That wasn't the worst of it. It was hardening. We ran to the sink and started washing it out of our hair laughing hysterically. And I learned, I learned that sometimes stuff happens."

Now everyone was laughing. Amione flushed, pleased that her memory of him was making everyone smile. He would have loved that.

She sobered a bit as she came to the last memory. "I hadn't seen him since I left Titan. I would talk to him via vid whenever conditions were right, but the Academy was so far away, and he insisted that I take full advantage of all of it. He said he would be there when I graduated, but he wasn't. I was looking forward to coming home and connecting again. I-- I'm sorry."

She felt comforting arms go around her as Curphay came up to the podium with her. The feeling of being exposed increased. She hated losing her composure in front of others. It didn't matter that people understood. It felt chaotic, wild, painful, and destructive.

"Do you want to stop?" Curphay asked softly near her ear.

She shook her head, wiped her tears away, and pushed back her curls from her face. Curphay stepped back, recognizing that Amione was determined to complete the task.

"I learned that sometimes love means sacrifice. My Da sacrificed a lot to make my dreams come true. He's gone, but he is still here." She placed a hand over her heart. "I will do whatever I can to make sure his sacrifice was worth it."

She stepped back, and allowed Curphay to lead her back to the box. She didn't bother to keep the stream of tears from pouring down her face. Her nose ran and she sniffed loudly. A handkerchief appeared before her eyes which she took gratefully. The rest of the ceremony was a blur. Several people got up and said a few words, and told a story about John. Some were sweet and others were funny. She kept thinking about how much he would have loved it.

Finally, it was over and Amione was exhausted. So many faces, giving her their condolences. She wanted to hide in the apartment and sleep for years. She was about to tell Curphay that when she spotted her mother watching from the edge of the gathering.

She excused herself and pushed her way to where she had last seen her, but she was no longer there. Had she imagined her presence? Was it wishful thinking that her mother would attend her husband's memorial ceremony? No, she was there, but didn't want to engage with the rest of the community. She understood on some level, but on another level resentment grew. She should not have to shoulder this alone.

Chapter 6

Insouciant

"The Universe is insouciant to the plight of its occupants. It is grappling with the fabric of existence. It's not its job to make sure you feel better about yourself."
Ira Beaman, Codification of Existence

In the time, Oal and the Entity figured out how to communicate. It still felt alien to them, but the companionship was welcome in the midst of space. Oal learned the Entity's species was called Sadool.

"What are the Sadool?" Oal asked, curious about his companion's origins.

"We are perfect nothingness," it said.

Oal couldn't conceive of an existence of nothingness. He had heft, and weight. Everyone he knew had something to them no matter how small.

"Why did you come to me?"

The Sadool replied, "I was curious." Simple and true.

"I suppose I am curious too, but to go into a place of nothingness is terrifying to my kind," Oal said.

"Why?"

"Since we are made out of matter, how could we ever exist in your place?" Oal explained. "We would cease to be."

"And that is terrifying," the Sadool said.

"Well, yes."

The Sadool thought on that for a moment. "But we are moving through mostly nothing now, and you are still here."

"That is true." The Sadool had a point. None of his kind had ever ventured this far out from the galactic plane. He could feel small particles brush by, but they were few and far between. Instead, there was something else there, faintly teasing against his senses, but still out of reach.

Another particle hit the Sadool and for a brief moment, Oal could see the Sadool more clearly before it reverted back to its shadow state.

"Mmmm. I feel strange whenever that happens," the Sadool said.

"Strange how?"

"I can feel your presence more strongly when it happens. It is brief, but interesting."

"I wonder why that is?"

"I don't know, but I want to find out."

"How do we do that?" Oal wasn't sure it was wise to encourage his companion, but quickly squashed the thought. What harm could come from innocent exploration?

"More particles."

"All right, the next particle I see, we will head toward it and see what happens," Oal conceded.

"Agreed."

The next particle Oal sensed, he steered toward it. The Sadool matched speed and continued to revolve around Oal.

"Here it comes," Oal warned, both excited and filled with trepidation.

It smashed into the Sadool and a larger reaction occurred. Oal was able to see the Sadool for a longer period of time, then the effect dissipated.

"Well?"

"That was...pleasant."

"This isn't a common experience for your kind."

"Just as you did not venture to Darkness, we do not venture to Light. Now I am wondering why."

"None of you have ventured to my side?"

"It isn't that simple."

"Then how is it that we exist like this?"

"I don't know. It is very curious. I want to continue to see if I can figure it out. This could be good for both our kinds. We could visit Light and you could visit Darkness."

Oal shuddered inwardly. He wasn't sure that he would want to visit Darkness. It was Darkness for a reason. There were so many wondrous things to see in the galaxy. Stars forming, stars exploding. They were all made from star stuff, but the Sadool wasn't. It was the opposite. What powered such beings that were not made from star material? How did they get their energy? Were they really completely made of nothing or was there another force at work?

He wanted to divorce himself from this creature, and yet he wanted to understand more.

They continued to travel together. Until they reached a part of space where there were more particles to consume. Even knowing that the impact would be greater than the last time, Oal was still caught off guard by the increasing strength and length of the change in the Sadool. It was like the Sadool was there, substantive, as real as Oal was, then faded just as quickly. If small pieces of matter had that kind of effect, what would something larger do?

Chapter 7

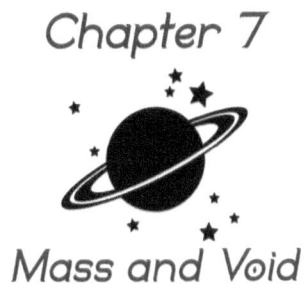

Mass and Void

"We become aware of the void as we fill it."
— *Antonio Porchia*

The next day Amione woke to a message from her mother on the wave screen in the living room. She stared at it for a good hour, wondering what it contained. Dread and anxiety spiraled until it was all she could think about.

She wanted to erase the message and pretend that it had never arrived. She quickly discarded that idea. Her mother would expect a reply and when it didn't come, she would end up at Amione's door, demanding an answer. Amione wanted to avoid that if at all possible.

"You know I can hear you pacing, right?" Curphay's muffled voice came from the couch.

"Oh, Curph! I'm sorry." She ran an agitated hand through her hair. "I'll be quiet." She set a mug of warm tea on the counter, preparing to go back to her room.

"No, I'm awake now. You might as well tell me what's wrong."

She smiled at Curphay's disheveled appearance. He was always so meticulous. It always amused her to see him when he wasn't.

"I got a message from my *mother*."

He swung his legs to the floor. "I'm going to need some tea before we start in on this. Why don't you make me a cup while I freshen up?" He grabbed his carry bag and took it to the bathroom.

She opened the cupboard and went through the soothing motions of preparing tea. The Arboretum had some of the best tea in the Saturn

System. Since her Da was friends with the curator, he had a healthy supply always on hand. It was kept in a tin that was hundreds of years old. She wondered how many different teas had been kept in this tin over the centuries. She sniffed it appreciatively before plucking out a bag.

She set the percolator to boil water and placed a tea packet on the top. She leaned against the counter while she waited. Her mind wandered to her mother's message. She would want an answer about the position on the ARK Project. Amione did not like being rushed. She wasn't sure how she wanted to respond.

The orange scent of the tea tickled her nose. She knew the cup was ready before the beep sounded. Curphay came into the kitchen with his hair immaculately styled, his face fresh and his beard trimmed of all stray hairs. He wore a taupe-colored thermal shirt tucked into a pair of graphene cargo pants in charcoal. His feet were still bare, and Amione admired how they seemed to have a superhero quality to them. Like something she saw in ancient Greek illustrations.

He smiled his thanks as he took the steaming cup from her hands. He blew on the contents, then took a sip, sighing appreciatively. "This is some of the best tea I've ever tasted. So much better than that drivel at Academy."

"Well, Demeter is known for its tea."

"I know I'm going to regret this, but where does tea come from anyway?"

"It was an Old Earth beverage. I think they grew it in the mountain regions. It became a very popular drink for just about the entire world. When we started traveling to other planets, seeds were collected and sent to each colony in the hopes that one day we would be able to terraform these places."

His eyebrows raised as he took another sip. "Terraform? Really? Here?"

"It's not as insane as it sounds. Other species have been xenoforming planets for millennia. Places colder than Titan. We are just a very impatient species. So, while there are seeds still contained in the vault, one of our ancestors decided to start the Arboretum."

They stood in companionable silence for a moment as Curphay finished his tea. She looked in her cup and wrinkled her nose. She wasn't a fan of reheating already made tea, but she loathed getting rid of something so precious. She sighed and put the remaining liquid in the recycler and took Curphay's empty cup from his hands and placed them in the sonic cleaner.

"So." Curphay clapped his hands together. "Shall we open your mother's message?"

She glared at him. "I had just forgotten about it."

"Then it's a good thing I'm here to remind you." He smiled, eyes twinkling.

"Don't take too much enjoyment out of my discomfort."

His face grew solemn with mock gravity. "Never."

She growled at him, then pushed his blankets out of the way so she could sit on the couch. Curphay picked up the blanket and folded it. Amione waved and brought up the message packet to the forefront of the viewer. Her hand hovered over the packet.

Curphay reached over and tapped it.

"Curphay!" She slapped his hand.

He chuckled, clearly not intimidated by her fury.

Her mother's face appeared frozen in front of her, floating in mid-air. Mini emitters were scattered around the room, making the image before her possible. Her mother had the same grim set of her mouth, the same arched brow that seemed to give her a perpetual expression of disapproval, and the black eyes that cut through her. She touched the play button before she could change her mind.

"Daughter. I'm sure you are wondering why I asked you to join the ARK Project. One, because you are qualified. I have followed your academics and I know you are proficient. We need a paleogeneticist, and you are it. You asked why I need an answer so soon."

Amione nodded.

"We have reached a critical juncture in our project. The timing is delicate. If you don't accept the position, I must find another suitable candidate. I would prefer it if you would tell me today what you wish to do."

The message ended, returning to the default image which was copper sparkles drifting in space. She impatiently waved it closed, staring at the empty space for a moment before turning to Curphay., "What should I do?"

He snorted. "Take it."

She fidgeted with her hands.

"This is what you have wanted for a long time. Don't let your feelings for your mother get in the way of that."

Her jaw took on a mulish tilt. "I'm still asking that you come with me."

He sighed. "I'd argue with you, but you seem set on it. Not that I don't want to be there, but I would like to think they wouldn't need your stubbornness to accept me."

She grunted, then waved the viewer into existence and set it to record. She stared into the screen. "I accept. Curphay is coming with me. Find a position for him." She completed the recording and sent it to her mother before she lost her courage.

A return message popped onto her screen, no attachment. Only one word burned into her mind. "Understood."

Curphay decided he wanted to explore the rest of Demeter, and Amione took advantage of the time to visit Leto. He lived on the west quadrant where most of the single folks lived. Most singles bunked together in twos or fours, but Leto had lived here so long that he had his own room with a small private bathroom.

Several sets of curious eyes focused on her as she entered the common area. Amione folded her hands behind her back to keep them from shaking. She channeled her mother and kept a carefully neutral mask on her face.

A young woman smiled and held out a hand in greeting. Amione returned the gesture as she assessed the violet-eyed woman with slicked back straight black hair and dusky rose skin. She was attractive in the way most young women were attractive, and would eventually age into a more handsome version.

"Welcome. Is there something we can help you with?" Her voice was soft and lilting as she adjusted the belt over her coveralls. She was probably getting ready to start work on the surface. Copper light illuminated the surfaces in the common area and gave a metallic sheen to her hair.

Amione cleared her throat. "I'm looking for Leto."

"Ah! Well, you are in luck." She leaned in conspiratorially. "He should be out any minute. Jared! Go get the Captain!"

A blond youth lifted his head from a mini wave screen projecting from his wrist unit. He rolled gracefully to his feet and disappeared down a corridor.

"Come. Please have a seat while you wait."

"I'm fine standing. Thank you." Amione turned from the young woman, but not so fast that she didn't catch the quizzical look.

"As you wish." The smile returned, a little less genuine. "I'll leave you to it then."

Amione declined to answer and watched as the young woman returned to the group. Hushed tones let her know she was a topic of interest.

She flushed. As usual she misread the situation. Would it have been so terrible to join them? *Yes!* Her mind screamed. It was bad enough to be awkward with one person. It was tortuous to attempt an entire group.

Minutes dragged out as she busied herself looking at the portraits of smiling young faces. She recognized the picture of the young woman who had greeted her. Her name was Lakshmi Advoran, and she was a shift supervisor. She could see why. There was an ease in how she interacted with the others in her crew.

She walked over to another wall. Her heart jumped a beat when she saw the newly installed picture of her father. This was a smaller wall filled with portraits of ages past. All of these people had been killed on the job. Her father's portrait was brand new as well as another young man, Arvi Korgeran.

Her fingers brushed over her father's smiling face. She could feel tears prick her eyes.

"He was the best of us."

Amione looked up at Leto who had stepped up beside her without her noticing. He looked at her father's photo with sorrow deepening the lines on his clean-shaven face.

"It's good to see you, Amione." A ghost of a smile touched his blue eyes. "Would you like to come back to my room? We will have more privacy there."

She nodded, grateful that he understood her discomfort around other people, and followed him down the hallway. The panels were made from a stronger configuration of graphene that insulated the entire station and kept things at a temperature comfortable for humans.

She remembered what Lakshmi had said earlier. "Why do they call you Captain?"

Leto chuckled. "It was something they came up with. They do like their nicknames."

"But why Captain?" she pressed.

"Probably because I'm old and married to my work." He gave her an amused look over his shoulder.

She didn't understand the reference and cataloged it for later research. She knew it was an antiquated designation from Old Earth that had somehow made it to their century.

They walked through a door near the end of the corridor. Unlike her Da's quarters, Leto had everything in place, the bed was neatly made, no clutter, dust, or mess of any kind could be found anywhere. She assumed it was a necessity with a smaller living space.

Leto indicated the only chair in the space. She sat on the edge of the seat.

"You can relax, girl," he gently chided.

She slid further back until she could feel the back of the chair. She had the overwhelming urge to bounce her leg and to fidget, but she resisted. What she was about to ask was difficult and she had to remain calm, but it took a lot of effort.

"Tea?"

"Please." She forced herself to smile.

He went through the familiar motions of making tea. It made her feel calmer watching him go through the motions as if she was doing the task herself.

If he knew what she was going to ask, he made no indication. He handed her a steaming cup and took his own, sitting on the bed.

She blew on the contents and took a sip. She was so nervous she couldn't taste it. For all she knew, it was hot water. The rosy hued contents indicated Roseberry blend, her favorite. She was touched by the simple gesture.

The warmth of the mug did little to improve the circulation in her fingers. They still felt ice cold, made more pronounced with the contrast to the steamy warmth. She set the mug on the small table next to her and focused her gaze on her hands. She wasn't sure how to start.

"Amione." She looked up at Leto's gentle tone. "It's ok to ask. I've been expecting you to come here with questions."

She stared at his kind blue eyes and let out a pent-up breath. "How did it happen?"

He nodded and drew in a deep breath letting it out slowly. "It happened like the first one."

"Arvi," she clarified.

He looked at her with a furrowed brow and nodded. "Yes."

"I saw his picture next to Da's."

"Of course." He collected his thoughts before continuing. "We were breaking new ground. Your Da was adamantly against it. He maintained the equipment and knew it was in no shape to dig somewhere new. There were no specs!"

Amione knew enough about her Da's work to know that specs were important when breaking new ground. A complete metallurgical and geological workup were required so they could calibrate the machines accordingly. "But that's unheard of!"

"Exactly! That was a red flag, but then these bastards are known to change things at the last minute or try to cut corners if they think it will give them more profit." Leto twisted his mouth bitterly.

"So, what happened?" She leaned her elbows on her knees.

"At first it was a couple of injuries. The first was a fall causing Namy's suit to depressurize. Fortunately, she was able to get into the Cat and get back to base. We didn't think anything of it. Accidents are rare, but they do happen. We thought it was just bad luck." Leto spread his hands in a helpless gesture.

"And then?" she urged.

"Then Kenden was hit by falling debris. Again, not unusual, but to have both incidents so close together made people nervous. That rise had been checked like normal and everything was secure. It never set well with me. Maybe someone was trying to sabotage our operations. So, we grew more vigilant." He rubbed his chin absently as he stared into space, remembering the incident.

"Then Arvi."

He looked back at her; his mouth set into a grim line. "And then Arvi. He was inspecting the entrance to a new tunnel when it collapsed. He was crushed to death instantly. That's when your Da insisted that someone was trying to kill us. I thought he was crazy at first. I should have listened. He might be--" He swallowed hard.

She leaned forward and squeezed his hand. "It's not your fault, Leto."

"I should have listened." His blue eyes were rimmed red with unshed tears.

"No one could have known that this would happen," she soothed.

"Your Da did."

She nodded and set back in her chair. "True, but my Da was not your average guy."

"So, I'm average?"

That startled a chuckle out of her. She gave him a knowing look. "You know what I mean."

He smiled, the twinkle returning to his eyes. "I do. He was really special."

She paused. The silence grew awkward between them as she

prepared to ask the next question, they both knew was coming. "So, what happened that day?"

He gripped his knees tightly and looked at the floor. "It started out like most of our days. We joked and jibed each other on the ride down, got into our gear, and got our assignments. I was assigned to the spreader that day on the north side. Your Da was assigned to one of the machines near the new ground on the west side. Normal for the most part."

He shifted on the bed distressed by what he would say next.

"Are you sure you want to hear this part?"

She nodded. "I need to know."

"His communications were cutting in and out. Some sort of interference. He said he saw something moving on the next ridge and asked if anyone else was out that way. Everyone was accounted for. He said he was going to investigate and I urged him to wait for me. To not go alone. I don't know if he just didn't hear me or was being stubborn by going by himself."

Leto had a thousand-yard stare on his face. Whatever he had experienced next, he wasn't going to tell her, but she could tell it would haunt him until the day he died.

"He said there was definitely something moving over there. A shadow. It didn't make sense. I told him to wait for me. He yelled. I'll never forget that sound. I yelled and yelled for him, pushing the Cat to the limit to get to him. It still took me over 5 minutes to get there, by that time it was too late. He was gone." He fell silent, sitting completely still.

Amione shook. She wasn't going to cry here. She would wait until she got back to their apartment before collapsing. She just needed to know one more thing. "What do you think the shadow was?"

He looked at her as if he had woken from a coma. "I don't know. All digging has been halted on that side. None of us will go over there and there is no one else that knows the equipment like your Da did. We aren't sure what the company will do. Maybe we woke something," he mused, almost to himself.

"Something?" She raised her brow.

"Maybe."

"Are there cameras there?"

"On the equipment your Da worked on sure, but the company hadn't set anything up on that rise yet. There is no footage of what happened, no real way to know."

She nodded. She had hoped that there was something she could see. She needed to know what might have happened. She rose to her feet and Leto did the same. She hugged him and he hugged her back tightly.

"I'm sorry. I'm so sorry," he breathed into her hair.

She pushed back from his embrace. "You have nothing to be sorry for." She captured his gaze with her own, hoping he could see she held no enmity toward him.

He nodded.

She stopped in front of the door and looked back at him. "You have helped."

"I don't see how. What will you do now?"

"I've been offered a job. I think I will take it."

His head bobbed. "Good. Live a good life, Amione."

She nodded with a tight smile and exited his quarters.

On her way out, she thought about how Leto's story differed from the official account by the company. It was more than covering their asses. Something was wrong. The question was, how deep would she dig?

Chapter 8

Going Rogue

"Funny how quickly someone can stop calling you a miscreant and a rogue when they want your help."
Brandon Sanderson

Oal and the Entity came across a rogue planet. At first it looked lifeless, drifting aimlessly in the darkness. The atmosphere was thin and very unlike the world Oal came from.

There was potable water on the surface, presumably heated by some internal source deep within its core. Where there was water, life was possible.

"Shall we see what is on this planet?" Oal drifted closer, caution vibrated through him.

"Yes." The Sadool was eager, almost greedy, in its desire to find more life.

Oal's unease increased.

They drifted into the upper atmosphere and tasted the air. It was mostly composed of sulfur and oxygen. It wasn't impossible to sustain life in that atmosphere, just not life as he was used to. He could feel the exterior of his shell burn and he quickly pushed his way back out of the atmosphere.

"What is wrong?" The Sadool growled.

"This planet is not suitable for me." Oal was relieved the burning dissipated.

"I don't understand. This is made of mass. You are mass."

"There are many kinds of mass, Sadool." Oal wasn't sure how to explain the difference.

The Sadool's confusion was palpable. "In Darkness there is no place unsuitable to my kind."

"How fortunate for you," Oal stated dryly.

He could feel the longing of the Sadool to explore the planet below.

"Do not let me stop you from exploring. I can wait in orbit," he assured it.

The Sadool hesitated a moment longer, then a sense of excitement enveloped the curious entity. It quickly dropped out of sight as it descended deeper and deeper into the planet's atmosphere.

Oal contemplated leaving the entity on the planet below. It would make things much easier. He did not like how the entity made him feel uneasy. What if his association with the entity unleashed something that would devastate the galaxy? He dismissed it. Neither of them were so great that they could decide the fate of galaxies.

Once it had fulfilled its curiosity, they could continue their journey to a place more suitable for Oal. He was curious what the entity would find in such an inhospitable place. Despite Oal's misgivings there was one thing he and the Sadool had in common, curiosity.

Oal orbited the rogue planet, contemplating what direction they could go once the Sadool returned. Regularly, he would peer down to see if he could find the Sadool. Sometimes he had convinced himself that he could see it, but his senses weren't as strong without the Sadool's presence.

There were occasional light displays, but that could be explained away as part of the weather cycle of the planet. Like the water cycle, sulfur oxide would condensate, precipitate, then it would heat up and start all over again. Plumes of thermal clusters could be seen around the equatorial region contributing to the replenishment of the atmosphere.

He searched all the previous memories of his parentage and none of them had come across a rogue planet like this one. Most had an overwhelming drive to find a planet like the one they were seeded on. He felt the same compulsion, burning within his consciousness.

Just when he thought he would need to move on to the next place without his strange companion, he saw the Sadool lazily climbing into the higher atmosphere. It danced on the convective cycles over and over. Eventually, it reached orbit. Oal wasn't sure, but it looked like it had grown, nearly imperceptible, but definitively larger.

"What was it like?" Oal neglected to cover his envy.

"Different. It had a certain...taste." The Sadool hissed in pleasure.

Oal contemplated the entity's choice of words. "Was there life there?"

"Yes, but different from the small thing we encountered before."

"Different how?"

"I'm not certain. It tasted different. Made me buzz with energy for a full second." It rotated around Oal faster.

Oal squelched the alarm he felt. Again, he wondered what kept the entity from consuming him. "You ate life here?"

"Only a small amount. I had to see if it did the same thing as before. There is not much life here. We should continue to another place." The entity tugged on their bond, and Oal complied.

Oal remained silent regretting his decision not to leave. This is not what he had imagined when he struck out away from the others.

They turned toward a star and pushed onward. There was no guarantee there would be life in that system, but he felt compelled to move toward it anyway.

Chapter 9

Synthesis

"We are approaching a new age of synthesis. Knowledge cannot be merely a degree or a skill... it demands a broader vision, capabilities in critical thinking and logical deduction without which we cannot have constructive progress."
Li Ka-shing

After leaving Leto's, Amione crossed the Arboretum in deep thought. She absently wound through the immaculately tended Titian stone paths, and unconsciously brushed by plants that hung over the barriers on either side. The liquid smell of water was filled her nose. Beautifully crafted waterfalls cycled water through the entire system, humidifying the normally dry air of the station, watering the plants, and providing an atmosphere of tranquility.

She read that running water was everywhere on Old Earth before the Cataclysm. There was something instinctive in a human's genetics that draws them to running water. She knew, intellectually, that it was an evolutionary component to their DNA. They were hardwired to respond to the sound, but how it made her feel was the curious part. How could she feel such an affinity for something she had never experienced firsthand?

Titan and now Mars were the closest thing to Old Earth in their solar system. Titan had a weather cycle involving methane and ethane. She had been on the surface enough times to hear the plinking sound of rain on the roof of the structures. It gave her a feeling of pleasure to hear it.

On Mars terraforming had progressed to the point where small weather systems were created successfully. Once the degraded magnetic field was addressed, and they accounted for the smaller size, terraforming was able to get a foothold on the red planet. Another thousand plus years and it would resemble the arid regions of Old Earth. It was a fascinating process, and one that was generously shared by their Alliance.

The Alliance was made up of five species including Humans. The Tromfelds, a long-lived mycologically based sentient species, was one of the founding members along with the Nouris, a colorful species of high intellect who sported wings and possessed some telekinetic abilities. The Ingvar joined later. Their planet was 85% water with two distinct species. The larger group evolved in the oceans and the smaller evolved in river and lake systems. The Ngs were Silicon based entities that made their home on a volcanic planet in the Tygr system.

The Alliance was the architect of the greatest scientific cooperative in the sector called the ARK Project, the very same project her mother insisted she join. The mission of the ARK Project was initially a water finding project. When humans joined, it gained a new urgency.

Colonizing the moons and planets in the sol system were not sustainable for humans in the long run. Mostly because of the gravity problem. Humans originally evolved with heavier gravity on Earth. None of their colonies came close. It had caused mutations such as visual impairment, and problems with the circulatory system and brain development. Current technology could only do so much.

Reclaiming Earth was definitely in the works, but it would take millennia to bring it back to pre-cataclysm standards. There was another planet that might give humans a new lease on life. One that was nearly ready for inhabitants.

Amione assumed they wanted her to be involved with that part of the process. Something that exited her greatly.

But first she had to finish Academy and she needed to know what happened to her Da.

She ran into a solid form. "Oh! I'm sorry," she apologized, trying to step around him. He blocked her path.

She recognized the man from the ceremony. He had an unusually heavy build with broad shoulders that strained the seams of his jump-suit. A dark shock of hair dipped down into his eyes which were a star-tling hazel.

There was something unsettling about him. She took another step back, prepared to flee the other way if he meant ill.

A tense silence welled up between them. She was about to turn and run when he spoke. His voice was deeper than she expected. "The answers you seek are down on the surface."

She frowned, balling her fists at her side. "What did you say?"

"You will find your answers on the surface." His brows knit together in frustration.

She shook her head in disbelief. "Answers to what?"

"To your father's death." He took a step forward and she took a step back.

He unfolded his left hand, a data crystal glimmered in the dim light. His hand was large and muscular with long fingers. They were rough similar to her Da's but scarred from injuries she could only fathom. He didn't look like a resident of Demeter. He looked like he belonged on the oldest city on Titan, The Derelict.

"What is that?"

"Answers." He stated, his eyes willing her to understand.

She turned her attention back to the crystal. Did she dare take it? She licked her lips. It might hold the answers she needed. Didn't she owe it to her Da to know what killed him?

"How did you come by this?" She kept her eyes glued on the data crystal.

"I worked the security system on Yenoa."

She looked at him in surprise. "Aren't you from the Derelict?"

He ignored her question. "Please, take it. Make sure you are the only one that sees it and destroy the crystal when you are done."

She carefully plucked the crystal out of his hand. "Thank you?"

"Don't view it on your wave. Find a secure device, or they will know you saw it and kill you," he urged.

"Who are *they*?" Her heart thundered in her chest.

His head turned at a sudden sound, and as quickly as he appeared he was gone. She wondered what spooked him. All she could hear was the running of water, faint laughter from other residents in another part of the Arboretum, and the gentle whirr she associated with the machinery of Demeter.

She looked at the data crystal in her hand before tucking it into a hidden pocket in the waistband of her trousers. She wasn't sure if the knowledge was real or not, but her gut told her to be careful. She would keep this safe until she could find a secure wave screen.

She wanted to tell Curphay everything that transpired, but she held back. He was as supportive friend as one could want, but she could tell that he was humoring her. Would he be supportive if he knew this? Probably rationalize it like he rationalized everything that seemed a little wonky.

She continued her walk and watched the surrounding paths with open eyes. She wasn't one to give in to paranoia, but with the question of her father's death looming, she had to believe that there might be people who wished her ill.

As her days grew busier, she debated whether she should view the data crystal. If it was as dangerous as the man said, she shouldn't watch, but then he had gone to a great deal of trouble to get it to her. In the end she had to know.

The Academy had given both her and Curphay permission to complete their degrees remotely since there was only a month left. The Dean assured her that their remaining possessions would be shipped back on the next transport. Most of the things she cherished were in Demeter anyway.

"Are you ok with your things being left at Academy?" She asked Curphay.

"Honestly, I carry the important stuff with me. The rest are just tablets, pillows, and blankets. Maybe some clothes. Besides, it will give me an excuse to go shopping. When are we going to Yenoa by the way?" He batted his warm brown eyes at her.

She chuckled. "Such a clothes horse."

"A clothes what?"

"Nevermind. Fine, we can go in a couple days. I have to finish this paper."

He groaned. "You always do the right thing. When are you going to let loose?"

She gave him a secret smile. "This is about as loose as I get." She squinted at the wave screen in front of her, trying to decipher a base pair sequence.

"Have you learned nothing from me?" He gasped.

She deflected. "Don't you have a paper due? Something about thermodynamics and the something something?"

"The lack of thermodynamics as it pertains to dark matter filaments. It's mostly written," he hedged.

"Where? Can I see it?"

"Well, it's written here. Technically." He tapped his temple.

She rolled her eyes and threw a pillow at him. "I never could understand how you do that. You have absolutely nothing, then the night before it's due you produce an impeccably written document with perfect references. Like magic." She snapped her fingers.

"It's a gift." He grinned as he smoothed his ruffled hair back into place.

She looked at him sidelong. "You could get your paper written, then help me."

"Blech, genetics? Ugh, boring. It lacks the elegance of physics." He turned up his nose.

She shrugged off his insults. "Understanding the cosmos is all well and good, but *my* work will change the world. Literally."

He sobered up. "I believe it will. So..." He twisted the fringe on the pillow in his lap. "What are you going to take to the ARK? And what will you do with this place?"

She closed the wave screen. There was no way she could take it all with her. She was allotted two trunks, an antigrav bag, and a carry-on. That was hardly enough room to pack her bedroom, much less a lifetime of memories. She could purchase new clothes on the ARK and other more mundane items which would free up room for other things.

"I'm not exactly sure. I know I can't keep it all. Honestly, I want to just seal the door and preserve it exactly as it is."

"A museum. That seems true to form." Curphay's mouth quirked at the corners.

"Yes, a museum." She rolled her eyes again. "But that's obviously not an option. Space is limited on Demeter, and I'm sure a growing family would appreciate the room. Da considered moving in with the Bachelors anyway when I graduated. He told me he was condensing his possessions and giving things away."

Curphay looked around in amazement. "This was *after* he culled his possessions?"

"Well yeah. That corner over there was stacked to the ceiling with old books, and boxes of artifacts."

"Wow. It's just so weird. I never realized how austere your life at Academy was compared to this. I thought your dorm was always so cluttered."

"I used a lot of restraint."

"Apparently so."

"I think it's strange not to have anything," she said, and immediately regretted it.

Curphay's face sombered. "You know there isn't much there to begin with, much less anything I want to remember."

Curphay grew up on Mars Colony in the largest community of Ares V. His parents were diplomats to the Ingvari. Curphay spent much of his time getting into mischief with his older brother bailing him out of scrape after scrape.

Something happened and Malchem died. Curphay never talked about it and Amione never pried. His parents rushed home, their cruiser was attacked by Sadool and they were considered lost.

Curphay was alone with a sizable trust fund to care for his every need. He was searching for purpose in his grief and found physics. The boy who had done so poorly in school for most of his life found his passion. That he was gifted in that passion was a bonus.

Amione met Curphay on the first day of Academy in their physical science course. Both hated it, but it was a prereq for both of their fields of interest. Since their names were next to each other on the roster, they were paired as lab partners. Little did they know that Dhager and Dhau would become almost inseparable in the years to come.

"Well, as long as we are together, I guess this stuff doesn't matter that much." She picked up a figurine of a butterfly and gently put it back on the table.

"Just don't wait too long to start. You have a lot to go through here."

Grief pierced her heart as her eyes burned. The unexpectedness of it caught her off guard and hot tears poured down her cheeks again. "I'm so tired of crying."

She heard Curphay get up from the chair and sit by her on the couch. She leaned her head gratefully on his shoulder. He squeezed her arm and kissed her on the head. "You will get through this." His voice was husky with emotion.

He would know what he was talking about. "It doesn't seem like it."

"It's only been a couple of weeks. Grief comes in waves and all those firsts without your Da are going to feel like walking on broken glass for a while. But eventually, you will learn how to ride those waves and maybe even smile when they come."

She sniffed. "That's a really nice analogy."

"It wasn't mine. My caretaker told me that a long time ago, when Malchem died." His voice sounded hollow.

"Thank you for sharing it and thank you for being here." She looked up at him, and he smiled down at her.

"You know I would do anything for you." He kissed her cheek.

"I'm very lucky to have you as my friend."

"Of course, you are. No one has a friend like me." He bounced to his feet. "I'm hungry. Do you want me to fix anything?"

"I'm not hungry." She stretched and yawned.

"You are never going to finish that unless you put some food in you. You know that," he chided her.

"All right! Maybe just a salad," she relented.

"That's better."

She leaned back against the couch and watched as Curphay pulled plates from the cabinet and ingredients from the chiller beneath the sink.

He rinsed the lettuce and the sound of vegetation being pulled apart was soothing. She fidgeted with the waistband of her pants and felt the hard edge of the data crystal. She still had not found a secure wave to view it on. Not that she had been exceptionally motivated to do so. She wasn't sure if she wanted to see what was on there.

Leto's recounting of her Da's last day was disturbing. She had nightmares of Da's last moments and wondered if he had suffered. She imagined she was him on more than one occasion and woke in a cold sweat.

She pulled up the news feed and a headline caught her eye.

ANOTHER WORKER DIES AT HESPER MINING CORP

She stared at it, stunned. It happened again. She felt her body grow cold as anxiety washed over her.

"Amione? You grew two shades lighter. What's wrong?"

Curphay hastily put down the plates on the table in front of them and sat next to her. She pointed a shaky finger at the headline. Before she could stop him, he opened the link. A picture of Leto blinked into view along with a three-paragraph synopsis and a video. She stared at Leto's smiling company photo. She had just seen him. Just talked to him.

Curphay hit the video.

A young dark-haired man stood in a pressure suit near the sight of the incident. A rain system was moving in pelting the intrepid reporter with liquid methane.

"I'm here at Hesper Mining Corp's newest operation. Hesper has been a staple of Titan's economy for nearly 300 years. Only a handful of deaths have been recorded in that time. Today marks the third death in two months. We don't have many details other than a worker, Leto

Brown, was working on a drilling machine when he was pulled into part of the machinery depressurizing his suit and killing him."

The camera panned the scene and Amione saw a blue tarp in the background. Part of the tarp lifted exposing a boot, Leto's boot. Her vision tunneled.

"We will keep you up to date when we know more, Grant--"

The viewer shut off.

She glanced at Curphay and saw he was disturbed as well.

Her leg bounced as she assimilated the information. She needed to find a secure viewer and watch the security footage.

"This is insane." Curphay shook his head. "What is going on?"

"I don't know, but I need to find out. Do you still have a secure viewer?" She leaned an elbow on her knee as it continued to bounce in anxiety.

"I still have my parent's diplomatic one. Amione, why would you need a secure viewer?" His mouth dropped open at her out-of-character request.

"I can't tell you that. I just need it." She glanced at him, then wrung her hands.

He sat very still. "What aren't you telling me?"

Should she involve him any further than the viewer? "Can I use it?" She leaned in, pressing her will on him.

He went to his bag and pulled out a viewer. His fingers tapped on the edges of the older tech as he assessed her. "I don't think you should get involved."

She looked at him incredulously. "I'm already involved. My Da and now Leto. Something is down there, Curphay."

He hesitated, then handed her the viewer. "The password is DhauDhager82/987g."

She nodded thanks and went to her room.

"I'm here, Amione, when you are ready to talk," he called after her.

The door slid shut cocooning her in the safety of her room, but even this space felt exposed. Copper light poured in through the small window near the ceiling as she activated the lights around her bed.

She sat cross-legged and stared at the viewer in her hands. She waved her hand over the device and the holographic display sprang up in front of her. A cursor blinked waiting for her to enter the password. She entered it and the viewer opened showing several applications. Most were unrecognizable, she wondered what Curphay used this thing for.

It was not uncommon for Mars to have encrypted hardware at their fingertips, especially if they were the son of a diplomat. It was completely outlawed on Titan. It had something to do with corporate espionage. Mars was a free confederation, with laws and a republic. The citizens decided who would represent their interests through a fair election.

But on Titan, the corporations ruled. It was a social contract between the workers and the companies. They did their jobs, and the company would provide food, water, shelter, and health care. They had no say in how the company did things or what resources they could or could not use. If you could work, you were provided for. If you couldn't, then your family was responsible for you. If you had no family, you ended up on the Derelict.

This life was all she knew until she met Curphay. She hadn't realized there were other ways of being. Which was better, she could not say. The Mars Colony gave the illusion of free will where none existed. At least on Titan they understood the terms of the contract. They could either abide by them or go somewhere else.

She shook herself. She needed to focus on the task at hand. It took a moment to find the correct app. She pulled the data crystal from her waistband. Cursing when it fell to the floor.

On hands and knees, she searched for it finally finding it behind a chair leg. She returned to the bed and inserted the crystal with a shaking hand.

Blinking lights and images flashed on the screen as the crystal downloaded its information packet. A single file labeled "Camera 43" appeared on the screen. She wiped sweaty palms on her pants and licked dry lips before tapping on the file.

The camera had a full view of the machine and the tunnel they were creating. Her heart pounded when she recognized her Da's pressure suit. It had a small bird painted on the top right side of his helmet. He said it was a reminder of why he did the work every single day. The camera was clear except for a bit of dust on the lower left side.

The desolate plains in the area spread out for kilometers each way. Small rises indicated a Tinorium deposit that ran through the region. It was what gave Hesper its wealth. Tinorium was used to fuel near light speed ships that traveled from system to system. It was highly valued and highly sought after. This newest vein would last the corporation for decades. Except, people were dying over it.

She ached as she watched his familiar movements. There was a certain elegant design to his maintenance kit. He was so sloppy in all other aspects of his life, but his work was different. He prided himself on his resourcefulness and his efficiency. He said it was because he was too lazy to do it the other way. Less energy wasted on a repair the better.

She couldn't see what he was working on from that angle. A distortion marred the viewer for a moment and was gone. Her Da turned toward something just beyond the view of the screen. He absently placed a tool on his maintenance kit and took a step toward whatever was claiming his attention. He stepped halfway out of frame, shifting from one foot to another.

He flew back into frame and hit the machine with his back. She cried out, covering her mouth. Her heart rate increased. Stunned, her Da struggled to get to his feet. Something grabbed his foot and yanked him beneath the machine. He clung to the wheelbase in desperation. Tears streamed down her cheek as she watched. A shadow flicked over his form, pulling him out of the frame.

She waited for several minutes for him to reappear, but he never did. She sobbed into her hand, looking but seeing nothing. S shadow flicker in and out of the frame before the video cut off.

She stared at the blank screen, taking gasping breaths as she tried to calm herself. She wished she hadn't seen it. But she had, and it was nothing like the official account given to her. They said the machine had malfunctioned and that he was crushed beneath it. There was no evidence to support their story.

She watched it again running it through several verifications to make sure it was a real recording. It was. She focused on the details replaying it over and over.

Setting the viewer aside, she paced in her room, trying to assimilate what she was seeing. Why were the two accounts different? At first, she assumed it was because Hesper didn't want her suing them, but this indicated something far more insidious.

Titan's gravity was lighter than Old Earth's. It was very difficult to throw anything with great force. What could have thrown her father like that?

She brought the viewer back onto her lap going through the recording frame by frame. She advanced the recording frame by frame until she saw something that didn't belong.

There! A shadow, just barely in the frame in the upper left corner. What was that?

At first, she thought it was the shadow of a person coming into view, but the sun angle was all wrong. The incongruity bothered her. How could you have a shadow that isn't being cast by something? The simple answer was that it couldn't.

The shadow flickered into view, then out of the frame. Her Da stepped half out of frame, then he was thrown. She flinched. She reversed the feed, then moved it forward again and again. There was no one there. No explanation on how he was thrown. She zoomed in on the point of impact and cocked her head to the side when she saw something dark pushing against her Da's chest, then retreating. It looked like a shadow, but if so, this was no ordinary shadow. It didn't seem to have form or shape, and yet it was obvious that it had enough substance to push a man forcefully several meters in low gravity.

She forwarded through her Da's struggle to stand and slowed it down to a frame by frame. His foot was yanked from under him, and he was pulled under the vehicle. She went back and zoomed in closer to his foot. At first, it was just a slight darkening around the ankle. Then the shadow grew more substantial as it snaked around her Da's ankle and pulled.

"What the hell is *that?*" she whispered into the silence of the room.

She moved the image forward and backward several more times before stopping. The video would give her nothing more to work with. Whatever was down there, it was not friendly, and it was decidedly not human. It was not like any species she had ever seen before. What was it? Was it sentient? And what was it doing here? Was it native to Titan? Or did it come from somewhere else? She many questions, and wasn't sure how to get the answers she needed.

Chapter 10

Decoupling

"There are times when I doubt everything. When I regret everything, you've taken from me, everything I've given you, and the waste of all the time I've spent on us."
David Leviathan

Oal and the Sadool had traveled for some time since the rogue planet. They diverted their path whenever something interesting passed nearby, but mostly it was empty space. Oal wasn't sure who was directing who. The fact that Oal could change his heading at all was still new, and he wasn't sure what to make of it.

Most seedlings were at the mercy of interstellar space. Small deviations could occur, but wherever the current went, that is where the seedling went. The journey ended when they reached a planet or moon.

Each time the Sadool consumed a bit of matter, it grew stronger, and Oal grew with it. He was able to stretch his senses further than he should have been able to as a seedling. He owed the difference to his constant shadowy companion.

Oal found this both troubling and exciting. Symbiosis meant there was a dependency. Could he separate from the entity when he chose? Or were they forever connected? None of his parentage could help with these questions. There was no precedent. He suspected that the Sadool had no frame of reference either.

"Have you noticed that we strengthen each other?" Oal asked.

"There is something about you that compels me to stay. I don't know why. I have had several opportunities to go back to Darkness on this Journey, and yet, I don't seem to have a will to do that." The entity shrugged mentally.

"As a seedling, I shouldn't be able to direct my movements, and yet, we are heading to that star system. I did that. I directed us, but that shouldn't be possible."

The entity mulled over the new information. "I'm sure there is an explanation, but I can't tell you exactly why these things are happening. Maybe we shouldn't question and just enjoy it."

A ripple of eagerness warped the link between them. Oal did not like the edge in its thoughts. Despite his trepidation, he enjoyed the ability to control his destiny. If the Sadool was eager to provide the benefits, then who was he to fight it? But a niggling doubt scratched at the corners of his mind, reminding him that one day he would want to separate. When that day came, would the Sadool allow it? Would he even want to? It was a disturbing thought, and one he didn't want to entertain.

What would the parentage think of this new information? Eventually, he would be required to connect with the rest of the network. His greatest fear was that he would be shut out of the network forever for the radical things he encountered, and his willingness to pursue them. It had happened in the past. Seedlings grow and reconnect with the network, and if the information contained was too disruptive, they were cut off from the collective forever.

The thought of never reconnecting, to be exiled, was frightening. To contribute to the Continuum of Knowledge was the highest purpose for any Tromfeld. If he could not do that... He pushed his worry aside and focused on getting to the next star system and seeing what it might offer. Worrying about something that might never come was a waste of energy. Energy that could be better spent acquiring knowledge.

They found another living particle and the Sadool consumed it. Again, Oal's range increased. Would he retain that strength once the entity was gone? As time passed, the desire to uncouple grew less and less. They continued to marinate in their comfortable existence.

Oal saw the creature first. It was not much larger than Oal, but then they hadn't seen anything this large since they began their journey together. It was amorphous in shape. He couldn't tell exactly where the thing began and ended, just that it was there.

"What do you see?" the entity asked.

"I'm not sure. I think it is alive." Oal tried to gain more information by taking in its electromagnetic resonance. It vibrated at a low frequency rosy hue.

"We should go investigate." The Sadool barely contained its eagerness.

"No, we don't know what it is. It is larger than both of us put together. And it could be hostile." Oal tried to push forward, but the Sadool resisted.

"I want to know what it is."

"And consume it," Oal stated dryly.

"That is a possibility."

"This isn't like the other small life forms we encountered. Those are mindless things that aren't aware of their existence. This one could be aware and if so, it might bring others."

"Good. I will consume them as well."

"No, you won't," Oal pushed back.

The Sadool remained silent.

Oal wasn't sure if it was chastised into silence or if it was working out a reason to get Oal to agree with it. Oal tried to move forward again, and the entity resisted. "What now?"

"I promise not to consume it."

Oal relaxed.

"Unless it attacks me." The entity added its condition.

Oal fumed. He should protest, but it seemed he couldn't move forward until this was resolved. The creature changed course to intercept. There was a subtle shift in color from rose to copper. He had no idea if it meant curiosity or animosity. It moved fast, faster than they could escape if the entity had any interest in doing that. Oal stayed trapped by their bond helpless to do anything but watch.

"It seems like the creature has decided for us," the Sadool cheerfully noted.

"It seems so." Oal tamped down the anxiety that filled him as he prepared for first contact.

Chapter 11

Anathema

"Darkness was anathema to the Shadows."
Steven Erikson

Amione exited her bedroom in a daze and into the living area. Curphay read on the couch, when he noticed her, he closed out his viewer. He looked at her with trepidation.

"Are you alright?" He ran a hand over his beard.

She didn't answer right away. Instead, she took a seat in the chair opposite and stared at the floor, trying to figure out a way to explain everything she had seen and what she wanted to do next. She noticed there was a hole in her stalking and wondered absently how long it had been there.

"Amione."

Her head popped up. She had forgotten he was there for a moment. She frowned at him. "Why do you look so disheveled?"

He barked out a laugh. "I just woke. You know it is morning, right?"

She looked at the timepiece over the door. Her eyebrows rose. He was right. She had been watching that video over and over all night.

"I need to go down to the surface." She stood up and paced, needing to expel nervous energy. She drew the shades back from the window and viewed the copper haze and ever-present Saturn on the horizon.

"You need to, what?!" Curphay sat up straight. "Why would you want to do that?"

"I need to know what happened to my Da," she stated rubbing her sleep deprived eyes with her right hand.

Curphay's eyes narrowed. "What was on that crystal?"

She shook her head and buried her face in her hands before pushing her hair back. "I don't know for sure, which is why I need to go down there." She returned to the chair, sitting heavily.

"What do you think it is?" He waved the viewer closed and drew up a knee.

"It's not a species I've ever seen before." She leaned back in the chair resting her head on the back.

"What makes you think you can do more than what the authorities are doing?" He walked to the window and looked out over the copper clouds. In the distance the city of Yorea floated, light reflecting off its communications array.

"I don't know, Curphay. I'm not asking you to go with me." She sighed in resignation.

He gasped in offense. "You think I wouldn't go with you? Of course, I would. I just don't want us to get killed in the process."

She looked at him helplessly. She didn't know how to convey how important this was to her, and she was too tired to explain.

"We will talk about this when you have had some rest." He offered his hand to her and she accepted it. He led her back to her bedroom. "Lay down." His tone brooked no argument.

She laid down, pulling the covers up. "Can you lay with me for a while?"

His expression softened. "Of course, I can."

She scooted over so he could lay next to her. She used his arm to pillow her head and held his hand. "Thank you."

"Sleep." A smile played on his lips.

She sighed, grateful for his warmth. It didn't chase away the images she had seen, but it helped her feel safe enough to fall asleep.

She woke to find Curphay had left. She sat up, rubbed her eyes and pushed curls back from her face. Her mouth felt dry. She had forgotten to clean her teeth before going to sleep. She looked at the timepiece over her desk. She had slept six hours. Not great, but she felt better than she did this morning.

She tied her hair back. She reached for the viewer on her desk. It wasn't there. She lifted various items, but no viewer. She knew she had put it on the desk. Cold washed over her as she realized Curphay must have taken it.

The sphere... She opened a compartment on the underside of her desk and sighed in relief. It was still there.

She held the small object in her hands running her thumbs over the unblemished surface. She couldn't be sure, but it felt warmer. The electromagnetic resonance had changed slightly. Instead of an ultraviolet low-key emanation, it looked blue. She wasn't sure what that meant. She traced the lines on the surface that petaled out from the center. She wasn't sure how the sphere fit into the big picture, but her Da thought it was important.

She returned the object to the compartment and changed into clean clothes. She placed the soiled ones in a bin built into the wall, which were then reconstituted into their organic components and made into something else.

She padded to her door hesitating. If Curphay had the viewer, he saw what was on the crystal. That was stupid. Of course, he would look. She wanted to keep him out of this, but it her subconscious had other plans. Once he saw what was on there, he would insist on going.

She opened the door and went to the bathroom, glancing briefly at Curphay who was standing by the living room window fully dressed. A vest was pulled taut over his back. Long sleeves fit over his arms in a pleasantly rumpled state. His pants were perfectly fitted, pleated and fed into a pair of boots.

She ducked into the bathroom before he turned toward her, and washed her face, cleaned her teeth, and combed her hair. She stared at her image in the mirror. Her eyes looked large in her thin face. She had bags under her eyes, and her complexion looked sallow in the anemic light. She wiped her image from the wall in front her.

She felt like she was coming undone slowly, insidiously. It was insane to go down to the surface when whatever killed her Da and the others was down there waiting.

Finally, she walked out of the bathroom. Curphay studied her, his eyes unreadable in the copper light.

"You have seen the crystal," she said.

He nodded.

"Then you know why I need to go."

His eyes stabbed through her. "You should be running from this place and never look back."

"Then you saw it too." Her gaze eagerly raked over his pinched expression.

"Whatever it was, it is dangerous." Fear flickered in his eyes.

"It killed my Da and it's going to keep killing until I find it," she said, trying to convince him that it was the only reasonable path.

"It could kill you too. You aren't being rational. The best thing the Company could do is abandon that site and bury it." His voice was rough with emotion.

She shook her head with a mulish set to her jaw. "I have to go down there."

"What about the ARK? You haven't started packing yet." He drummed his fingers on the windowsill.

She let out a noise of frustration, pacing between the living area and the kitchen. "I can't move on with my life until I know."

Curphay grew still. "What if it's unknowable? Do you stop living your life?"

Amione looked at his mournful eyes and knew that this was not about her, but his loss. Her heart ached and she grabbed one of his hands in her own. "I have to try, don't I?"

He hung his head and nodded reluctantly. "Fine. But you aren't doing this alone. That's so much worse. If you must seek answers, I will be with you at your side."

She squeezed his hand again, grateful that she didn't have to go alone. "There are two SCIS in my Da's locker and I can requisition a shuttle. I don't know how long we will be down there. We will need supplies.

Food mostly. Some water, but the work shed has potable water too. Extra clothes, patch kits, oxygen, and a crystal burner. I want images of this thing. Maybe if I can get a clear image the Company will have to do something." She rummaged through the cupboards looking for things to pack.

She glanced over her shoulder and could see Curphay had not moved.

"What is it?" She gently placed a ration pack on the counter.

"Just realizing that we are really doing this." His face was two shades lighter than normal.

She felt her stomach dip in guilt. "Being my friend isn't easy, is it?"

His lip quirked in amusement. "No, but it is always interesting. I've known you long enough to know that when you decide on something, you won't let it go until you have solved it to your satisfaction."

Her uneasiness increased. "I'm being selfish."

"No." He walked around the back of the couch and flopped onto the cushion. "You are being who you are. It's what makes you such a dogged scientist. That determination has gotten you far."

"It's gotten me in trouble plenty of times," she stated gruffly.

"Only because the people here don't understand what you are." He nodded with a surety that she wished she felt.

She raised an eyebrow. "What am I exactly?"

"Fucking brilliant." He grinned.

She didn't feel brilliant, but she played into the compliment. "Of course, I am."

The tension ease in the room and she turned back to sorting through ration packs. Why her Da kept so many, she didn't know, but it was coming in handy right now. She chalked it up to his eccentricity. She popped two cups of tea in the percolator and continued sorting.

"You know, there was something odd about the shadow." Curphay went through the viewer again, examining it frame by frame.

"I couldn't put my finger on what it was, but yes, I noticed something was off, too."

"It's like it was there, and not at the same time. I thought it was a glitch in the footage, but if that was the case, there would be glitches in other parts of the video and there is none. Just the shadow." He swiped through another frame and back again.

She walked two steaming cups of tea to the table in front of the couch. Curphay swung his legs to the floor. He picked up his mug and absently sipped from it, hissing when he burned his tongue. She looked at him in amusement.

"What can be there and not be there at the same time?" she wondered.

"Maybe it is just a trick of the light." His tone said otherwise.

"Which is why I want to go down there. That reminds me, I need to pull out Da's weapons. We might need protection." She looked toward the locker secured by the front door.

Silence reigned in the small room. Only the whirr of Dino's agitators could be heard as the little robot dutifully cleaned every speck from the floor. It looked ordinary; the steaming cups of tea, two friends working on a project, the service robot cleaning as it did every day. It could never be ordinary again with her Da gone. His death had to mean something. She needed it all to mean something.

"Um." Curphay's apprehensive voice punctuated the silence. "I don't know how to use anything like that."

"It's easy. Just point it at whatever you want to shoot and pull the trigger." Amione shrugged.

Curphay's Adam's apple bobbed as he swallowed hard. "If you say so."

She patted his knee. "It won't come to that."

"I hope you are right."

She moved the frame back and forth looking at where the shadow had made contact with her Da's chest. It looked solid enough. It wasn't a hand, more like a tentacle. Then it seemed to evaporate as it moved back out of view. "Do you see this?"

Curphay leaned forward. "It just disappears. Do you think it is native to Titan?"

"Wouldn't the surveyors have noticed something like this?"

"Not if it evaporates into air. It's not a natural phenomenon. There seems to be intent behind its actions."

She noticed that too. She didn't want to make assumptions, but it seemed to know that there was a recording device trained on that area. It went around and pulled her Da beneath the machine. Unless there was more than one. Either way, the cameras were avoided. If it was intelligent maybe it could be reasoned with. If it had form, she could kill it.

The viewer disappeared.

"Hey," she protested.

"You are obsessing. You won't know more until you get more information." He gave her a knowing look.

An alarm sounded. They looked at each other, then brought up the main viewer. A message tracked across the screen backed by flashing red light. "An unauthorized person has been found on the station. Keep all cabins locked and answer when the authorities ping your door. We will end the alert once the person has been apprehended. Thank you for your patience." The message repeated over and over again. She closed the viewer.

"What is that about?" Curphay's eyes were wide with alarm.

"It doesn't happen often. Demeter tracks people's movements to and from our city. Occasionally we will find a stowaway from the Derelict, but that hasn't happened in a very long time." Her mind went to the man who had given her the data crystal.

"The Derelict?"

"It's the oldest city on Titan. It's smaller than Demeter if you can believe that. It was built to house 500 workers comfortably. But there are over 5000 people there now."

"The conditions there..."

"Are horrendous. It was never meant to have that many people. Over the years, residents have expanded it, but it's not safe. Truth be told, it should have been decommissioned years ago."

"Then why hasn't it?"

"Two reasons." She held up two fingers. "One, the Company can't agree on where to rehome these people. No one wants them and they can't agree on how many each remaining city would take."

"And the second?"

"Most don't want to leave. It's their home as imperfect as it is. So, the Company provides materials for repairs, food, medicine, and leaves them to themselves." She shrugged.

"Have you been there?"

She shook her head. "No. It's not like it is a destination like Yorea or Caiphus. I think Da went there a time or two to deliver supplies. He said there was a pathos to them, and yet underneath it all was a resilient set of people who, if given the chance, could make a good life for themselves."

Curphay rubbed his chin. "Why don't they build a new city?"

She laughed. "Oh, that was a plan for a while, but it went nowhere. Mainly because of money and mostly because the rest of us aren't inconvenienced enough to do anything about it. It's easier to throw some supplies at them and think that they are doing their part."

Curphay turned his cup in his hands looking pensive. "On Mars, we had places less well off than others. But it's different there. The Colonies aren't run by corporations, they are run by a central government. We all pay a little to be used to improve places."

"Well corporations are in charge here, and if they don't have to pay for something, they won't. It's in their interest to provide for Demeter because that is where the majority of the workers come from. We build up a little extra from trade in the Arboretum which reduces the cost the corporation needs to put out for the city. That little extra helps our less fortunate citizens. Everything is carefully monitored. And it works for us, but I always felt like we were one disaster away from becoming the Derelict or worse."

"Do people here realize that?"

"Those that do the monitoring do. Da used to talk to them on a regular basis. He would trade his time to do repairs and that was how he was able to afford my tuition to the Academy. But I think most of the people here are clueless as to how precarious our place is here on Titan."

"Do you think that will change?"

"Not anytime soon. I'm not sure they are doing anything about these deaths. Other than covering it up." She resumed packing supplies.

"Because it would affect profit."

"Exactly."

They worked side by side in silence each deep in their own thoughts.

"Are you ready?" Amione slung a pack over her shoulders.

"What? Are we leaving now? But the alarm said stay locked in our quarters." Curphay stopped turning his cup and stared at her.

Amione smirked. "It always says that. But this would be the best time to grab a shuttle when most of security is occupied elsewhere."

"But won't they be watching the shuttles?"

She almost laughed at his gaping expression. "Yeah, but I know the guy. He won't have any issues with me taking a shuttle. The alarm couldn't have come at a better time."

"Fine." He sighed in exasperation. "At least let me change into something less... nice. I just got this vest."

She laughed and checked his pack again. She noticed the viewer with the data crystal in it. She extracted the crystal and put it in the pocket on her waistband. Then she slipped on a pair of compression socks and wrapped her boots around her ankles, cinching them tight. She wrapped a grav belt around her waist.

She dug around the table to see if she could find her Da's spare belt. Triumphant, she lifted it to the light and examined its condition.

"What is that?"

She jumped at Curphay's voice behind her. He was dressed in a worn pair of skin tight pants, a long john shirt, and held a pair of boots in his hand.

"It's a grav belt."

He frowned. "What is that exactly?"

"The surface gravity is lighter down there. This will help keep your footing."

"Oh." He sat on the couch and put on his boots. She helped him put on the belt and cinched it as tight as it would go. Curphay was thinner than her Da, but it would do the job.

She grabbed a jacket and zipped it over the pack. Curphay mimicked her actions. Tentatively, she opened the door and looked up and down the corridor. Red lights lit the hall in a repeating pattern, but no alarm was heard. It must be a level one alarm. She slipped out, closely followed by Curphay and locked the door behind them.

She held a finger to her lips and beckoned Curphay to follow. She could hear his clothes rustle, but there was nothing to be done about it. Curphay wasn't used to stealth. He wasn't used to a lot of things she was used to.

At the end of their corridor, she looked both ways before turning left. This path would take them around the edge of the Arboretum, past Medical and out into the trading platform. This path also avoided all surveillance. The platform was near the shuttle bays so that trade was sequestered from the rest of the community.

She glanced at Curphay and watched red and blue light flash across his skin leaving his eyes in shadow. His brow wrinkled in worry or concentration. She wasn't sure which. She peered around the corner and saw a doctor walking to Medical. She pushed Curphay back against the wall and waited for the man to pass.

The heels of the Doctor's boots clicked on the graphene tiles briskly. He didn't give the hallway a glance as he passed. Amione let out the breath she had been holding. She peered around the corner and saw the Doctor enter Medical. They turned right to continue down the corridor leading to the trade platform.

Groupings of potted trees blocked them from view. She observed the platform, scanning the open area and making sure there weren't any guardians. Curphay squatted next to her.

Her heart pounded as adrenaline surged through her veins. The electromagnetic fields made everything feel hyperreal. She could taste the colors floating in the air, metallic with a hint of lemon. It was a side effect of her optical implants, happening to 10% of recipients. She was one of the lucky few.

The trading platform was abandoned except for a couple of vendors who entertained a visitor.

They kept an eye on the vendors while making their way silently across the platform. They reached the hallway to the shuttle bay.

The sky darkened as Saturn eclipsed the sun. True night was falling on Titan. She never got over how beautiful the rings looked during true night. The other moons of Saturn hovered at different points in the sky.

They reached the end of the corridor. She peered around the corner, and smiled in relief when she saw her friend in the shuttle control booth. Making sure he was alone, she walked confidently up to the door and tapped the glass.

Reikan Vejar jumped, then his violet eyes warmed in recognition. They had been schoolmates for most of their lives, and one of the few people who liked her quirky chaotic ways. He pushed his raven black hair off his forehead and his golden cheeks warmed to a rosy hue, giving interest to an otherwise ordinary face.

He punched in a code and beckoned her into the booth. "Amione what are you doing here." He grinned, then gave a quizzical look at Curphay.

"I need your help." She moved to the corner of the booth where no one from the outside would see them and sat on the floor.

Curphay followed suit, looking at Reikan with interest. Reikan blushed a deeper shade of red. Amione watched the exchange with a raised brow.

"Uh, sure. What can I do for you?" Reikan gave her a perplexed smile.

"We need a shuttle to the surface."

Reikan sat on a stool and folded his arms across his chest. "We are on lockdown."

"I know that, Reikan. Which is why I need your help." She gave him a pleading look.

He shifted nervously.

"We would really be in your debt if you could help us." No one could resist Curphay when he chose to turn on the charm.

Amione looked at her friend and stifled a laugh when she saw him bat his eyes at Reikan.

"Well...I could do a workaround. But Amione, why are you going down there?" His violet eyes were filled with trepidation.

"I have to see it, Reikan." Her voice grew soft and serious.

Realization made his cheeks pale. "I'm not going to be able to talk you out of this, am I?"

She shook her head, pressing her lips together in determination.

He sighed, and gave her a bemused shake of his head. "Ok, Amione. Go to Bay 3. I'll make the necessary prep. When you hear the calipers unlock you can board. I can't promise that you won't be detected, but by the time you are, they won't be able to do anything about it. You will have a lot of explaining to do when you come back though."

"What about you?"

He smiled crookedly, then blushed again when he noticed Curphay looking at him. "I'll be alright. The calipers are always malfunctioning in that bay."

"Thank you, Reikan. I owe you!"

"You definitely do." He smiled, shyly glancing at Curphay.

They slipped out of the booth and made their way to Bay 3.

"You are incorrigible." She laughed.

"Reikan is cute. Why didn't you tell me about him sooner?" Curphay accused.

"I didn't think he was your type."

"Tall, dark hair, and gorgeous violet eyes? What's not to like?"

She sighed and turned her attention back to their destination.

It was one of the original bays before the city was refitted with five new ones. The markings were pockmarked from repeated pounding from shuttle engines over the decades. It had been ages since this one was refurbished. Like most things the Company maintained, it was the bare minimum. The bay doors could be activated from the booth, but since this was an older bay, the mechanisms also responded to shuttle controls.

The shuttle itself was a standard Dracon class. It held two pilots, and 12 passengers. Normally it was in near constant use, but since Titan was going into true night, it sat idle. A fine film of Titian dust covered most of the exterior. A vacuum system got most of it, but there seemed to be a perpetual yellow hue embedded into the hull.

She pulled on one of the suits and indicated that Curphay follow. They were orange with dingy white reflective straps. She helped him pull the suit over his head and buckled and fastened everything into place. He did the same for her. She placed her helmet on and latched it, checking the indicators as they sparked to life on the inside of her visor. Curphay had trouble getting his to latch. So, she pounded it until it finally complied.

"Do your indicators work?" she asked.

She wondered if he had heard her until she heard static in her auditory.

"Yes."

"Good." She pulled her gloves on and made sure the seal was in place. She checked his gloves and gave him a thumbs up.

The calipers clicked open, releasing the shuttle.

"That's our cue." She couldn't keep the excitement out of her voice.

"Goody." Curphay's voice sounded flat.

She ignored him and exited the booth into the bay itself. She punched in a code on her forearm console and the shuttle doors unfolded. She purposely walked up the ramp and inside the dark shuttle. Lights sprang to life on the consoles. Once Curphay was inside, she closed the doors. She seated herself in the pilot's chair and Curphay took the other seat.

"Have you ever flown a shuttle?"

"I haven't flown anything before."

She grinned at him irreverently. "Don't worry, I'm a professional."

"Great. I feel so much better." Curphay rolled his eyes.

"You need to buckle up buttercup, we are going for a ride." She couldn't keep the excitement out of her voice as she slid the restraints into place and tapped on the panels in front of her. The engine hummed to life. She saw Curphay hastily pull on his restraints. She hit the control to open the bay doors. Alarms blinked to life, warning anyone in the bay that it was about to be depressurized. The doors opened at a slow deliberate pace.

She fidgeted in her seat, waiting for the doors to be open just wide enough for her to slip through. Her screen indicated that the forcefield was in place and no atmosphere leaked out of the bay. Finally, the doors were open wide enough, she tapped the panel and the shuttle shuddered into the air. She could hear Curphay draw in a sharp breath.

She punched the engines. They screamed out of the bay doors and out into the mists of Titan. Once outside of the City's influence the shuttle dropped as it adjusted to the change in pressure. Curphay yelped and she chuckled.

"Hold on!"

She barrel-rolled through the canopy and pulled the nose up once they were through laughing hysterically. A surge of adrenaline made her heart skip as she felt the controls respond to her seamlessly.

"Not funny, Amione!"

She glanced over at Curphay who had his face covered.

"It was kind of funny."

"I almost threw up!"

"Ah. It has a good filtration system in that helmet."

"Not that good."

"Oh, so you are in the habit of throwing up in your suit?"

"Ha ha. Smart ass."

She checked her monitors and kept communications off just in case a patrol tried to raise her. She programmed in the destination. It was several kilometers west of where Demeter was orbiting. Overhead she could just make out the shadow of the Derelict. It looked like their orbit had decayed again because the stabilizer poked through the canopy. The last time that happened they had to scramble to give it an orbital assist.

She pushed it out of her mind as she flew towards the Company's main mining facilities. Since night was coming, there would only be a couple people there to keep an eye on things. Her Da used to have to do night watch from time to time when she was little. She hated it.

True night wasn't the best time to go to the surface, but it was also a time when very few people were on the surface. She had a feeling that whatever she found, she didn't want any witnesses.

Chapter 12

All-Consuming

"It's good to have put yourself in someone else's skin. It's all-consuming."
Natalie Imbruglia

As the creature moved closer, Oal noticed several things. It was round in the center with undulating fins around the midsection. A long fleshy tail trailed behind it, stablizing its path in difficult interstellar medium.

The Sadool tried to intercept the creature. It took all of Oal's will to keep them exactly where they were. He had no intention of allowing the entity to devour the creature before they could ascertain if it was a friend or foe.

"Let me go to it," the Sadool hissed.

"If it is sentient, others might come if you kill it, then our journey would be over." Oal prayed that would be enough to make it pause. It worked. Oal felt the tension between them ease.

The creature slowed to a stop. For a while nothing happened. Then it switched from color to color with bands of black delineating each color. It cycled faster and faster until Oal became dizzy from observing the it. Oal sent a quick warning to his companion before the creature struck.

The creature released an electromagnetic pulse, pushing him away, and ripping the Sadool from his orbit. His momentum took him further and further from their position until the creature was only a blip. He could not "see" the Sadool, but that was not unusual. The Sadool was a creature of darkness. It would have repelled the wave and remained behind.

Oal tried returning to his previous position, but without the Sadool he was helpless to combat the interstellar currents. He saw the creature strobe and flash. Then it was swallowed by darkness. A small bit at first, then more and more of the creature disappeared from sight.

The Sadool had consumed it after all. They had agreed! Well, ok. Maybe agreed was much too strong a word.

Oal tried to get back to his previous position again, but all he could do was keep monitor the space he had last seen the creature. The interstellar currents were gentle but persistent, and despite Oal's best efforts, he slid further and further away. He resigned himself to the fact that he would just drift to the next place wherever that might be.

Space seemed colder, and certainly lonelier. He was startled to find that he missed the Sadool. For a massless being it sure had made an impact on his life. He was convinced he needed to be away from it, but now that he was. All he wanted was for the Sadool to return.

Particles grew denser as he passed near a small star. There weren't any habitable planets in the system, and he continued to drift. Having control over his own direction had been intoxicating. To be able to determine every single move he made, was novel for his kind.

He wondered what his parentage would think of his adventure so far? Probably disapprove. It was not exactly Tromfeldian what he and the Sadool shared.

He sensed the Sadool before he saw it. His form was more substantive. The edges of its being glowed a bioluminescent blue. Faint, but definitely there. It gained on him steadily. It had adopted the round center of the creature, but instead of undulating fins, tentacles reached out searching, sensing.

"Found you." Its voice came out slightly off key. Oal shivered. The decoupling was short lived. The most distrubing thing was that he wasn't sorry.

Chapter 13

Thermodynamics

"Scientists have long been baffled by the existence of spontaneous order in the universe. The laws of thermodynamics seem to dictate the opposite, that nature should inexorably degenerate toward a state of greater disorder, greater entropy."
Steven Strogatz

Amione heard a pop and felt the shuttle shimmy beneath her fingertips. Something had broken on the little ship. They were descending much faster than they should be.

"Uh oh."

"What 'uh oh'?" Curphay's voice sounded strained in her helmet.

She tapped on the console to see what the problem was. It looked like the manifold had completely given out.

"What is it? Are we going to crash?" Curphay's hands gripped the arms of his chair.

"Not if I can help it." She yanked the panel open and pulled out the manual aperture. She would have to land this thing the old-fashioned way.

Rain pummeled the window in front of them. Thick sheets of liquid methane made looking out the window impossible. She would have to rely on her instruments to land. She had never been more grateful for the flying lessons Leto had given her.

The sound of liquid crashing against the hull became deafening. Another alarm blinked to life. She shut it off. The entire cabin shuddered as she pulled the nose of the craft up to slow their descent.

She glanced long enough at Curphay to see he had his eyes squeezed shut, gripping the arms of his chair. She pushed her boots into the console on either side of the manual steering and used all her strength to keep the nose up.

She glanced at the instruments. They had decelerated down to 100kph. Still not enough to land safely. If she could get below 80kph she could switch to hover mode. It would be a rough landing, but they would be in one piece.

More alarms went off. She banked from left to right and back again, hoping to bleed off more speed. She heard Curphay groan.

"Sorry Curph. I need to slow down or we will both be pancakes."

Curphay was silent, not that she was expecting a reply.

"Just a little more..." She gritted her teeth. She saw on the map they overshot the ground base. She adjusted the plan. There was an outpost ten kilometers from the ground base. She should be able to get close to it.

Calling for help was not an option. She would have to explain why they were down there, and she didn't feel like answering their questions. Not when she had plenty of her own.

The speed indicator hit 80kph. She reached for the hover control panel and quickly initiated the engines. The shuttle shuddered again as it switched from orbital to hover. She set the shuttle down on a flat area. She referred to the topographical map, locating the outpost five kilometers from their position.

It landed with a thud. She powered down the systems and rechecked their position.

The rain sluiced down the window in slow moving rivulets reflecting the copper and blue lights inside the cabin. She could see a perimeter pylon's red light refracted through the liquid methane. True night was quickly descending. They didn't have long to get to shelter. It would get much colder before night ended. The outpost would have food, and a CAT, a all-terrain vehicle specifically adapted to the Titian terrain.

She heard Curphay scramble out of the restraints and move to the back of the cabin.

"Are you alright?" She glanced back.

An incredulous laugh buzzed her ear. "We could have died."

"I'm sorry, Curph." She busied herself with shutting down the rest of the systems and setting others on idle.

"No, you're not."

She looked over her shoulder at his tense back. She realized she might have crossed a line with him. "I was just--"

"You were showing off," he said flatly.

She remained silent. He wasn't wrong. Whenever she was dealing with particularly dark emotions, she would do something that made her feel alive. The increase in adrenaline brought her out of her depression on more than one occasion. Maybe there were better ways of coping, and maybe, she was addicted to the sensation of careening out of control.

"You need to promise me something."

She swiveled to face him. "Anything." She wanted to be sure he saw how earnest she was.

He stared at her assessing her intention and nodded. "Do not take unnecessary risks once we go after whatever killed your Da."

She sat very still. Could she promise that? "I will try to restrain myself."

"Amione, what *was* that?" He wasn't ready to let it go.

She sighed and swiveled back to the console. "My chaos."

"You've never done anything like that at Academy." He sat in the chair next to her and stared at her profile.

"That's because Academy is structured, predictable, and it has been the best time of my life."

"Explain."

"There is a reason why residents on Demeter think I'm too chaotic to be a scientist. After my mother left, I would seek out reckless entertainment." She grimaced. That was putting it mildly.

"What does that even mean?"

"It started out small. Climbing the trees in the Arboretum. Then climbing the walls inside the Arboretum. Once I even constructed a glider, so I could glide down to the city center." She chuckled at the memory.

"How old were you?"

"Nine or ten."

"Amione! If I was your Da, I would have been scared."

"Oh, he was. He also recognized why I was doing it. So, he found ways to channel that chaos. Mostly it worked. Sometimes not. Flying was one of the things he and Leto taught me. He also taught me Aikido. His father taught him, and he passed it on to me."

Curphay stared at her with his mouth open. "It's like I don't really know you."

"You know me, Curphay. You know me better than anyone alive." Her voice caught on that last word.

He placed a hand on her shoulder and squeezed. "If you feel chaotic, let me know. I'll do my best to help. Or at least steel myself for whatever you come up with next," he stated dryly.

She looked gratefully at him and was about to say more when the communications console chirped to life.

"Shuttle 36. Alpha Ceti over. You have made an unauthorized trip to the surface. Return immediately."

She contemplated whether or not she should answer. They would come sooner if she didn't at least answer. Maybe she could buy them more time. "Alpha Ceti. Shuttle 36. Negative. We need to do repairs."

There was a long pause. Her leg bounced anticipating what would come next.

"Shuttle 36. Do you need assistance?"

"Negative. We have it handled."

Another long pause made her antsy. They weren't going to let it go. She could feel it. Traveling to the surface had never brought this type of attention before. It could be innocent, or it could be that the Company knew something and wanted to be sure no one went looking for whatever it was they were hiding.

"Shuttle 36. We are sending down a crew to help with repairs."

Fuck. "Acknowledged. Shuttle 36 out."

They didn't have much time. Once they knew who she was, they would be down there fast. So much for a leisurely rest. They would have to get the CAT and go to the site immediately.

She pushed herself out of the chair. "Time to go."

Curphay followed her. "Aren't you going to wait for the repair crew?" She patted the side of his helmet. "Dear Curphay, they aren't sending a repair crew."

His eyes widened. "What does that mean, exactly?"

"It means we have to hurry." She checked her pack, then checked his.

"Wait, are you sure it's worth the trouble? We can still turn back." he asked, as he patiently waited for her to finish her inspection.

"More now than ever. There is definitely something here the Company doesn't want us to see." She patted his shoulder letting him know she was done. Then went to a compartment and rummaged through the equipment.

"But the shuttle…"

"We'll do a visual inspection. I suspect we will need to get something from the outpost in order to fix it. Here, put these on."

She handed him helmet beacons used by the miners to see in the dark tunnels. She showed him how to click it into place on the top of the helmet. It took him a couple tries, but he put it together. She tested her pair and adjusted the intensity using the display inside her helmet.

"How did you do that?" He nodded toward her beacons.

"It should be showing up on your display." She tapped her visor.

"Ah, there it is." Curphay scrolled through the settings.

She pulled two packs out of the compartment under the seat. Additional supplies they might need while down here. Extra food, water, dry clothes, first aid and other things that might come in handy since it seemed they would be down here longer than a few hours.

"This is a lot of stuff just to get a part."

"It's always good to be prepared. Ready?"

He nodded.

She waved a hand over the door panel and watched the doors unfurl. The rain plinked against the metal hull and splashed into the soft ground covered in rounded pebbles no larger than her hand. Most of this part of Titan was covered with them. A little annoying to walk over, but at least they weren't jagged. They had been gently worn down by the near constant rain during the warmer months. She gingerly stepped off the ramp and sank a few centimeters into the detritus between stones.

"Careful. The terrain here isn't like Tor'an or Mars. It's a bit slippery if you aren't careful."

"Got it." Curphay wobbled, then righted himself. He gingerly took additional steps.

She made her way back to the engines to see what might have happened to destabilize the shuttle. One of the panels to the engine housing was crumpled. She pulled a tool out and peeled back the housing. She adjusted the light to a narrower beam and examined the engine. It didn't look too damaged. One of the drives was broken, but nothing else seemed affected. If all went well, she could just replace the part and it would be almost as good as new.

"So, what's the verdict?"

"I think we just need to replace a part and we'll be good." She pulled the damaged panel over the housing uncrumpling it as much as possible so the internal mechanisms would be protected from the rain.

"You think?" He quirked a skeptical brow.

"I won't know until I replace it. They have spares in the outpost." She hooked a thumb towards the pylon with the red eye.

"And you'll fix it before we set out for this place, right?" Curphay's voice was filled with anxiety.

"I told you I would." She grew annoyed.

"I would rather not spend any more time here than we have to." He scanned the deepening darkness.

Titan was now behind Saturn effectively blocking the sun as the moon transited past Saturn's dark side. The only light was what shone through the great rings encircling their parent planet. Trillions of stars filtered through the hazy sky. It was the only time in Titan's revolution that you could see the night sky without Saturn competing for the light.

"It's beautiful, isn't it?" She sighed, looking at the vastness of the cosmos. Humans and their alliance companions had only just grazed the surface of what exists in their sector. There was so much more out there they didn't know.

"Lovely," Curphay said.

She scoffed, "You are a physicist, I thought you would be enamored by the night sky."

"From the safety of my lab, I don't want to actually interact with the cosmos."

She laughed. "You are so odd."

"And you are so anemoic." He chuckled.

"What the hell is that?" She wasn't sure if she should be offended.

"Nostalgic for a time you have never known," he recited with amusement.

She thought about that for a moment. "I suppose I am. Doesn't everyone feel that way, at least a little?"

"Nope. Just you."

It was times like these that she realized just how different she was from most people. Most people didn't wonder about times past and how they were living now. She had yet to meet another person who remotely thought as she did. "Why do you spend so much time with me if I'm so odd?"

"I ask myself that every day."

"Ah ha ha." She laughed sarcastically.

"So where is this outpost?" He shifted in his boots, careful not to step in a soft spot. The rain continued to pelt their suits, but it was freezing into sleet as the temperature dropped.

She closed the hatch to the shuttle and consulted her display. "It's this way. Just a couple of kilometers." It was closer to five kilometers, but she wasn't going to tell him that. Bad enough that they ended up off course. They would just need to make the best of it.

She set out in the direction of the outpost carefully navigating the field of stones until they reached a cleared roadway. Two tire tracks bifurcated the land on either side. A slight rise graded upward several meters to the right, and continued to slope away from them on the left. She couldn't have found a better spot to land in an emergency. They should be able to take off quickly once the shuttle was fixed. After that, she didn't know where she would go.

She set her sights on the pylon. Pools of liquid ethane dotted the road, liquid splashing against her boots as she slogged through the freezing muck. She looked over her shoulder, but the shuttle was already out of sight as the road curved around the hillside. Curphay followed close behind, concentrating on his feet.

On some level she knew this trip was foolhardy, but the desire to know what happened burned in her chest. The death of her Da and Leto couldn't have been for nothing. If anything, she wanted to find wrongdoing on the Company's part. If she found proof, they would have to admit that they contributed to their deaths. At the very least, it would save more lives. Mostly, she needed to know for her own peace of mind.

The pylon rose up several meters overhead and below it was the outpost. It was a longhouse composed of graphene, dendrite, and cormaline. It had been there for at least a couple hundred years. At one time it was painted a bright turquoise. The rain had worn down the paint bit by bit and the Company didn't feel it was important enough to repaint.

The red light of the pylon reflected dully in the liquid ethane that coated the roof and walls. Empty containers dotted the landscape. A human size door had a dim light over it and the larger doors were used to accommodate the CAT.

"Finally," Curphay said under his breath.

She smiled inwardly as she examined the panel on the door. It looked new. She frowned. It looked really new, like it had just been installed. Were these new security measures? She hadn't considered that.

"What's the matter?"

She couldn't see Curphay's face clearly through the helmet, but she could tell he was apprehensive.

"New security measures."

"Great." He leaned against the wall by the door. "Should we go back to the shuttle?"

"No, I have an idea. Stay here."

She went around to the side of the building. All of these old outposts had a back entry that very few people knew about. She betted that the Company security didn't know about it. She moved an empty container out of the way and opened the trap door at the back.

Perfect! She carefully made her way down the slick steps to the bottom where a grate drained away the excess liquid. Just as she hoped, this door was seldom used and probably long forgotten. She yanked on the handle and didn't feel it give. She set her feet and gave it another yank and felt the door shudder open. She didn't need it all the way open, just enough for her to slip inside.

Once she had enough room to slide in, she shut the door behind her. Ethane sublimated off her suit in the warmer atmosphere. She went through the enviromodulator until all of Titan was left outside and the earth-like atmosphere stabilized. She took off her helmet and shimmied out of her suit. She went to the control area and punched the panel that unlocked the front door. The two-hundred-year-old analog control panels always amused her. They could have been replaced by the newer wave tech, but true to form, Hesper lived by the adage, if it ain't broke, don't fix it. Which is why the new security upgrade was so curious. They never gave the outposts a second thought before, why now?

Curphay peered inside with sheets of rain pouring behind him.

"Get in here already."

Curphay slid inside the enviromodulator chamber, then peeled off his suit and entered the cabin.

"And people work in those things all day long? How can they stand it?" He held the suit between his thumb and forefinger in disdain before letting it drop unceremoniously to the floor.

"They get used to it. You can get used to a lot when you have to." She shrugged.

He rolled his eyes at her, then examined the interior. The CAT stood ten meters high in its stall. Another stall was empty which was not unusual. They maneuvered CATS all over the site on a daily basis. These were easily a hundred years old. Some were probably older. Nothing got done without a CAT, and in this case, her mission couldn't be completed without one.

The control panel sprang to life once she entered the booth. Displays showed the computer monitoring seismic events, the weather, and others showed a real time map of the area. Copper and blue readouts lit the interior of the cabin, compiling mass amounts of data in a matter of moments. The system was designed on an old quantum computing structure. It was much too slow for the zepto computing capabilities in other places, but then a mining operation like this didn't need the fastest computer, just one that could take a beating from time to time.

She scanned the displays and plucked information from one area to add to her main viewer. At least security wasn't upgraded on the computers yet. Weather maps, seismic activity, reports of unusual activity, maintenance logs, production reports, crew manifests, and production numbers were at her fingertips.

"What are you looking for?" Curphay peered over her shoulder.

"Anomalies." She expanded a log of all unusual instances. There was nothing but a smattering of reports, nothing unusual. Until she got to this year's logs. The number of unusual reports increased exponentially. She looked at the production schedule and matched the increase of incidents with the opening of a new mine.

"We know there was an increase, otherwise why would your Da worry?"

"True. It's not a coincidence that these incidents started going up when they opened the new mine. They disturbed something there." She pressed a finger to her lips as she continued to read through the report.

"All the more reason to let it sleep."

"I don't think the Company has any intention of letting whatever this is, sleep. No, there is something valuable there. Something they know, but won't tell anyone else."

"Then it is only a matter of time before they come for us." Curphay paced away from her.

"Which is all the more reason we have to see for ourselves and take that proof to the Counsel. They can't deny evidence if it is laid out before them." She directed her comment to his back.

"Your faith in people is...refreshing." He looked at her with a mix of wonder and pity.

She glanced at him confused. "Why would someone deny evidence like that?"

"Not everyone has scientific minds like ours. Haven't you noticed that some people simply aren't curious about how things really work?" He gestured in frustration before folding his arms over his chest.

"I suppose so." She thought about Mrs. Cormac and the other residents of Demeter. They were only concerned with how things looked and not how things actually were. "I really don't understand how a person can go through life like that."

"Which is why your home is not on Demeter. It's why you were selected for the ARK, and why you will travel further than any of those people up there. You are designed to see the universe in a certain way. And while those people will never appreciate your brilliance, you have found people who do." For a moment he reminded her of her Da.

She swallowed the lump in her throat. "I'm glad I found you too."

He kissed her on the forehead. "I know you are, Darling. It's one of the many reasons why I love you."

She rolled her eyes at him and continued to pour through the information. She hacked into the camera system. She gave a sound of frustration when she discovered the files she wanted were erased.

She instinctively touched the data crystal hidden in her waist belt. Apparently, she had the only copy. It was good that she hadn't destroyed it at the stranger's insistence. She would use it to convince the Counsel.

"All the video from the attacks were erased."

Curphay frowned. "Are you sure it is the Company that is doing this?"

"I have no reason to believe otherwise. Why?"

"I don't know. Something is not adding up."

An alarm sounded. She quickly brought the map into focus. An orbitor icon descended toward their ship.

"That didn't take long."

"What do we do now?" Curphay asked.

"Eat up and drink something." She pulled a pack from her suit.

He looked confused.

"We won't be able to repair it. I thought we would have more time. We'll have to push on to the site before they can stop us." She closed out screens, downloaded the data onto another crystal and attached that to her suit. At least she had more information than she had before. It wasn't enough, but it was a start.

"They will know what we are up to."

"Hopefully we can talk our way out when they do finally catch up to us." She handed him a ration pack.

"You talk your way out? You wouldn't even plead your case with the instructors. How are you going to talk your way out?" He took the pack from her, looking at her as if she was a stranger.

"The stakes weren't high in those instances. This? It's not the first time I've had to talk my way out of a situation." She wasn't sure how to explain it any better.

"I will have to see that. I'm more comfortable in academia. This is crazy."

"Do you want to go back? You can always say I kidnapped you."

"Not a chance! I'm not going to miss this for all the stars in the universe."

"Good. Because I uploaded a copy of these files to your viewer. It would have been difficult to sell the kidnapping story." She erased all traces of what she accessed and wiped down the board. "Do you know how to fuel up a CAT?"

"Nope."

"I'll show you."

It had taken over an hour to bounce their way down the road toward the new mining sight. She wished she could run without lights, but that would be suicidal. Her only solace was that whoever was following them would not have access to a CAT. That would buy them some time.

The rain had stopped. A rusty haze settled over the surface, making the headlights useless. She switched to night vision, but still had trouble finding the road. Soon that haze would crystalize as the temperature dropped.

Despite her earlier bravado, she was scared. She fidgeted making the steering to wobble. Curphay placed a steadying hand on her arm. That small gesture was enough to quiet her nerves.

The final pylon and its red light pierced the gloom. She headed towards it confident they were close. She wasn't sure how far behind their pursuers were. She pushed the CAT as fast as she dared without sacrificing safety.

Large mining equipment came into view. Peeling white letters stood out starkly against the yellow painted behemoths. Some were taller than buildings. Others had articulated appendages used to extract and remove excess Titian soil. Large hills of detritus were silhouetted against the faint light of the rings.

She maneuvered the CAT behind a large drill on the other side of the clearing. She stopped the CAT. She scanned the clearing. All seemed quiet.

The image of her Da being thrown flashed through her mind. She recognized the configuration of the machine. It was the same machine her Da worked on when he was killed. Her body shook uncontrollably as she blinked back tears and swallowed the sob that threatened to burst from her throat.

A small lake fed into a cave system on the far side reflecting Saturn and the stars. It looked so peaceful, not the site of three brutal murders.

Heavy ethane mist clung to the surface of the pool. Signs of weathering could be seen in the riven cliff walls. The spring months were particularly wet in this part of the moon, and the convective cycle was energetic during this time of year.

She put the CAT on stand-by. The familiarity of the task allowed her to master her emotions. The mine shaft yawned before them. The darkness that lay there was almost enough to make her turn back. Another part of her urged her forward. The answers she was seeking were there. She was certain of it.

"Last chance to eat, drink, and use the privy," she announced.

"Is this it? I can't tell. It looks different from the video."

"This is the place." Her tone was flat and assured.

They opened the doors and climbed out. Amione hopped from the bottom rung to the ground. She shut the door and turned to the site, flicking on a flashlight and examining the terrain before moving forward cautiously. A small weapon was laced to her hip not that it would do any good against whatever had killed her Da. If she was right, it was some sort of semi-corporeal life.

"What if it is a Sadool?" Curphay stepped up next to her.

Images of news feeds flashed through her mind. The Sadool threat was not new. Every couple of years, one would attack a transport and it would be lost. No one had actually seen them. They blended into the darkness so completely, that the only evidence that anything was wrong were the frantic maydays that went out just before the complete destruction of the ship.

"I've never heard of a Sadool doing something like this. Just ships, no people." In truth, she wasn't sure.

"Maybe."

"I have a feeling this is not going to be what we expect."

Curphay snorted. "You don't sound like a scientist right now."

"Maybe not. Maybe I sound like a grieving daughter." She set her mouth in a grim line.

Curphay sobered. "I'm sorry, A."

"Don't be. I know you are anxious, and that's how you deal." She patted his arm.

"Still, I shouldn't--"

"Forget about it." She stepped forward and examined the ground. The rain and wind had obliterated whatever evidence had been there long ago. She squinted at the machine, trying to see if there was any evidence that a man died there. There were none. It stood there, stoic against the night sky unmoving.

She touched the cold metal and closed her eyes. She didn't want to keep seeing that image in her head anymore. He was gone. This was where it happened.

She understood the how. She needed to know the why.

She squared her shoulders and headed for the mine opening. "This way."

She heard Curphay follow. They closed the gap in companionable silence. Only the occasional drop of rain beat on their helmets. The rest was as quiet as death.

The maw into the hillside opened before her; the drilling machine sat idle next to it. Support struts were built into the tunnel walls. As she neared the opening, copper lights blinked to life, illuminating the slick surface. As they walked inside, lights blinked on, others behind her would blink off as they passed.

She checked her display for seismic activity in the last 48 hours. There was a minor trembler yesterday as the workers were leaving. Not uncommon especially when land was disturbed.

"Will these things hold?" Curphay ran a hand up one of the struts.

"They have been using them for the last fifty years or so. I imagine they are as safe as one can expect." She shrugged.

"You know how to make a man feel better," he replied without humor.

She ignored the last jibe and moved deeper into the tunnel. The hard stone beneath her boots reverberated up her spine and did little to quell the anxiety pooled in her stomach. Usually feeling solid ground beneath her feet was an almost spiritual experience, but right now, she was wondering if she was dooming them both.

She looked behind her and saw that the mouth of the tunnel was obscured as they moved deeper inside. A new light would blink on and another would blink off. Several side tunnels branched off the main one. She ignored the first three, but paused in front of the fourth.

"What do you see?"

"There is something different about this tunnel." She examined the stone. There was a change in resonance. It looked much older than the newly created tunnel they stood in.

"It looks the same to me."

"No, it is definitely older. It's sepia toned. Very different from the blue aura of the new tunnels."

"I'll have to take your word on that."

She had told him about her augmented sight the second year at academy, which he tested on everything he could find. She found his excitement amusing. Eventually, he grew to rely on her judgement.

She stepped into the side tunnel. It narrowed. She contorted her body sideways and slightly bent to thread herself through the fissure.

"I didn't pack my spelunking clothes. I need to go back and get them." Curphay joked.

"Get in here. It's already widening."

She was rewarded with a long-suffering sigh.

Her persistence paid off. On the other side was a lattice structure that looked distinctly organic. Its lacy appearance made it look fragile. She expected that it was anything but.

She searched through the logs to see if there was any mention of this configuration. There wasn't. Either no one noticed, they didn't want to report what they saw, or they did report it, and like all the other incidents, it was hidden from the public by the company

She switched her display to infrared.

"There is heat coming off of these structures." She stepped closer.

"Heat?" Curphay grunted as he squeezed through the small opening and into the strange corridor.

"Switch your display to infrared." She ran her glove over the structures withdrawing it quickly as the entire structure reacted with wave after wave of color.

"You are right. There is a definite heat signature. Does Titan have volcanic activity?"

"It does, but not typically this far north. None of the geological surveys have indicated there is one, but that doesn't mean anything.

Their ground penetration tech isn't that sophisticated. The most it has uncovered is occasional seismic activity and thermal expansion and retraction depending on the time of year."

"I'm not geologist, but this doesn't seem like volcanic activity."

"I agree. Whatever this is, I have never seen anything like it," she mused.

She switched to a metabolic scan just out of curiosity.

"Whoa!" A myriad of colors bloomed.

"What is it?" She could hear the edge of hysteria in his voice.

"Switch to the metabolic," she urged.

"What? That doesn't make sense." He fiddled with his display settings. "What the hell?"

She glanced at him and saw his mouth agape. "Definitely not seismic."

"Is it alive?"

"It must be."

"But there is no life on Titan."

"Also, incorrect. We are looking at it." She waved her hand toward the structure.

"The Company had to have known about this. It's not like the tunnel is hidden." Curphay reasoned.

"No, but all record of it is missing. They are trying to cover this up. This is exactly the proof we need in order to convince the Counsel to shut Hesper down." But it didn't answer the question of what killed her Da, and why.

She walked further into the cave carefully stepping around the delicate structures.

"We have your proof, Amione. We should go back and show our findings."

"We have nothing yet," she insisted. "We have some non-sentient life growing in a cave. This is no more remarkable than the butterflies we use to pollinate the plants in the Arboretum. Whatever killed Da had a mind."

"It would be enough to get the Company shut down for good."

She gave him a feral look. "It's not enough for me."

She saw Curphay step back, unsure how to proceed.

She switched to night vision. Colors faded from view, replaced with a detailed look at the terrain. She located another opening on the far wall, large enough for her to crawl through. "I'm going in deeper."

"Amione--"

"You can stay here if you want." She examined the opening. There was a larger chamber on the other side. She turned sideways and put her leg through the opening, then her shoulder and finally the rest of her body. The indicators on her display showed a ten degree increase in temperature.

Curious. Maybe there was a cryovolcano somewhere nearby.

She heard Curphay scramble behind her. She was relieved he was still with her. She would have to make it up to him somehow. She knew she was being terrible, but something drew her in deeper. She knew the answers she needed was close.

The ground was softer inside the cavern. She felt her boots sink into the muck up to her ankles. She pulled an expandable staff from the forearm of her suit and snapped it into full length. The last thing she needed to happen was to sink into a hole up to her neck. Curphay snapped his staff behind her.

"Which way are we going?"

"Stand next to me and we will test the floor in a semicircle."

She looked at the cavern ceiling several meters overhead. Bulbous stalagmites hung down occasionally meeting a stalactite on the floor. It had an almost spiritual feel to it.

Remnants of fallen stalagmites littered the floor and were partially buried in the hydrocarbon sludge. She wasn't sure how deep these things went, and carefully probed the sludge until she was sure there were no issues.

She checked the chronometer on her display. Two hours had passed. By now their pursuers realized their shuttle was in need of repair and know they had taken the CAT. The tracks they left would be easy to follow. She and Curphay might have another hour before they reached the tunnel.

The cavern floor rose above the sludge. She kept the staff handy just in case and poled her way to the top of the rise. Below she saw what looked to be another organic structure. This one looked like a tree. Scans showed it was not the same composition as the lattice, but it was definitely organic. It grew out of the ground with large curling branches filling the space.

She looked at Curphay.

"Is it alive?" he asked.

She switched to the metabolic scan. "It's definitely alive."

"But how? Is it native here? Or is it something else?"

She felt an overwhelming urge to touch it, to be near it. This wasn't the shadow that killed her Da. It was the opposite. A light emanated from within that grew brighter the closer she got.

Curphay pulled on her sleeve. "What are you doing?"

She tugged her arm out of his grip.

"If this thing is here, the Shadow is likely to be here too. What are the odds that there are two distinct entities here?"

She scanned the cavern, but didn't see any indication that there was any other presence. Then she spotted several spherical shapes on the ground around the entity. She gasped, and quickly made her way down the slope to the base of the tree. She knelt and picked up one of the spheres. It looked exactly like the one in her desk on Demeter.

"What is it?"

"I don't know," she replied.

She turned the sphere around in her hand, noting the tell-tale markings. She switched to her normal sight and like the other, it had an ultraviolet energy signature. The markings varied somewhat from sphere to sphere. They littered the ground beneath the entity. More dangled from the curled branches. They looked like seeds similar to the trees in the Arboretum.

"It looks like a tree of some sort."

"What is a tree doing under the surface of Titan?" Curphay picked up a seed and examined it. "These markings are unusual."

Her Da had been here. The sphere in her room was proof of that. It was likely that was the reason he was killed.

She carefully stepped around the seeds until she was face to face with the trunk. It looked pale in the glow of her helmet. Her display was unable to get much of a reading from it other than it was alive. Though unlike any life she had ever seen. She lifted her hand, hesitating a moment before pressing her palm against the trunk.

A presence slammed into her mind. Images of the stars, various planets, a shadow and a planet filled with millions of trees just like this one, inundated her mind. It was ageless and new. White light enveloped her, blinding her to her surroundings.

The next moment, she stared up at a white-faced Curphay who was shaking her shoulder.

"Amione!" When he saw her eyes were open, he hung his head in relief. "You scared me!"

She tried to push herself into a sitting position and slipped in the muck. "What happened?"

He helped her up, and was startled to see she was approximately thirty meters from where she had been standing.

"You went up to the tree and then, Bam! You flew across the cavern."

Energy hummed in her fingertips. Several images lingered in the forefront of her mind. "I think it was trying to communicate with me."

Curphay looked dubious. "It seemed more like an attack or maybe some kind of defensive barrier."

Her impression of the images might be an aftereffect of the energy. "You may be right. It would seem logical that it would have some kind of defense. I wonder if my Da saw this. There was no indication in his logs."

"Would you put something like this in your logs? If this Company is as heartless as you say it is, they would have exploited it. Still might if they find this place."

She checked the chronometer. "They should be in the tunnels by now. We don't have much time. This tree is obviously not the one who killed my Da."

She shone a light at the cavern ceiling and thought she saw a shadow that didn't belong to the rock formations, but it could have been a trick of the light. She gave the tree a wide perimeter and walked to the back side of the cavern.

"We need to keep going."

Curphay reluctantly followed.

Chapter 14

The Moon

"Behold the mighty rings on our moon's horizon. Changing, and never changing. Only we change as we orbit its mighty girth."
Ardue Glinath, poet from the 23rd Century

The system Oal and the Sadool had been drawn to was small by galactic standards. The accretion discs showed planets in various states of formation; smaller rocky worlds closer to the star, and larger gas planets that grew larger with each revolution.

Objects moved at incredible speeds, hitting, splitting, and moving in different directions until they accreted together to form larger objects. It was violent. It was thrilling. Only a few Tromfeld had ever experienced something similar, which made Oal feel justified for going against the wisdom of his parentage.

After much time, the intense bombardment abated. One planet in particular called to him. Several bands of rings encircled its girth along with several moons. The largest moon had a thick atmosphere and reasonable amount of gravity for his purposes.

He had considered the third and fourth planets, but it would be a long time before the effects of their formation quieted. Besides, his feelings toward this moon went beyond practical and into the spiritual.

Tromfeld's were a spiritual species. For all their knowledge, they believed that something much bigger than the universe drove their existence. Each new bit of understanding gave them awe. Everything worked together in a beautiful convergence of science and magic.

Everything was connected. Everything.

"Are you sure of this place?" the Sadool asked, doubt shading its voice.

"There is plenty of organic material for you to consume. If we remain below the surface, we should be able to weather the worst of the climate," Oal assured the entity.

"Very well," it conceded.

"I need to start becoming more. I can't do that without significant gravity."

"How do you know?"

How did he know? His parentage could have explained it in more succinct terms, but for him it was instinct. There were somethings that he just knew. He tapped into the Continuum and searched for the knowledge that would rationalize his vague assumptions. "Something from my parentage's memory. It is a fact that my species needs gravity to thrive."

"It's an interesting concept and something we share, if only a little."

"How so?" It was rare that the entity shared anything about its existence in Darkness.

"Electromagnetic forces don't seem to affect us, but we live for gravity. You are drawn in by it, but we feel the need to push against it time and again. It's why we live on the edges of galaxy and are not drawn in by them."

"Except for you."

"I guess I am an exception. I was curious. Curiosity is not a common trait for my species."

Oal wondered aloud, "So I feel a pull to this place. Do you feel the opposite?"

"Yes, I feel like pushing away, but I am curious as to where this will lead. Doing the opposite of what is expected has its benefits. I am content to remain here as long as you need.

It was an oddly reaffirming statement. In all the millennia they had traveled together, Oal was still suspicious of the entity's motives despite these moments of sentimentality.

They curled around the edges of the heliopause for a while, observing the continued changes in the system. The inner planets were still being bombarded by asteroids and comets. The impacts sparkled in the darkness. There were a couple of large impacts which created a moon on the third planet and two lumpy moons on the fourth as material was sheared away from the northern hemisphere. Another large impact turned the seventh planet completely on its side.

Oal imagined what his offspring would think of his memories. They were unique. No one in his parentage had witnessed a planetary system form like this.

When the worst of the bombardments ceased, Oal and the Sadool entered into orbit around the largest moon of the sixth planet. It took some time before they located a suitable cavern beneath the surface. And longer yet to find a way inside.

The Sadool's non-corporeal state made the process easier than it would have been otherwise. Armed with Oal's specifications, it finally found a suitable cavern. It led Oal to a crevice in the rockface, and through a series of twists and turns.

Already, he could feel the pull of gravity on his shell. He could not remain in the elements and have a healthy transformation. The moment he broke from his shell he would be at his most vulnerable. Without the Sadool, he might have perished.

"Through here," the Sadool coaxed.

Oal's shell crack painfully. "I can't go much further," he gasped.

"We are close, I promise."

Finally, Oal shimmied through an impossibly small crevice and landed in a large cavern. Hydrocarbon sludge covered the bottom of the floor in a thick slurry that the Sadool delighted in tasting. He could see the entity grow more substantial and felt it wrap itself around his shell and carry him the rest of the way.

"This rise should be ideal."

Oal couldn't speak, the pain became overwhelming. The Sadool gently lay him on the rise, then hovered above him as he went through his change. Each snap and crack caused pain to crash over him in wave after wave. He expanded outward relief replacing the pain. New limbs unfurled. The petals on his head flexed and curled. Relief made rest possible and so he slept.

Chapter 15

Aether

"Luminiferous aether, aether or ether, meaning light-bearing aether, was the postulated medium for the propagation of light. It was invoked to explain the ability of the apparently wave-based light to propagate through empty space, something that waves should not be able to do."

There was change in the atmosphere before Amione noticed anything tangible. Wherever the light touched, shadows retreated, and when the light left the darkness filled the void. The cavern's cathedral ceilings gave the space a spiritual feel, a reverence to whatever presence filled it.

She placed a staying hand on Curphay's arm, pointing to a particularly dark spot on the far cavern wall. At first it looked like any other shadow. Then it moved, slowly, sinuously, down the side of the wall. A mass of black tentacles enveloped, caressed, and slunk across the surface. It used the stalactite to pull itself around the rocks.

She took an involuntary step back and felt Curphay tighten his grip on her shoulder. It was a nightmare come to life. One moment it was real and solid and the next it was phasing into shadow. This is what she saw on the video. This is what killed her father.

It paused. She couldn't be sure, but it felt like they were being examined.

Curphay tugged on her arm, but she resisted. She felt his arm snake around her waist as he lifted her off the ground and started running back the way they came. It followed, disappearing into the shadowy ceiling of the cavern.

They dropped to their knees on the slushy floor. She pushed herself to her feet, pulling Curphay up. They continued to run, hoping against hope that there wasn't a soft spot in the middle of the pool. She looked up expecting to see it dropping on top of them, but there was nothing.

"Faster," she yelled hoarsely.

Her body screamed in protest as she pushed harder toward the entrance. There was no way they were going to keep up this pace. Halfway across the pool, she saw the shadow materialize into something humanoid in shape. Tentacles draped across its shoulders like a cape. A face forme. Glowing red eyes stared back. It held up a tentacle.

Curphay and Amione slid to a stop arm in arm, watching the entity. She searched the cavern to see if there might be another way out, but if there was, she couldn't see it. She turned her attention back to the creature.

It glided forward, looking from her to Curphay. Amione shook.

"I'm sorry, Curphay." Regret pulled at her words.

"It's ok, Amione. If I didn't want to be here, I wouldn't be." His voice was hushed, trembling at the last word.

"Still...I shouldn't have been so impetuous."

Tentacles reached out, one for her and one for Curphay. It made contact with her helmet, then through the shell as if it wasn't there. It materialized and pressed against her bare forehead. Red eyes bore into hers.

The tentacle did not feel wet or slippery as she expected. The touch was gentle, almost like a caress. She relaxed when a stream of images filled her mind. She involuntarily closed her eyes. She thought she was screaming, but everything was muffled as if she was underwater.

Stars, planets, the tree, and an endlessly deep void poured through her mind. Images of her own childhood, sights, sounds, feelings were drawn out like a torrent of water pouring over the waterfalls in the Arboretum.

The exchange slowed to a trickle, and she slumped to the ground unconscious.

She woke laying on her side, but she was not in the shallow pool of methane where she expected to be. Instead, she was on the rise where the tree stood. Her mouth felt dry. Her neck ached from being in an unnatural position within her suit.

She checked her display, but nothing worked. Her heart skipped a beat. It wouldn't work because they were on power saving mode which meant they had been in there much longer than she intended. They had to get back to the outpost or they would suffocate.

She pushed herself up, grunting at the effort. All of her limbs were stiff. She looked around quickly locating Curphay. He lay on his back near a cluster of seeds. She crawled to his side and looked inside his helmet. His eyes fluttered and she sagged in relief.

"Curph! Wake up." She shook him, he didn't move. "Curphay!"

"He will sleep for a while longer. It will give us time to speak." A disembodied voice floated through her helmet.

She looked around for the source. "Who is this?"

"Who I am is not important. You have something that belongs to us." The voice was not human although it was a reasonable facsimile. It had a staticky quality as if the voice was piped through a shoddy radio receiver.

The sound seemed to come from the tree, but that was impossible. Trees were not sentient. *But maybe this one was*, she conceded. "What could I have that would belong to you?"

"The other human, your parent, took one of my seeds."

Her mind flashed to the sphere hidden in her desk. "You mean these spheres?"

"They are my offspring. It is important that they remain with me until it is time for them to transform." The tree was definitely alive. She could see the electromagnetic resonance change.

"I don't know what you are talking about."

The resonance changed again. "Yes, you do."

Amione clamped her mouth shut. "How do you know that?"

"My companion exchanged thoughts with you. It was not difficult to find the memories."

Amione pressed her lips together. "What else did it read?"

"We were only interested in the location of my offspring." It said.

She was not convinced, but it didn't seem as if it would matter anyway.

"I need a promise that you will return with my child," the tree insisted.

"I could leave and never return," she countered.

"You could do that, and there is nothing I could do about it. But... your friend would stay, and I don't think your suits will keep you alive indefinitely even with my interference."

She looked in horror at Curphay. She couldn't let her friend pay for her mistake.

"What if I won't leave without Curphay."

"Then you would both cease to be," it stated.

She cursed under her breath as she thought over her options. The damn tree was right, she had nothing to bargain with.

"We are a long-lived species. It doesn't matter to us how long we wait. Eventually the child would find its way back to us, but I would rather it was sooner."

"There are people searching for us. What happens if I'm prevented from coming back?"

"You have proven yourself to be resourceful. I am confident you will prove yourself again. But to answer your question, we do have the means to sustain this human's life beyond what your normal physiology would normally allow. And my companion has agreed to bond with you, so that you can accomplish the task."

"Bond with me? What does that mean?"

"You, however, do not have the luxury of time. Maybe a few days. Your environment will run out of the atmosphere you desperately need. You are incredibly delicate creatures. How you have managed to acquire sentience, we don't know."

She bristled at the condescending tone in its voice.

"I would go now if I were you."

The decision seemed to have been made for her. She couldn't let Curphay down. She could either do as the tree asked, and get the seedling, or she could remain by Curphay's side and die. There wasn't really a choice. She had to go back.

She pressed her helmet to Curphay's and whispered, "I'll return. I promise."

She pushed to her feet and stared at the tree that was not a tree. Resentment for being in this situation bubbled up. She needed answers. "I need to know one thing, tree."

"Oal," it interrupted.

"What?"

"My name is Oal."

"Fine, Oal," she conceded in exasperation. "Did my father really take one of your children?"

"He did."

"He didn't know." Amione's replied in outrage. "Why did you kill them? Why did you kill my Da?"

"We didn't."

She turned from the tree and made a sound of frustration. "But I saw the shadow. It had to be you."

"It was not us."

"If not you, then who?" Amione couldn't believe it. Her Da, Leto, the others were dead, and she still didn't have answers.

"We don't have the answer you seek, but perhaps we can help."

"I have more questions."

"I promise to answer them once my child is home again."

Amione hesitated a moment longer. She hated being manipulated, but wouldn't she be just as ruthless if it were her child? She went down the rise and onto the path out of the cavern again.

She still felt adrift. All the anger she harbored, dissipated into a black despair.

She had to get the seedling and bring it back so Curphay could leave. She wished she had left well enough alone. Now everything was wrong.

Her Da and Leto's death was wrong, and Curphay had been taken hostage. If she didn't come through, he would die. A sob escaped. Curphay was in this position because of her.

The entity glided into view on her right.

"What do you want?" She glared at it.

Its red eyes flickered within unnamed emotions.

"I go with you," it intoned. Its voice was raspy, as if it had not been used in a very long time.

"I would rather go alone." She walked down the rise toward the cavern entrance.

"You will need me."

She increased her speed. "Haven't you done enough?"

"No. It was my inattention that allowed one of you to take the seedling. I must make it right."

She was surprised by its desire to make amends.

"Won't that happen again if you aren't here?"

"No. I was careless. I have placed new barriers to keep your kind away."

"Can't you just materialize in the City and take the seedling?"

"It doesn't work that way. I must be attached to a willing being to do that. Our natural state is the noncorporeal."

Her eyebrows raised. "Noncorporeal?"

She started forward again with the Shadow trailing next to her.

"I need to do this for Oal." The Shadow didn't have human emotions, but she could swear that she heard regret in its voice.

She continued to trudge through the deepening muck in silence until they reached the opening to the mining tunnel.

"I can go no further with you unless you are willing to accept me." It floated next to her phasing from substantial to a near invisible mist.

She looked at the shadow entity dubiously. "No thanks."

She went to step through and was blocked by the entity. "You will not complete your mission without me and your friend will die. You will need me." Its red eyes bore into her.

She stepped back and assessed its intent. The low oxygen indicator blinked on distracting her. She only had twenty minutes of oxygen left. It would take longer than that to get back to the CAT. If she died, then Curphay died.

She growled in frustration. "Fine, but as soon as this is done, you leave."

The creature lifted a tentacles. "Good. I will provide air for you so you can return safely, and I will help you when you run into obstacles."

"When?" She raised a brow at its choice of words.

"The probability is high."

"What do I have to do?" She spread her arms out in resignation.

"Do not resist."

"Why? What's going to happen?"

"It will be easier if you do not resist," it clarified, its tentacles flowing around its form.

Remembering her Akido lessons, she shook out her limbs and cleared her mind. She drew in a deep breath and let it out slowly, trying her best to ignore the low oxygen alarm. She drew in another breath. "Ok. I'm ready," she exhaled, even as a knot of anxiety grew.

It moved forward, then phased out of existence. Shadowy mist filled her helmet. She felt as if she was breathing in something wet and heavy. She panicked, but willed herself to remain calm as the presence curled itself around her consciousness. She felt its presence waiting in the back of her mind.

"Now what?" She noticed the low oxygen indicator no longer blinked.

"Now we go to your home." Its voice sounded hollow in her mind.

She stepped through the opening and among the latticed creatures that filled the previous chamber. The main mining shaft remained in darkness. If someone had passed through, they were gone long enough for the lights to turn off. Maybe she would be able to skate by them and take their craft back to Demeter.

She worked through several scenarios. Maybe she could elude them long enough to make repairs and return the shuttle to Demeter, or she would get caught and find a way to get out of the inquiries. Somehow.

None of these scenarios were appealing. The need to get Curphay back to safety was all that mattered.

She paused before the opening into the main tunnel. She listened for anything that sounded out of the ordinary. There were no motors, no voices, and no footfalls. She had expected them to be crawling all over these tunnels, but nothing. Where were they?

"Any suggestions, Shadow?" She wasn't sure what else to call it. Shadow seemed appropriate.

"You are worried the lights will come on when we walk out of this tunnel. They won't."

She was confused. "Why not?"

"I have disabled them."

"How? They are on a closed circuit."

"It is a simple manipulation of the molecular cohesion of this structure. Easy."

She laughed to herself. "Piece of cake."

She could feel Shadow's confusion. "What does an edible confection have to do with it?"

She mentally shook her head. "Nothing, it is an Old Earth saying."

"Old Earth." It sounded out the name carefully, curiosity filtered through their connection.

"Later, Shadow, we need to leave this place." She slid out into the shaft and as Shadow had promised the lights did not work. If it could do that, what else could it do?

What she really wanted to do was to become invisible. If someone happened upon her in this tunnel there would be nowhere to hide. She could hear dripping ethane toward the entrance. She picked up her pace.

A figure appeared around the corner. Their face was illuminated by the helmet.

She froze. They were staring right at her. Panic bubbled to the surface. She had barely gotten out of the side tunnel, and her trek was in jeopardy.

"Remain still," Shadow whispered.

"What?"

"Don't move."

She had every reason to run, but she stayed still anyway. The man in front of her did not acknowledge her. He didn't see her. How was that possible? Her helmet was the same type of design. He should have definitely seen her. She held her breath as he walked past her down the corridor. Lights flickered on and off as he passed.

"What just happened?" she asked Shadow. She was thinking about being invisible, then she became invisible.

"I concealed you from his eyes."

"But how?" she ran her hands over her body. The Shadow's explanation was inadequate. She didn't feel any different, and yet her entire perception of what was possible was changed forever.

"I will explain later, but for now you need to move. More will be coming this way from one of the side tunnels," it urged.

She bit her tongue and pushed forward to the entrance, glancing down the side tunnels as she passed. She could see faint lights flicker on the sides, but no one was in sight. She moved on eager to get to the entrance and into the CAT.

Once at the entrance, she scanned the clearing. The Pylon's glowing red eye blinked calmly in the slushy rain. Liquid rattled down gutters. Puddles had increased in size since she was down there. Their consistency had changed since the sun had gone down. The temperature dropped 40 degrees. Methane covered every surface with a think sludge. There was a reason why no one worked during a Titian night. Even the best heated doors would eventually freeze shut. She had to get to the CAT before that happened.

"I don't see anyone." She said.

"They are there." Shadow said.

Power returned to her helmet and her infrared display clicked into place. "There."

The silhouette of a man stood next to the CAT.

"I'm not going to be able to sneak into the CAT without him noticing. Invisible or not." She looked over her shoulder nervously, expecting to be found out as she figured out how to get in the CAT without being detected.

"Then we will use other methods," Shadow stated.

"What does that mean?" She was getting frustrated with the entities lack of candor.

"Do as I say. Walk to the front of the CAT. You will be mostly invisible. There is nothing I can do about the rain, but I can get you close."

"Then what?" Her breathing increased.

"I will instruct you. Go."

She stepped into the sleet and carefully navigated the growing puddles in the middle of the clearing. She tried to keep the sounds of her steps at a minimum, but it was nearly impossible in the slush. She wondered how she was going to make repairs on the shuttle under these conditions.

Out of the corner of her eye, she caught sight of a Runner. They must have brought it with them on their shuttle. The sleek lines looked fast next to the cumbersome CAT. It would take half the time to return to the shuttle. She had never driven one, but it couldn't be that much different from the other vehicles she had used.

"Change of plans, Shadow." She indicated the Runner to her right.

"Can you maneuver it?"

"I think I have to try." She was already looking for data on Runners to download into her visor. There were a surprising number of variations of the same vehicle. She picked one that looked the closest to the version in front of her.

"So be it."

She checked on the guard's position and skirted around the CAT until she was on the backside of the machine. She trembled. She wasn't a big girl and Akido was only going to take her so far in low gravity.

"Don't worry. I'm with you."

She felt strangely reassured though she wasn't sure how the entity would be able to help her. She didn't have time to wonder long, the guard walked back to the Runner. She stepped out from behind the CAT and lunged low with a kick, dropping him to his stomach with a grunt.

He bounced to his feet, sliding a couple feet away from her and simultaneously drawing his energy weapon.

She dove behind the CAT just in time to avoid being hit and drew her weapon. She aimed for his hand and willed it to hit its target. The weapon flew from his hand, and she advanced on him intending to wound him. He kicked her weapon out of her hand and they grappled in the sludge. Being bigger and heavier he easily threw her to the ground.

Shadow pulled something from within her. She stumbled, watching as smoke filled her helmet, expanding outside of her suit. Curling tendrils of smoke took on more substance, reaching for the man standing over her.

Tentacles snapped out and wrapped themselves around the man's arms and legs, yanking him to the ground. The man screamed, desperately trying to get out of the tentacles' grips. Each one drew tighter and tighter. Bones crunched and the man's screams went up an octave.

Her father's death flashed into her mind. She moaned.

"Stop," she called out. She wanted to get away, but was riveted to the spot. "You need to stop. You're killing him!"

Shadow's tentacles stopped compressing the man's legs. "He will come after us." The man's screams were muffled by his helmet, but she could still hear the pain and terror in his voice.

She swallowed back the bile that had risen to the back of her throat. "He is in no shape to chase us. Quickly, the others heard him. We need to go." She slipped in the icy sludge before she was able to stand. Her legs were weak with disgust and terror. Her stomach turned when she saw his misshapen arms and legs. The bones were crushed, but he would live although he would never be the same.

Maybe she should have allowed the Shadow to finish what he started as a mercy, then shuddered at the thought. She wasn't going to stand by and allow it to kill. Images of her Da flashed through her mind.

"Is this what you did to my Da?" Rage built to a frenzy burning away her fear.

"It was not us."

"Then it was something like you. I saw it." She ran as fast as she could skidding to a stop next to the Runner.

"Then there is another. After all this time," Shadow murmured.

"Another what?"

"Another one of my kind. It's been a very long time since I've seen another. They don't venture away from Darkness."

"You did."

"I was unusual."

"I guess you inspired another to do the same." Her mouth was set in a grim line. She hated to think what an army of shadows could do.

"Perhaps."

"What you did to me, could that be done to another?"

"It is the only way we can take form. It must be--"

"--a willing host. Got it."

She examined the entry panel. Fortunately, it was not encoded.

"You won't do something like that again without my permission."

"What I did to the human?"

"Yes. Never again, understood? Or I will undo whatever you did."

"The bonding."

"Yes. Is that understood?"

"Yes. I will not harm the humans unless you wish it."

Whenever she solved a mechanical issue, she found light conversation actually helped her problem solve more effectively. "So what did you do to me anyway?"

"The bonding?"

"Yes, that." The door clicked open. She scrambled up the ladder.

"Oal and I were bonded. We knew it was the best way to accomplish our goal."

"The tree and you were bonded."

Shadow paused searching for reference. "He is not tree. More of a mycological entity."

Amione laughed. "So, he's a mushroom."

"Correct. A mush room."

"What does that make you?"

"Not a mush room," Shadow replied.

Amione laughed again. For a noncorporeal being it was actually kind of funny in a horrifying bone crushing kind of way.

"Why do you make that sound?"

"What sound?"

Shadow mimicked her laughter.

"Because you are funny."

"Funny?"

Flashes of light danced at the mine's entrance.

"We need to go," Shadow urged.

She took one last look at the man lying in the rain. She waved her hand over the panel to close the cockpit, hastily orientating herself. A red button blinked. How quaint. She pushed it and the Runner hummed to life.

People ran out of the mouth of the mine, heading toward her. She turned the Runner onto the road back to the shuttle. Then engaged the thruster which threw her back against the seat as it accelerated.

She set the guidance to find the shuttle and watched as the road sped beneath its tracks. Sleet pelted the windshield, providing low visibility. Her monitors cut through the interference with no issues. She wished she could keep the Runner. It was much nicer than the CAT. The seat hugged her in the right places. The controls were adjustable. It had a vintage feel to it that reminded her of some of the Old Earth machines she had seen.

And it was fast. It would take less than an hour to get back to the shuttle. She needed a plan.

She found the controls to the scrubber and hooked her suit into the system to replenish her oxygen. Her mind turned to Curphay lying beneath the tree in the cavern. Mushroom. Whatever. What if he wasn't alright? What if this thing was using her to get off the surface?

"I assure you; we will keep our word."

"Can you read my mind?"

"You have very distinct thoughts."

She shook her head involuntarily trying to shake Shadow from her mind.

"I'm afraid that won't help," Shadow calmly explained. "When you accepted me, we were bound together."

"I don't remember agreeing to *this* level of intimacy."

"Nonetheless, you did. I can't bond with an entity unless they are willing. And you are very willing to help your friend. I can understand that. I am willing to do what I can for my friend."

"I don't feel comfortable with any of this," she growled.

They hurtled past the outpost which looked deserted. Exactly how they had left it hours before. It wouldn't be long before the landing site came into view. She powered down the Runner to half speed and looked for a place to conceal it until she decided how to get to the shuttle without being detected. She located a rise just above the site and guided the Runner off the road. The CAT should be several minutes behind them, and that's if they don't stop off for first aid at the outpost.

She powered everything down and slid far enough forward to view the site below. The sleet had stopped, allowing her to see that the shuttle was exactly where she left it. She telescoped the viewer to get a closer look, then panned to the sleeker, faster shuttle from Yorea. Two crew members stood at attention weapons drawn, looking up the road where they expected her to be. Except she wouldn't be there.

She looked over the panel in front of her. "Computer, locate scattering effect." The appropriate control lit up. That should at least scramble their infrared scanners. "Computer turn off transponder." Another indicator switched from green to red.

She panned the viewer back to her shuttle and drew in a sharp breath. There was someone there. She sharpened the resolution. She gasped.

"What is it?" Shadow asked.

"Who the Hell is that?" She switched displays to a graded view.

"He is not part of the crew," Shadow observed.

"How do you know?"

"The way he is moving. He does not wish to be seen."

She knew who it was. His build was unmistakable, but what was he doing down here? "Well, that solves one problem, but brings up another."

"I do not understand."

"Whoever he is, he is fixing the shuttle. One problem solved. But if I don't get down there before he finishes, we might be left here."

"Can you walk from here?"

She looked out the windshield and saw more weather coming in. It wouldn't be long before it turned into ice and eventually snowfall. It wasn't impossible to walk in the stuff, but it wouldn't be fun.

"It looks like I don't have much choice."

She unclipped her helmet.

"What are you doing?"

"Unlike you, I *need* sustenance. You know. Eat. Drink."

She pulled off a glove and pulled her pack around to the front. She brushed off the residue from the outside and opened it. She pulled out a protein pack and a bag of water and quickly downed them both.

"It's a curious method for consumption."

"Is this your first-time meeting a human?" She was very aware of the absurdity of making casual conversation with a noncorporeal entity that casually broke bones and moved through rock like butter.

"No. I have observed you before. You are very fragile."

She tried not to picture her Da again, but the image came unbidden. She pushed the feeling of loss away. She couldn't give in to her grief. Not right now.

"You keep seeing the same image over and over." She felt Shadow move at the back of her mind.

She scowled not liking the intrusion into her private thoughts. "He was my Da."

"Your parent."

"Yes," she grounded out.

"Your...attachment. It is unusual."

"You don't have parents?"

"No. Oal has parent, but it's not like yours."

"How do you procreate?"

"We just are."

Amione mulled that over as she finished off the last of the water.

"The tree is not fragile?" She changed the subject.

"No, Oal is quite strong. He has traveled millions of your years to this place."

"Traveled from where?"

"I do not know. I found him when I was exploring."

"Where do you come from?"

"Darkness." There was longing in those two syllables.

What must Darkness be like and what kind of creature was both corporeal and non-corporeal at the same time?

"Darkness. The space between the galaxies. It was postulated as a probability, but there was no way for us to know if it truly existed." She recalled some of the latest science papers she used to read in Academy.

"It exists. It is my home."

"This place must seem very strange to you."

"Strange, but interesting at the same time. It was quiet for a very long time before your kind came."

"Well, we have a habit of going places where we shouldn't." She returned her pack to its place and put her helmet back on. She replaced her gloves and checked her O2 levels and made sure her display was working. All systems were nominal. "Time to get off the surface and get you what you want."

She punched the control and the cockpit canopy folded open. She swung her legs over the side and slid down the ladder into the muck. She closed the canopy while scanning the site below. Nothing had changed other than the crew looked restless, nervously scanning the roadway.

The other man continued to surreptitiously complete repairs. She had a lot of questions for him. Like how he got to the surface, and what his connection to all this was. Did he know what she would find? She really wanted to know the answer to that one.

She slid down the rise far from the crew. She was never more grateful for the strange rock formations on the surface. They rose out of the muck as if pushed by unseen fingers. She wended her way through them until she was almost upon the shuttle. She wished she still had her weapon, but it was laying in the mud back at the mine.

She looked at the suit more closely. It was one of the suits from the shuttle. She switched her comms to connect with his suit.

"Hey mister, that's my shuttle you are working on."

He spun around and met her gaze, shoulder's tense. He relaxed when he recognized her. "It seemed like the thing to do."

"Are you done? In about five minutes a CAT will come barreling into the clearing. I would like to be well on my way before then."

"Then you are in luck." He grinned with a lopsided tilt of his mouth. "I just need to tighten this and we can go."

She looked over her shoulder, lights bounced along the horizon. "I'll go in and start the flight sequence."

She ran up the ramp and strapped into the pilot seat. She started the ignition sequence. A few seconds later she heard the man run up the ramp and close the doors. Weapons fire sizzled as it hit the hull. He slammed into the copilot seat and strapped in. Then proceeded to help her with lift off. More weapon's fire pinged against the hull. Not that it would do much damage. They would need something with more fire power.

The shuttle lifted off of the ground. As if on cue, a larger beam of energy seared past her window. Alarms went off, but it was too late. They were off the ground and heading to Demeter.

"We won't have much of a head start." She worried her bottom lip as she deftly guided the craft to a higher altitude.

Suddenly the sky lit up as a bomb detonated below.

He laughed. "You didn't think I spent all my time fixing the shuttle, did you?"

She gave him a sidelong glance. The difference in demeanor was not lost on her.

"I created a cascade failure. As soon as they used their weapon, it was triggered." He seemed extremely satisfied with himself.

She turned sharply toward him. "Are they..."

"Dead? I hope so, the bastards." His mouth twisted bitterly.

She snuck a glance at the hulking man sitting next to her. She hadn't paid attention to his appearance before now. Just that he was disheveled and he was much larger than anyone she had ever met.

His brown hair brushed his large forehead. Bushy brows framed sharp hazel eyes that missed nothing. He had a broad nose that bifurcated a chiseled face with a fuller lower lip. His movements were more purposeful than graceful.

He caught her staring and a smile quirked his mouth as his eyes warmed at her appraisal. She quickly looked away, hoping that he hadn't noticed how her cheeks warmed.

"What's your name?" she asked.

"Willan. Willan Gonzalez."

"Don't you want to know mine?"

"I already know that. You are Amione Dhau."

"What is your deal? Why the crystal? Why were you on Demeter?"

"Did you find anything interesting?" He deliberately changed the subject.

She scowled. "Yes and no."

Careful, Shadow cautioned.

Don't worry I have no intention of giving him information especially about you and Oal. She said through their link.

She flipped the comm system on. "I need to let control know we are returning."

He placed a hand over hers. "Not just yet. We need to make a stop on the Derelict."

Shadow shifted restlessly in the back of her mind. They didn't have time for a detour. "Why?"

"I assume things didn't go well because your friend isn't with you." She narrowed her eyes in suspicion, but his gaze held no subterfuge.

"No, it did not. I need to get back to Demeter."

"Do you think they will let you back on after stealing one of their shuttles and causing a very conspicuous explosion?" He clucked his tongue. "No, honey, you are as much a fugitive as I am. The best place for us at the moment is the Derelict."

She grimaced. If she went back to Demeter, they would detain her, then she wouldn't be able to get the seedling. She needed a new plan. "What is your plan?"

"I have contacts there that can help us get back on Demeter." He gauged her response before adding, "For a price, of course."

"Of course."

She turned her mind to Shadow. *What do you think? He's not wrong. I would be detained and we wouldn't get the seedling.*

We could use my abilities to get by.

No. We have already drawn too much attention to ourselves. I'm not infallible, and I suspect you aren't either. I die, and you will have a bigger problem.

Shadow contemplated her argument. *I could find another host.*

One as willing as I am? I don't think so. Her jaw tensed as they proceeded to puncture a layer of dripping clouds.

I can't fault your logic, Shadow conceded.

Then we go with his plan. Whatever that is. She wasn't entirely sure that was the wisest decision, but it was the best they had at the moment.

I would prefer to know it before agreeing to it. Shadow wasn't easily placated.

He was the one who sent me the video which led me to you. She pointed out.

All the more reason to be suspect of him.

An alarm tripped bringing her attention back to the cockpit.

"What's your decision? Because we are about to have company." The man flipped through several displays before settling on one that showed three blips closing on their position.

"Shit..." she breathed.

He chuckled softly at her expletive. "They will try to ground us."

"They can try," she said through gritted teeth.

She worked some of the controls to see if she could boost their speed and headed to the Derelict.

"So, you have made your choice." His baritone caressed her ear, making her shiver.

"It's not like I had much of one. Let's hope your patch job holds up." She nosed the shuttle toward the canopy, watching as the blips steadily gained on her. Weapons fire sizzled past her window as the lead fighter caught up to them. It was a warning shot. She wouldn't get another.

The comm pinged. She ignored it and barrel rolled back through the canopy with the lead fighter close behind. She could feel the pull of Gs on her chest as she pushed the engines to their limits, then pulled back on the throttle. All three fighters flew past her toward the surface then split off into three separate directions in the hopes of forcing her to ground.

Two fighters came from either side shooting at their shuttle. One grazed the top of the shuttle, causing the enviros to collapse. There was still plenty of oxygen in her suit so she wasn't concerned. She wasn't sure about her companion. She banked and avoided the fire of the other fighter. Then she headed straight for the lead fighter.

"Are you crazy?" He gripped the edge of the console, while trying to hammer down the enviros.

She ignored him and set her sights on the fighter before her. If they wanted her dead, they would have to hit her. They wanted her back alive. At least, that was her theory. She intended to play chicken with the fighter to see who flinched. She pushed the engines harder.

The fighter increased in size. She kept her focus. She couldn't change course even if she wanted to at this point. Either he would move or they would be dead. At the last possible second the fighter moved to avoid collision it's wing grinding with the hull of the shuttle as it passed.

She pulled up and watched as the blip of the lead fighter faded from view. The other two fighters broke off pursuit and she throttled down, returning their heading toward the Derelict.

"Fuck, that was intense!" The man looked at her with a mixture of awe and as a man who knew he had narrowly missed death.

She made sure she didn't react, but secretly she was pleased that he was impressed.

The comm pinged again, this time it was from the Derelict.

He opened the display. "This is Willan Gonzalez. Requesting permission to dock."

"Willan is that you?" A husky feminine voice crackled over the airway.

"It is, love. I've brought you a present."

"I can see that. A shuttle from Demeter? You shouldn't have!" She chuckled. "Dock on the leeward side. We'll get you squared away."

"I have pursuers from Yorea. Let the Magistrate know we need Scramblers to remind them that this is not safe ground."

"That was some fancy flying."

"I wish I could take credit. Can you let me know when they are launched?"

"You got it."

"Thank you. Can you get me into a Clean Room? A wipe down wouldn't be out of the question."

"I'll see what I can do. Derelict out."

"Clean Room?" Amione couldn't fathom what that meant.

"Washing up. Getting clean. I haven't had a decently clean thing since I escaped from Yorea to give you that data crystal."

"Why did you steal that data crystal?" Amione pinned him with a look before turning to the controls.

"All in good time, Amione. All in good time."

She scowled. She didn't like any of this, and she needed to get back to Curphay. A pang of anxiety fluttered in her stomach. What if she failed?

You won't fail. We will get the seedling somehow. Shadow would have sounded encouraging except there was an edge to its thoughts that she found disturbing. She could feel it slither through the back of her mind, waiting for any opportunity to complete the mission.

Let's see how this goes. Then we'll talk, she promised.

Chapter 16

Emergence

"Out of suffering have emerged the strangest souls; the most massive characters are seared with scars."
Khalil Gibran

Oal was no longer a seedling. Without his shell, he was vulnerable to the elements, but the cave provided protection. Though not as cold as deep space, his new body felt the effects of his new environment. New sensitivity brought a new appreciation for life.

This moon was not like the planet he was spawned from. That one was an oxygen nitrogen atmosphere. This one was Nitrogen and methane, so cold that the methane fell like water from the sky. It seeped through the rocks and created stalagmites and stalactites throughout the cave system. Strangely enough, he was able to sustain himself on a small amount of these complex hydrocarbons.

It felt good to dig his petals into the slurry and draw up whatever sustenance he needed. He quickly grew from just under ten centimeters to a full meter in relatively quick time. The Nitrogen was particularly useful to his growth. He breathed it in as quickly as he was able to breath out. The initial weakness faded replaced by steadily increasing strength.

The Sadool was enamored by the moon. It was able to consume organic material in greater quantities, and learned the pleasures of corporeal existence as well as its limitations. For the first time in its life, it understood what beings of Light experienced, and it wondered if life started in Light, or in Darkness as it had always believed. There was no way to know for certain.

He should have learned all there was to know about Darkness. Instead, he chose his curiosity and found Oal. It felt an obligation to regret the decision, but deep down it was glad that it had chosen this path. It was sure no Sadool had ever experienced corporeal existence. If they had, they would leave Darkness in droves.

One thing both the Sadool and Oal did not understand was this strange connection they possessed. One seemed to enhance the other's attributes and abilities. Things they should not have been able to do alone became possible whenever they were together.

"I should not be able to levitate any more once in this state, " Oal commented as he and the entity floated to the roof of the cavern.

"And yet you are. I should not be able to take corporeal form, and yet here I am."

They shared a moment of amusement.

"What do you think our parentage would say if they saw us?" Oal wondered.

"I imagine my elders would tell me that I am violating the sacred truth and that no good can come of it," the Sadool expressed wryly.

"Do you believe that?" Oal flexed one of his limbs.

"I have never believed it. It was why I chose to explore the Light instead of remaining in Darkness," the Sadool stated with conviction.

"You are doing more than exploring the Light." Oal couldn't keep the amusement from his voice.

"Perhaps." The entity was unwilling to abandon everything he learned no matter how true Oal's statement was. "What about your parentage?"

"We were taught to fear Darkness. That it would consume us." Oal imbued his words with reverence.

"Obviously not, I would have done it already."

"You what?!" Oal gasped. "Did you try to consume me?"

"Of course not." The entity stated in a way that suggested he had at least entertained the idea.

"You did! You tried to consume me!"

"I might have tasted you when you were hibernating. Once," the entity equivocated.

"You are unbelievable." Oal shook with anger.

"This was before I knew you well. I would never do something like that now." The entity reasoned.

"I'm not sure what to even say. I would never have tried to consume you."

"Hard to consume something that isn't corporeal."

"That is beside the point." Oal turned away from the entity.

The Sadool hovered close to Oal. "Are you mad?"

"A little."

"Are you going to stay mad?"

Oal turned on the entity. "I should! I should stay mad for at least a millennium."

"But you won't." The entity correctly assessed.

Oal's limbs drooped. "No. It was long ago as you said. It was just a shock to learn my fears were confirmed."

"We are both long lived species. I can't believe we have never met before." The Sadool wrapped a tentacle around a stalagmite and pulled itself across the cavern ceiling. "Perhaps that is why you cannot be consumed by us. You evolved in a way that makes that impossible."

"It is a big galaxy and an even bigger universe. We have only met a handful of beings and none were sentient by our standards," Oal concluded. "If my ancestors met a Sadool, there is no record of it."

"Perhaps those other species are so short lived that their civilizations rise and fall before we ever see them," the Sadool posited.

"Perhaps," Oal mused. "But we are here now."

"Yes. I could exist here for a very long time."

"Do Sadool die?"

"Die?" the entity swirled around Oal carefully lowering him to the ground.

"Cease to exist," Oal clarified.

The Sadool contemplated the question. "Not exactly."

"My people come from a seed, we grow, then we take root. Eventually we die after millions of years."

"It must be constrictive, remaining in one place for so very long."

"Strangely, no. We are designed with wanderlust for a short time, we find a place to take root, then we connect with the network to share our knowledge."

"And this is the place?" The entity wandered the cavern, testing its ability to become substantial.

"It feels like a good place to be. I could safely live here and eventually pass on my seed."

"Not for a while."

"No, not for a while."

"Then what shall we do?" The entity curled around the formations on the ceiling and drifted back down to Oal.

"I need to grow stronger, and then we shall explore everything this moon has to offer." Oal flexed his limbs and stretched them as far as they would extend. He needed to relish the sensation while he could. Eventually, his limbs would stiffen, and such movement would be impossible.

After a pause.

"I still can't believe you tried to consume me." Oal's limbs shook in outrage.

The Sadool ignored him and morphed through the cavern wall.

Chapter 17

Adhesion

"Out of association grows adhesion, and out of adhesion amalgamation."
Charlotte Bronte

The Derelict looked more fragile up close. The stabilizer had dipped beneath the cloud deck once again. The only lights she could see were the basic red lights that warned craft there was a city there. Modules not originally designed for the Derelict stuck out at odd angles. Thrusters would normally be enough to keep the city's orbit from degrading, but the new additions made the entire structure heavier and more cumbersome.

Several turrets housed phase weapons. It was one of the reasons Yorean patrols didn't try to venture into the city's air space. The Derelict had teeth, and they weren't afraid to use them to defend themselves.

As they approached the bay doors, a series of old-style crafts and a few newer models were tethered to the outside of the city in a precarious web. She handed control over to Willan. She was a good pilot, but she wasn't about to attempt to navigate this particular labryinth.

She watched him out of the corner of her eye as his brow furrowed in concentration. Deftly he maneuvered between ships that were stacked four high. He threaded the shuttle through them with practiced ease. Except, she knew it wasn't that easy. She noticed a thin layer of perspiration covering his upper lip.

He found a slot and docked the shuttle. She gave the bay a cursory glance. It looked like the original bay, which was completely open to the elements. A hatch extended covering the shuttle door.

Her knee bounced as they waited for the light to turn green green indicating the seal was good.

He powered down the shuttle systems. She followed suit grateful that she could expend that excess energy somewhere.

He looked at her for a long moment.

"What?" she asked.

"I'm wondering if you are going to be ready for this." His voice held a note of caution, and his hazel eyes were serious.

"Ready for what?" She could feel her anxiety rise again.

"I know that there are stories about Derelict being over populated, but I don't think you appreciate what that means. I need you to remain calm and stay at my side. Do you understand?" His eyes searched hers.

She nodded wide-eyed. She did not understand. Not at all. A small knot formed in her stomach. This was not what she had expected when she decided to find out what happened to her Da. A pang of sadness overwhelmed her for a moment as she wished he was there now to tell her what to do.

Misinterpreting her expression, Willan continued, "Don't worry. I can handle things. People know me here. They know not to mess with someone who is under my protection."

She turned away and unbuckled her restraints. She wasn't comfortable with this stranger attempting to read her. She wasn't comfortable with the situation period. Regardless, she needed to stay alert and remain calm. Someway, somehow, she was going to get through this.

Finally free from the restraints, she stretched her limbs. Fatigue draped over her shoulders, weighing her down. It had been a long several hours and she had not slept since before this started. She stood at the door next to Willan and braced herself for what was to come next.

He waved a hand over the door panel and the ramp unfurled. There was a tunnel leading into a crude enviro-modulator, which she had serious doubts actually worked. The ramp closed behind her. She wanted to run back onto the ship and fly away. Anything was better than facing the unknown.

She looked longingly at the closed shuttle door noting the scoring from phase blasts. It looked far more inviting than the city in front of her. She took a deep breath and caught up to Willan who stepped into the chamber.

It took forever for the enviro to pressurize. In reality, it might have been fifteen minutes, but in those fifteen minutes wild scenarios ran through her mind. What if they imprisoned her? What if they tortured her? She would never get the seed. She would never get back to Curphay. She would never know what this was really all about.

She felt Shadow move in the back of her mind. Just a subtle shift to remind her that she wasn't alone. Whatever abilities it gave her, she wasn't sure it would be enough to fend off a determined army of people.

The doors opened startling her from her reverie. They stepped down a ramp into the middle of a press of bodies. She heard the doors close behind her and fervently wished she was back inside the enviro.

Willan chuckled, making her fume. What did he find so funny all the time?

"Stay next to me." He lightly gripped her elbow and walked to the left toward a glass booth at the back of the bay.

People brushed by her and others pushed her gently out of the way. She could see they were all on their way from one place to another merging and diverging down several corridors that branched off of the bay. Everything was dimly lit by incandescent lighting. Nothing looked like it had been replaced in over a hundred years. Decades of scuff marks marred the floor which likely had not seen a cleaning bot in nearly that long.

They entered the control booth and she sighed in relief. At least there weren't hundreds of bodies brushing against her.

She looked around the booth. It was neat if somewhat cluttered with useless items. A display panel showed older style graphics

"It might be old, but it would be a mistake to think it is inferior." A petite woman with strawberry blonde hair and violet eyes challenged.

"I wasn't—"

"You didn't have to. It was written all over your face. This baby," she patted the computer console lovingly, "can track anything within the Saturn system, and can hack into almost any system."

"I'll take your word for it," she muttered.

The woman had already turned her attention to the man next to her. "Willan, I'm very glad you made it back. I was beginning to worry." The woman batted her eyelashes at him.

Willan removed his helmet, revealing a sweaty mop of hair. "You didn't have to worry, Layna."

"Oh yes, I did! I had a huge bet on you. I would have been pissed if I had to lose because you had gone and gotten yourself killed."

Her laugh was melodic and Amione found herself staring.

Layna hooked her thumb toward Amione. "And who is this?" Her violet eyes raked over her, calculating, before turning her bright smile back on Willan.

An unfamiliar feeling of jealousy rose up. She mentally shook herself. She didn't even know Willan.

Willan turned to her smiling reassuringly. "This..." he paused for dramatic effect. "Is Amione Dhau."

Layna looked at her as if she was a mouse and she was a cat about to pounce. "Ah, your name has come up a time or two. You can take your helmet off now. I promise the air here is just as clean as on Demeter."

Amione ignored the jibe and looked at her curiously. "What do you mean my name has come up?"

She narrowed her eyes. "Nothing beyond the usual chatter."

Amione blinked. Layna was lying. Everyone on Titan knew about her father's death. Was that how Willan got ahold of the video?

She removed her helmet, brushing back her curls while drawing in an appreciative breath. It was good to be back in air that was not recycled a hundred times through her suit.

Willan shifted from one to the other watching both women warily. "Is a Clean Room available? I would like to get cleaned up and I'm sure Amione feels the same."

Layna pursed her lips and nodded. "You can use 3. Nice to meet you, Amione." Her saccharine voice grated on Amione's nerves.

"Same to you." Amione kept her expression neutral as she followed Willan out into the fray.

He gently took her wrist in hand and tugged her behind him as he made his way to wherever the Clean Rooms were. She imagined they were exactly as advertised, a place to get cleaned up.

She felt Shadow shift restlessly in the back of her mind, making her anxiety rear up with a vengeance. Body after body pressed against her. Her breath got shorter. Perspiration dotted her forehead. An over-whelming pressure built in her chest. Sounds were muted. The edges of her vision darkened. Breath tore at her chest. Her helmet dropped from numb fingertips with a thud.

Willan turned toward her. His hazel eyes wide with concern. His voice sounded far away. "Amione? Are you ok?"

She couldn't answer him.

Recognizing she was in distress, he scooped her into his arms like she was nothing. "I've got you."

She pressed her face into his shoulder and clung to him for dear life as he pushed his way through the crowd. It seemed like several long minutes, but must have only been a couple. He carried her inside a small room and shut the door, blocking out the drone of people.

She held him tighter when he tried to set her down. Instead, he sat with her cradled in his lap, and brushed her curls back from her face. "Are you alright?"

She licked her lips and tried to breathe normally. She didn't want to open her eyes yet. She was grateful that he allowed her to just sit for a moment. She relaxed so much that she felt like falling asleep.

Her head popped off his shoulder when she remembered where she was and who she was with. She slid off his lap.

He chuckled. "I was starting to enjoy myself."

Embarrassment stained her cheeks.

"Not like that!" He held his hands up.

She wasn't sure what she was supposed to do, so she stood in a corner as far as she could get from him. "I'm sorry, I don't know what happened."

"I do. It's all these people. If you aren't used to it, then a panic attack is inevitable."

"A panic attack?" She had never heard of that combination of words before. She frowned.

He nodded. "You come from Demeter where the population is carefully controlled. I bet the Academy is the same way. Am I right?"

She nodded, folding her hands behind her back.

"So, it's natural to get overwhelmed here." He gestured, trying to ease her discomfort.

She was grateful for his kindness, but she couldn't help feeling like he wanted something from her. Shadow agreed. She nodded and looked around the space properly for the first time since coming inside.

It was a small room, no bigger than the bathroom in her Da's quarters. There was one bench near the door and several concealed compartments lining one wall. A small basin was set into the wall next to her. Behind her a Mirror showed her reflection. She looked gaunt in the strange green lighting.

"So, what does a Clean Room do?" she asked cautiously.

"Well, it doesn't actually clean you. But it has all the things you need to get cleaned up. Clean clothes, soap, water, and a little something to eat at the end." He smiled, rising to his feet.

The space was so small that they were almost touching again. She shrank further into the corner. The right corner of his mouth quirked and he winked at her.

He opened compartments to her right. She could smell sweat and dirt and something more as he moved closer. "So, first we gather our supplies. A cloth." He handed her a fluffy cloth and pulled one out for himself. "Soap. We have several to choose from." He seemed to be relishing the tour. "Personally, I like this one."

He opened one of the containers and held it out to her. It smelled of wood and green things, not unlike the Arboretum. He handed it to her and opened another. The spicey scent made her sneezed.

He laughed. "Ok, so not that one." He plucked another out and offered it to her.

She sniffed it tentatively, relishing in the wonderfully rich aroma. She took it from his hand. "What is it?"

"It's called vanilla. Something from Old Earth, long gone like most of these things. Somehow the artisans here have passed down the formula from generation to generation." He turned away, but not before he saw the pain of loss cross his face.

She cradled the vanilla and breathed in the scent as if it was the most heavenly thing she had ever experienced. She jumped when she realized Willan was undressing. "What are you doing?" She pressed herself back into the corner.

He held up his hands as if calming a skittish animal. "The only way to get clean in a Clean Room is to undress and get to it."

"Get to what?"

He sighed and ran his hand through his hair making it stand on end. "I forget that you do things differently on Demeter. I'm afraid there is no privacy in this place. Usually, this room is four people full, I was able to secure it for just us."

She narrowed her eyes at him, but nodded her understanding. Her gaze brushed over his well-defined arms and his stained gray tank top. She had never seen a man who was so large before. She remembered how easily he picked her up and carried her. Had she not been so overwhelmed she might have enjoyed the sensation.

She noticed a gash in his upper left arm.

"What happened there?" she indicated the cut.

He twisted his arm to look at the injury. "One of your security shot at me when I was leaving Demeter. It's just a graze." He peeled off the offensive shirt, dropping it into another bin near the door. He turned his back to her and she noticed several scars scoring his back. Whatever his life was like, it was certainly filled with more danger than she was used to.

He opened the container and started rubbing the contents over his face and neck and then over his shoulders and arms making them glisten in the dim light. Her mouth grew dry as she watched.

He looked over at her. "Um, it's customary to do your own thing, preferably over there. I promise not to stare."

She had the grace to blush and turned back toward the mirror. She watched to be sure he stayed with his back turned, then cautiously unbuckled her suit, pushing her arms out of it and down to her waist. Her long-sleeved shirt was drenched in sweat and she smelled foul. She glanced at the mirror to be sure he was still facing away from her before peeling it off her frame entirely. She gave an involuntary sigh of relief when the cool air touched her skin.

She opened the container and sniffed the contents again. She dabbed a little on her fingers and messaged it into her face, and over her neck. Her eyes fell close as she methodically worked the cream beneath her undershirt over her breasts and back again.

Willan asked over his shoulder. "Can you get my back?"

Amione froze. She had forgotten for a moment that she wasn't alone. She slowly turned and saw Willan holding the container, looking at her over his shoulder. She stepped toward him and took the container from his hand.

"Just take some and work it in there." He turned back to the wall.

She could feel the heat radiate off of his body. She felt like curling into his back and experiencing that warmth first hand.

What was wrong with her? She had never reacted to another person in this way, but then, she had never been in a position like this before.

She dabbed some of the mixture on her hand and tentatively touched his back which was firm and warm beneath her fingers. She felt a muscle jump as she smoothed some of it down his spine. She stopped.

"Don't be shy. You won't hurt me." He captured her violet gaze with his hazel one.

It was best to get this over with. She dipped her fingers into the container again and rubbed it more firmly into his skin. She traced each scar, plane, and divot at the base of his back marveling at how wonderful it felt to be touching another person in such an intimate way.

"Thanks. Your turn."

She flushed. "Um, I'm ok."

"Ah ah, every bit needs to be cleaned before we leave here. Those are the rules."

She frowned skeptical that was actually a rule. Her curiosity overruled her better judgement and she turned obediently away from him, holding her container out for him to take. She felt him take the container from her fingers and couldn't quell a shiver of anticipation when his hands smoothed over her lower back.

Willing herself to remain still beneath his ministrations, she watched him in the mirror as he gently rubbed the cream over her back. His brows were furrowed in deep concentration. She felt him lift her undergarment and massage the cream between her shoulder blades and the middle of her back, his longer fingers wrapped around her sides as he used his thumbs to work things out. She involuntarily gasped.

He looked at her, then met her gaze in the mirror. She covered her breasts with her arms. "Did I hurt you?" Concern flowed over his features.

She shook her head, unable to disengage from his gaze.

His hands dropped away from her, leaving her feeling bereft. He turned back to his own ministrations by shoving his suit the rest of the way off and tossing it into the clothing chute. Then his underwear followed showing her an exquisitely formed ass.

She quickly looked away as she pushed the rest of her suit off. He took it from her and dumped it into the bin. The sooner she got out of there the better.

"There are clothes that should fit you in the compartment next to you." He hooked his thumb to the right.

She opened the drawer and found an undershirt and underwear neatly folded inside. She quickly pulled the new one over the old then worked the old shirt off without exposing herself. She checked the mirror and saw Willan working the cream into his legs. So, she quickly changed her underwear and kept them in place while she administered the cream to her nether regions.

"Now, before you pull the other clothes on, you take your cloth." He walked to the basin and waved the cloth beneath a faucet, causing water to come out and soak the cloth. "Wet it, and go over everything again. Then you are clean." He smiled.

She flushed when she noticed he was still not clothed. His smile widened when he saw her looking. He turned away chuckling. Grateful that he wasn't so close, she wet her cloth and finished her ablutions, then quickly put on the rest of her clothes. A worn long sleeve tunic, snugly fitting cargo pants and a pair of ankle boots had seen better days, but they were clean.

She finger-combed through her hair, trying to get the curls untangled without much success.

"Here." He ran something through his hair which made it a couple shades lighter.

He squirted a dollop into her hand and she used it to run through her hair, making it more manageable than what it normally was. Her eyebrows raised at the transformation.

"One last thing. There is a particular way we wear our hair around here when it is long. Can I?" He held up his hands with a questioning gaze.

She shrugged.

He pulled her hair back off her shoulders and gently used his fingers to capture wayward strands from the side of her face and forehead. She could feel him gingerly tug on the back of her head and secure the strands with some sort of clip.

His fingers lightly brushed her shoulders, causing them to tingle. "There. All ready to face the world." He smiled sweetly.

There it was again, another odd phrase. She filed it away along with the rest of her observations about Willan. She looked into the mirror, turning her head this way and that, admiring his handiwork. She gave him a curt nod.

He handed her a tablet and popped one in his mouth. "This is to clean your teeth. Chew it until it completely dissolves."

She put it in her mouth and her eyes widened in surprise when she felt it fizz and give off a minty flavor.

"Are you ready?"

He placed a hand on the door. She secured the data crystals in her waistband, and pulled her pack onto her shoulders. "I guess so."

He held out his hand and she looked at it for a long moment before placing her hand in it. His long fingers wrapped around her smaller one giving her a reassuring squeeze. "Just squeeze my hand if something becomes too overwhelming. I won't let you go. Promise."

Her mind went to Curphay. It was something he would do whenever she felt anxious. It reminded her of why she was here and what she needed to do.

"Where are we going?" she asked.

"We are going to see the Magistrate."

"He will help me?"

"She will give you a deal." Something flickered over Willan's face. He had been completely open in the Clean Room, now he was keeping his expression closed. She wasn't sure if it was because of her, or because this was how you made it through a place like this. She didn't have that capability. Whatever she was feeling was there for all to see whether she wanted them to or not.

She nodded, steeling herself against the flood of people in the corridor beyond. As soon as the door opened, she wished they were back inside. The lights seemed too harsh, the drone of voices made her head ache and the close proximity of other people made her want to crawl inside of herself.

Shadow stirred within her. *Let me help you.*

Sounds and sensations were muted. It didn't alleviate everything, but it was enough to keep her from a full-blown panic. *Thank you.*

Whatever it takes to help you get the seed, Shadow assured her with steel backing its thoughts.

Willan guided her through the crowd keeping a firm grip on her wrist. Most of the inhabitants of the Derelict were human. Not just humans from Titan. There were humans from other parts of the system.

The clothing was an eclectic array of cultures. She recognized Martian style immediately, which reminded her of Curphay's easy style. Belters wore utilitarian clothing filled with buckles, pockets and loops meant to hold tools and whatever else they may need on an asteroid. Gany's from Ganymede wore baggy clothes that seemed to swallow them in fabric. Lunar wore tailored suits like her mother. Europans wore fur lined clothes, which she wondered how they could stand the heat with all these bodies in one place.

Alien races walked among the humans. The Nouri had elegantly long necks and wings folded neatly behind their backs. Their eyes were various shades of copper and oranges and glowed with intense interest.

Aechas were great horned beings. Their horns were iridescent and rippled with color beneath the Derelict's strange golden globes.

Cor'adas had long limbs to propel them forward with small bodies and compound eyes. They carried packs strapped to the underside of their bodies.

The sound in the corridors was deafening despite Shadows help. The constant drone rumbled through her mind and made her ears hurt. There wasn't one voice she could focus on, but several disjointed sounds and laughter punctuating the throngs of people.

They turned down an adjacent corridor that opened into the center of the Derelict. A tangle of ropes held banners of various shades, dingy with age. It connected from one balcony to another as it graduated its way to the top. Each banner fluttered in the atmo as it was pumped and recycled into the cavernous space.

Crammed into every available opening, vendors of all sorts sold various wares. The crush of people yelled out prices as they haggled for whatever they needed. Flashing lights, and chaotic music added to the mishmash of bodies. She gripped Willan's hand tighter. He looked over his shoulder in concern. She waved him on. She didn't want to stop in the middle of all this if it could be helped.

They reached the other side and waited in a line to use the lift. She watched as the carriage moved up and down in an agonizingly slow ascent and descent. Passengers unloaded and new ones were loaded. Ebb and flow, yin and yang. Then it was their turn.

The passengers unloaded and Willan stepped into the back of the lift. More people pressed in brushing her shoulder. She moved closer to Willan who gave her a reassuring squeeze. Everyone called out their level.

"Seven." Willan called out clearly.

Several passengers gave him and Amione curious looks. She surmised very few people went to that level. At each level people got off and more people got on. As they neared the higher levels, more people got off and fewer people got on, until it was only the two of them.

The doors opened to a quiet minimal corridor. Polished white floors stretched in front of them; so different from the chaotic dingy worn look from all the other levels. It was small compared to Demeter, but was appropriately opulent for a Magistrate's office. Groupings of succulents filled small planters as they passed, giving off a faint earthy smell. At the door two guardians stood sentry in the small hallway.

They were garbed in army green cargo pants with matching button up shirts. The pants were tucked into their worn boots. They had hard suspicious eyes as they looked at Willan and her.

"Gentleman." Willan released her hand and gave them a conciliatory bow. "The Magistrate is expecting us." He smiled magnanimously.

The one on the right with dusky skin, hard black eyes, and curly black hair gave him a condescending look as he tapped the badge on his chest. "Willan and his... companion to see the Magistrate." He gave her a sharp look.

She wanted to quail beneath his gaze, but locked her jaw and maintained eye contact.

"Send them in." The disembodied voice sounded authoritative and slightly exasperated.

The other guardian scowled and worked the controls to open the door. It slid open with a squeak and a hiss. She peered through the doorway, but could only see another door beyond. Willan nudged her forward with a hand on the small of her back. She took several steps into the small compartment trying her best to quell her apprehension.

Her claustrophobia returned with a vengeance, but Shadow sensed her distress and eased the worst of her anxiety.

Thank you.

The door closed behind them. She expected the opposite door to open immediately, but it didn't. She looked at Willan questioningly.

"They have to scan us. It won't take long," he assured her.

She didn't feel as if they were being scanned.

"What do we--"

He shook his head, warning her that this was not a safe place to speak.

She closed her mouth and folded her arms across her chest. *Shadow, are you there?*

I am.

Keep watch. I don't like this place.

Understood.

She could feel Shadow shift inside her mind. The weakness she had felt since stepping on the station was replaced with added strength. She hoped she wouldn't need it. Whatever deal this woman was offering, she had a feeling she wouldn't like it. Not that she had much choice.

The door finally slid open, revealing a room with windows on three sides looking out over the mists of Titan. Saturn loomed large behind her still in silhouette with the rings backlit by the sun.

Demeter's interior was all coppers and blues, but the Derelict was charcoal and orange with white accents. Everything felt aged, utilitarian, and built to maximize small spaces. A small desk was the dominant feature in the room. It was minimalistic, with a chair that fit snugly in place. To one side were compartments and shelves filled with data crystals, tablets, and a rare personal effect.

In the corner looking out over Titan stood a tall woman in a coverall cinched at the waist giving her svelte figure emphasis. Her sleeves were rolled up to her elbows and she had one hand pressed to the window and the other cradling her generous hip. Her blonde hair was in a messy bun with a headband keeping stray hair from her face. Her nose was long with a bump, bisecting high cheekbones and ending over a generous mouth. Her skin was alabaster in coloring, almost luminous in the dim light.

She turned at their approach, piercing green eyes assessed her before shifting to Willan with a slight frown. "So... the Prodigal Son returns." Her voice was soft like a velvet glove over steel.

Willan bowed slightly. "I have."

The Magistrate turned her attention back to Amione. "And you have brought a guest."

"This is Amione Dhau of Demeter. Amione, this is Magistrate Kone-stro, our supreme leader at the Derelict."

"Cadence. You know I hate that name," she sharply corrected.

"Of course. Leader of Cadence," Willan apologized with a slight smirk.

He was enjoying himself, the asshole. Amione's frown matched the Magistrate's.

"Did your mission go as planned?" The Magistrate got straight to the point.

She was different from the leaders at Demeter who simpered and pandered to each other with incessant small talk. Amione rather liked the straight, no nonsense approach the Magistrate offered.

"It mostly went as planned."

The Magistrate's brows rose. "Mostly? Do I want to know?"

"I doubt it. Suffice it to say, I was able to extract Amione from the surface."

"You did? I seem to recall I was the one who was doing the flying." Amione blurted out without thinking.

"You wouldn't be flying if I hadn't repaired the shuttle." He looked at her pointedly.

She had the grace to flush.

"So, you found something." The Magistrate's green eyes looked from one to the other.

Amione clamped her mouth shut. She wasn't going to reveal her deal with Shadow. She quickly calculated what she would reveal.

"I sent her the footage. It was interesting. In fact," He stepped in front of Amione and removed the data crystal from her waist. "This will show you the same thing."

Amione grabbed his hand. His eyes pleaded with her to trust him. He could have easily taken both data crystals, but only took the one he had given to her. She pushed her indignation aside, for now.

The Magistrate waved the viewer into existence and inserted the data crystal into her console. Amione kept her eyes on the floor. She had watched it enough times that it was seared into her memory. She didn't need to see it again.

The Magistrate played the video forwards and backwards several times and enlarged sections of the video for a better look before waving it closed. "Did you find whatever that was?"

Amione could feel Shadow tingling in the back of her mind, urging her to use caution. "No, Ma'am."

The Magistrate narrowed her eyes at Amione as if she didn't believe her before turning to Willan. "Did you see anything?"

"No. I was at the shuttle when Amione and her friend went to the site. She came back, but he didn't."

The Magistrate leaned against the window, then took a seat at the desk tenting her fingers as she worked through the scenario. "Why would you leave your friend?"

Amione pressed her lips together before replying, "I had my reasons, and I need to go back for him."

"That will be difficult. You both caused quite a stir. We saw the explosion from here. Yorea will retaliate." She rose from the desk and went to the window again. "We are barely hanging on here. You know that, Willan."

"I know. I'm sorry."

She gave him a sharp look. "Either I give them the perpetrator, or they withhold supplies from us again."

"What are you planning to do?" He lifted his chin.

She stared at him, then replied, "I will select one of the less fortunate, and pay their family extra rations."

"Or you can send me."

"No. You are much too valuable." She turned back to the view.

Amione listened to the exchange in horror.

"It's a lot harsher here than you imagined, isn't it." She directed her gaze to Amione.

"There is no other way?"

The Magistrate shook her head in resignation. "No. The sacrifice of one helps the many. We are waging a quiet war, and we are losing."

Amione didn't know how to respond. She looked at Willan who was lost in thought. All the cockiness he had before was gone.

"How do you plan on getting back there?" The Magistrate pinned her with her green eyes.

"I don't know," she replied.

The Magistrate nodded. "Finally, an honest answer." She sat back down, and leaned back in her chair. "We might be able to help you with that, but we require something from you first."

Amione shifted uncomfortably beneath the Magistrate's gaze. She looked at Willan who gave her an imperceptible nod. She had to get back to Curphay, which meant making a deal she might not like. "What do you want from me?"

The Magistrate gave her a tight smile. "Nothing big, just a bit of larceny."

Chapter 18

Hard-Won Trust

"To be trusted is a greater compliment than to be loved."
Unknown

O al was enthralled by this place; its changing seasons, its proximity to such an interesting planet, and the ever-changing topography. During warm months, Oal and Sadool explored vast stretches of the moon without worry. Oal's plates had hardened sufficiently that he was protected from the worst elements.

He grew at a steady rate. Eventually he would take root within the cavern he and the Sadool had found. For all of Oal's many attributes, the winters here were too cold.

Occasionally, the Sadool would wander off for days, but Oal noticed he was doing this much less frequently. "Why are you nearby more often, Sadool?"

"I have explored much of this moon's surface and it doesn't interest me like it used to."

Oal worried. "Does that mean you wish to move on?"

"Absolutely not! Your path is my path," the Sadool assured him.

Oal was relieved. He wasn't sure when it happened exactly, but he had grown quite attached to the dark entity.

One day the Sadool returned quite agitated. "You must come see. I have found something unusual."

Oal unfolded his increasingly lanky frame. "What is it?"

The Sadool floated through the air tentacles twitching in excitement.

"Come." It led the way to a crevice Oal had previously explored, but had stopped part way through when another path looked more promising.

Oal's plates twitched as he followed. Curling appendages fluttered behind him, the tips brushed with a rose color, marking it as new growth. Soon he would be too large to fit through these crevices. He walked through the crevice and carefully navigated the hydrocarbon detritus and stalactites. Some of the passage was incredibly narrow and required careful management so he would not snag on the walls.

They traveled for several hours and Oal wondered if the entity knew where he was going. "Are we almost there?"

"Nearly. I'm sorry it is not comfortable for you, but I promise it will be worth it. I forget how long it takes you to get somewhere."

"Not everyone can walk through walls. I must admit that is a handy way to travel."

The Sadool's form glowed a faint blue, a sure sign that they were close. A faint glow emanated from the other end of the tunnel, then exited into another chamber.

He had thought he had seen all that the moon had to offer, but again, this place surprised him. A cavern opened in front of him filled with honeycombed structures that gave off a faint iridescent glow. "What is it?"

"It is alive."

"Alive?" Oal trained his rose quartz gaze on the entity. "But how? We have been here for centuries and we found no indication of life before. How did we miss this?"

"I don't know, but it is here now."

Oal examined the floor of the cavern and detected a heat source. It was warm enough to melt some of the ice. It must have been enough to allow life to from.

Oal walked among the lattice. They looked delicate at first sight, but upon closer inspection they were surprisingly strong. He ran his feathers over the honeycomb of light and was rewarded with a wave of color that spread through the entire structure.

"It responds to my touch," Oal stated with wonder.

The Sadool hovered over the structure, but refrained from touching it. "It feels primitive."

"It isn't sentient. Maybe some form or figot, or genevan. Still, this is quite a find. We passed so many quiet planets and moons."

"And yet, life persists here."

"I will consult my parentage and see if there has been anything like this in other places, or if this is something entirely new." Oal brushed his fingers over the lattice again and watched as waves of color drifted up the honeycomb to the roof of the cavern and down other lattices in other places.

"I knew you would appreciate it." The Sadool's voice was filled with smug satisfaction.

"Thank you. This will provide some interest as my time to take root grows nearer."

"How much longer?"

"I'm not sure. It is different for each Tromfeld. No one has ever been on a moon like this with these conditions. Your guess is as good as mine."

"Will the parentage know your outcome?"

"Eventually. We have traveled very far from the next Tromfeld. It may be millennia before I receive an answer. In the meantime, I will continue to gather more data."

"Will they know about me?" The Sadool's voice sounded wary.

"Only if you want me to tell them."

"I do not wish it."

"Then I will omit it from my experience. Though you should know that alone will make them curious."

"Let them be curious."

Oal nodded and returned his attention back to the lattice. He was reluctant to return to their cavern, but the hydrocarbons were in limited supply here. What he needed was sustenance to keep him fulfilled until his transformation was complete. Until then, he would meditate on the meaning of this new find.

Chapter 19

Diffraction

"Light propagates and spreads not only directly through refraction and reflection, but also by a fourth mode; Diffraction."
Francesco Maria Grimaldi

Willan took Amione back into the corridor. She started to say something and he lifted a warning hand and pressed a finger to his lips. She clamped her mouth and followed him to the lift. She wasn't sure where he was taking her next. She watched him warily as she leaned into the corner of the lift.

What had she gotten herself into? Her anxiety tugged at her stomach painfully. Every hour she was away from Curphay agitated her more. She would do anything to get back to him. She just hoped it didn't take her soul in the process.

Shadow stirred. *If that is what it takes.*

She scowled at the entity, wishing she had never sought it out. Her gaze shifted back to the man next to her. He was the reason she had pursued it further. No. That wasn't exactly true. It was Leto's death that had pushed her over the edge. Willan just gave her information wouldn't have gotten otherwise, confirmation for what she already suspected. Though she never imagined it would this strange.

She looked at him again. Why did he risk his life to get that recording? What did he get out of all this? Who was this guy?

The door opened, allowing more passengers on the lift as they descended further into the city. Instead of going to the ground floor, Willan tugged her wrist and they exited on the fourth. He quickly turned down a corridor until they were in the outer ring of the city. Doors lined the walls on either side, presumably living quarters.

She balked. "Where are you taking me?"

He glanced at her. "To my place. We will be free to talk there. Don't worry, I will behave myself." He laughed at her look of alarm.

She felt a flutter of excitement at the idea that he might try something. She quashed that. She needed answers and she couldn't afford to be distracted by a man, especially one as tempting as this one.

He stopped in front of a nondescript door and waved his wrist over the panel. How quaint. He had an embedded crystal. Something that had not been in use at Demeter in over 20 years

He gestured for her to go before him. She walked into a cramped space that was a living area, kitchen, and cleanmat all in one. There was a curtained off section in the corner. There was a funky odor coming from the room that she couldn't identify.

"Is that you, Willan?" A high tenor voice called out from behind a curtain.

Amione's mouth hung open when she realized there were feet sticking out from beneath the curtain with pants around their ankles. Apparently, that was what passed for a bathroom in this place.

"It's me, Rollo." Willan sent an apologetic look to Amione.

He guided her to the door furthest from the front and invited her inside. The room was smaller than the Clean room. There was a bunk built into the wall facing a small window that looked out of the leeward side of Titan. She could see a million stars dotting the night sky just above the mists. Modules hung above and below the window, making it feel as if she was looking out of a tunnel.

There was a small table and chair nestled beneath the window. Next to it was a wave and a very old replication unit. A cup, bowl, and multi utensil sat on top of the rundown machine. Several containers of water were stacked beneath the table as well as ration packs.

A fine layer of dust covered most of the surfaces. She saw that his bed was unmade, with a sad looking pillow and threadbare covers. Three drawers lined the bottom of the bunk presumably where he kept his personal items.

The walls had once been a deep blue, but they had long since faded except for the back wall of the bunk which looked relatively new next to the older walls.

Willan waved another light on. "As you can see, space is at a premium here."

She nodded. She had known that the Derelict was overcrowded, but to see it first hand was shocking. It made her Da's cabin look grand by comparison.

Willan chuckled. "Actually, this is one of the better rooms. At least I have a window to look out of. Most will live their days never seeing beyond their walls. A bitter twist of his mouth indicated there was a lot more to that statement. "Needless to say, I haven't been here in a while. I apologize for the mess." He pulled the covers up on his bunk and indicated that she be seated.

"You don't need to apologize." She sat gingerly on the bed.

"But I do. See, me finding you wasn't an accident." He fidgeted giving her a nervous glance.

Her heart jumped. She leaned forward. Now she would get some answers. "What do you mean?"

He sat in the chair across from her and his long legs nearly touched her own. He looked at his hands, wondering where to start. "I was told that I needed to find you. To help you."

"Told by who?" She stared at his profile as he searched for words.

He shifted uncomfortably. "That's not important. What is important is that I found you and that I set you on this path."

She wrapped her arms around her chest. "What path?" She could feel Shadow's interest piqued.

He shook his head. "I don't know. I only know the first steps. That it is important and that you could change the course of this system and many other systems."

She shook her head confused. "What? Like I'm some sort of Chosen

One?" She gave an incredulous laugh. "I don't know what you are talking about. I just want to get my friend off the surface."

"And I will help you, Amione." He met her gaze.

"How? By stealing something?" Remembering the conversation with the Magistrate.

He ran a frustrated hand through his hair. "If that is what it takes."

"I don't steal," she stated bluntly.

He smiled. "Really. And you acquired that shuttle how?"

"That's different. I was going to bring it back," she cried out in indignation.

He chuckled, shaking his head. "No, you just benefit from what I steal," he challenged.

She winced and looked at her feet. He wasn't wrong. She had known the data crystal was stolen. "Fair enough," she growled.

"The Magistrate is desperate and she sees an opportunity in you. A way to make things better here." His hazel eyes pleaded for her understanding.

Damn him. Why did he have to be so attractive? She wanted to say no unequivocally, but then Curphay's face floated into her mind and Shadow gave her a mental nudge. There was too much at stake to rely on her moral judgement. "Do you know what she wants?"

He nodded. "Seeds."

Her heart jumped at the mention of seeds. Shadow replied, *He means the seeds from your Arboretum. Not the one we need.* She took a deep breath and calmed her nerves.

"Seeds?"

"Specifically, ones that are fruit bearing. There is a shortage of Vitamin C here. We have not been successful in obtaining it from other sources and it is notoriously hard to replicate. We are in danger of running out. Some sections already have and they are seeing the effects."

"Have they gone through proper channels? Why doesn't the Counsel help?"

His mouth twisted bitterly. "The Counsel...They would, for a price. Nothing comes for free from those people. Nothing."

Amione remained silent. It was true, the Counsel required a lot when Demeter asked for something. The Leaders and the residents debated about issues long and hard. She remembered her Da saying, "If they wanted to cripple us, they could easily do it. All they need to do is cut off our means of trade, and that would be it. We would become the Derelict."

Sometimes they accepted the Counsel's help and other times they would secure trade elsewhere. It was like balancing on the edge of a blade. One wrong move and Demeter would be lost.

"The seed vault would be nearly impossible to reach." She finally broke the silence.

"Then we need to harvest them ourself."

She blanched. No one was allowed to walk off the path into the stand of trees that grew in the far corner. They would surely be seen. Plus, there were cameras everywhere. "I don't know if that is possible."

"Leave that to me."

"You?"

"I have been able to successfully elude security before." He shrugged.

Her mind ran through several scenarios. "How will I explain my presence on the surface and what happened to Curphay?"

"You were taken hostage."

"But I wasn't--"

"Yes," Willan's eyes lit up as he fleshed out their story. "I kidnapped you and had you show me where the mine was. I needed things for the Derelict and it was the only way I could get them. Curphay was accidentally left behind."

"That would make you a fugitive." She worried despite herself.

"Oh, honey, that ship has sailed a long time ago. The Counsel has been after me for years. They haven't managed to catch me yet." He smiled with a wicked gleam in his eye.

She couldn't help but smile back. Whatever Willan was, he was charming. She mentally shook herself. She had to stay on mission. Curphay was depending on her. "So, what is the plan?"

"You get sent back by the Magistrate. She will tell them that you were rescued from this rogue, and that in good faith, she will send you back home. With the sincerest of apologies, of course. Simple."

Amione looked at him, mouth agape and hands on her knees. "Yeah, simple. I can see a whole host of things going wrong. We need an actual plan."

Willan blinked at her innocently. "Like what?"

"Like what?" She looked at him incredulously. "They find out who you are. An alarm goes off. The Council decides to pay a visit. They don't believe my story. You can't hack the cameras. I run into someone I know and I am delayed. They detain me. Which, by the way, is the most likely scenario." She ticked off each possible scenario on her fingers.

He held up his hands laughing. "Stop! You are borrowing trouble."

She glowered, folding her arms across her chest again. Another odd phrase she had never heard before. In fact, he said a lot of odd things that she had never heard before.

"We will work it all out, but there are a lot of things that could go right. You have to admit it."

She rolled her eyes at him. "So, when are we doing this thing?"

"Tomorrow."

Her heart skipped a beat. "Tomorrow?"

"If we wait any longer than that, the timing will become suspicious." He reached under the table and pulled out a water offering her a swig. She shook her head. He upended the bottle and drank, wiping the excess moisture from his lips.

She nodded curtly. Tomorrow seemed simultaneously too fast and too slow.

It will work. Shadow whispered in her ear, causing her to relax a little.

At least she wasn't alone. If need be, Shadow could help. She could feel fatigue weigh at her shoulders. The events of the past several hours had finally caught up to her.

"You look like you need rest." Willan examined her face.

"No, I'm fine," she insisted.

"You can barely keep your head up. Lie down for a while."

She looked at him in alarm.

"I'll go into the front room. You can have my bed." He put the cap back on the bottle and placed it under the table.

She nodded. "Very well." She waited for him to leave.

He examined her a moment longer, then went to the door. "Sweet dreams, Amione."

The door slid open and closed behind his bulky form. She stared at the doorway for a moment, then kicked off her boots and lay on top of the bedcover. The pillow crackled beneath her head. The faint smell of earth and growing things wafted up from the pillow making her feel soothed and happy.

She ran through the events of the day. Only this morning she and Curphay were together laughing, arguing, and going about their day. Then the trip down, and what they found in the cavern. She recalled the images Oal had sent her. Pictures of places she could never hope to reach, an agelessness that went beyond her understanding, and a promise extracted under duress. She tried not to picture Curphay's too still face as she left him behind. How could she leave him like that?

Anxiety made her heart pound harder. She was tired, but her mind was fully awake, wondering if there was more she could do to get back to Curphay faster. After a thorough assessment, she concluded she was, but she didn't like it. Regret pulled at her heart. She should never have allowed him to go with her.

She sighed. She would never get any rest if she kept thinking about what she couldn't change. She shifted her thoughts to Willan. He wasn't beautiful like Curphay, but there was something compelling about him. Realization hit.

"I know why I'm drawn to him," she muttered kicking herself for not realizing it sooner. The reason she was so drawn to him, is that he was like her, chaotic. She laid her head back against the pillow. It made perfect sense. The thought of connecting with someone so like herself excited her.

His hazel eyes flashed into her mind. He knew what she was too, and liked her for it. She wasn't sure what she would do with that information. Likely, they would finish this mission and go their separate ways. She hoped not. Her eyes drifted closed and she was asleep.

Amione woke on her stomach with stray locks of hair over her face. She pushed the strands back, taking in her surroundings, forgetting for the moment where she was. She looked out the small window at the sea of stars and recalled that she was on the Derelict.

She sat up gingerly and took one of the water bottles and opened it. The water tasted bitter and salty, but it was water and she needed it. She chugged seven swallows before gasping and wiping the excess moisture on her sleeve. She carefully closed the bottle and put it back with the rest.

She sat in the chair and stared out into space. *What am I supposed to do, Shadow?*

Shadow stirred and separated itself from her body. *I have been giving it some thought. You must do what is necessary to get back to Demeter and the seed. My friend and yours are depending on it.*

Agreed. But I don't like this plan, or lack of one. She scowled.

Then we need to change it.

How?

We will find a way down to the surface without Willan.

There was something undefined in Shadow's voice. It sounded jealous. Could a noncorporeal entity feel jealousy? It's such a human emotion; it was hard to imagine. Perhaps it was time to get to know her reluctant guest.

Tell me something, Shadow. How long have you lived in this place?

We have been here for millions of years.

I can't fathom living so long.

I can't fathom living such a short time.

How did you two meet? She lightly tapped her fingers on the table's surface.

By chance. He was set free to travel to other systems from his home system. We came upon each other and something odd happened. Something unexpected.

What?

Symbiosis. We enhanced each other's existence. He was at the mercy of interstellar currents and I gave him direction. He gave me substance.

And you have been together ever since.

We have. I have been his protector. I owe him for this existence. Without him, I would always be a being without form.

How were you able to connect with me so easily?

I'm not entirely sure. All I know is that you need to be a willing host. Shadow's attention diverted. *I must return. He is coming.*

She briefly contemplated not allowing the entity back into her mind. She would have, but she still needed its presence.

Ok.

Amione closed her eyes, allowed Shadow wrap itself around her shoulders, and into the base of her skull. It felt comforting like being wrapped in a very soft blanket.

The door slid open and Willan poked his head inside. "Good, you are awake. We need to get supplies before we leave. Are you hungry?"

She was about to say no when her stomach betrayed her.

"I'll take that as a yes." Willan grinned.

She entered the front room and saw two individuals sitting on a couch, playing a game. Their pants were rolled up to their knees exposing shins spotted with red and blue marks, the hallmark of vitamin deficiency.

Willan opened a ration pack and handed it to her. She quickly devoured the tasteless meal. Grateful for something to boost her energy, she kept an eye on the two in the front room who were giving her equally suspicious glances.

"Let's go."

They exited into the crowded corridor. "Friendly bunch."

"Don't mind them. They are just sore that I got a room with a window."

Children were running up and down the corridors wearing not much more than a shift and a pair of weighted shoes to keep them tethered to the floor. Several of the children were blind. If she hadn't been looking for it, she would have missed it. They seemed to have adapted without the aid of sight. This could have easily been her if she hadn't had the benefits of Demeter's medical accommodations.

Willan nudged her elbow. "I was wondering when you would notice."

"Why haven't they received augmentation?"

He looked at her with somber hazel eyes. "You know why."

"It's not right. There is no reason why these children should remain blind. What if I never--" She couldn't complete the sentence. To not know the light? She didn't want to imagine it. Instead of grateful that she was born on Demeter, she was disgusted by the callous treatment of these children.

"But you weren't. You were born on Demeter through no fault of your own. Just as these children were born here through no fault of their own. The fault lies with those bastards at Caiphus." Willan growled. He guided her past the children and back to the lifts. "In spite of their lack of access to medical facilities, they have adapted remarkably. In some ways they have superior abilities to the sighted."

Amione looked back at the children thoughtfully.

"Let's go." Willan urged.

"Where are we going?" Amione tried to tamp down her anxiety.

"While you were asleep, I got orders from the Magistrate. She has figured out a way to get you back to Demeter."

"What about the inquiry?"

He looked apologetic. "I'm afraid you will still be subject to an inquiry. There was no way to get around that."

She could feel Shadow shift restlessly. "That could take days."

"She has it on good authority that it won't."

She clamped her mouth shut. She didn't like it, but would go along for now.

He steered her back to the Clean Rooms. She could feel her panic rise as more and more bodies pressed closer to her. Willan sensed her unease and placed a protective arm around her shoulders to shield her from the worst of it. She didn't want to feel grateful, but did anyway.

They ducked into a Clean Room and shut out the cacophony outside.

She breathed a sigh of relief and went to the basin to pull out a cool cloth. Her cheeks felt hot, but in the dim light, she looked pale. She swiped the cloth over her face and caught Willan studying her in the mirror.

"What?"

"Are you ok? Will you be able to do this?"

She leaned against the counter not taking her eyes off of him. "I will have to."

He nodded and turned to a pack near the door.

"What's that?"

"Provisions."

He pulled out a Yorean uniform and began stripping.

Amione turned away, listening as he methodically undressed and slipped the uniform on.

"Where did you get that?"

He grinned at her. "I can't give up all our secrets."

"Humph." She glanced over in time to see him zip up the front. "Why do you need a Yorean uniform?"

"You didn't think I would leave you to the dragons?" He gave her an amused wink.

Dragons? She filed it away with all the other odd words and phrases he used. "I don't know what to think, to be honest. I still don't understand what you think you will get out of all this."

"I told you. Seeds."

Her heart skipped a beat. He didn't know about the seedling, but the connection was still much too close for her comfort. She would indulge him, and at the first opportunity she had, she would bail and make her way back to Curphay.

She convinced herself that it was because she didn't trust him, but in reality, she didn't trust herself. She was feeling more than a passing attraction to him.

She looked back in the Mirror and realized her hair was still pulled back from Willan's earlier ministrations. She started tugging at the clip and let out a hiss of frustration when it became tangled in her curls.

166

"Here, let me."

She glanced at Willan's outstretched hand and up into his eyes. That was a mistake. Why did he have to have such fascinating eyes? She could feel heat rise into her cheeks as she dropped her arms at her side and stared straight ahead.

He stepped behind her. The close quarters made it difficult to remain distant as the tops of his thighs brushed against her buttocks. Even though he was no longer touching her, her body was aware he was mere centimeters away.

She felt a gentle tug as he worked the clip out of her curls. She snuck a look at him and saw that he engrossed on the task.

She allowed her eyes to fall close. The clip gave way and Willan set to the task of untangling her curls. His fingertips brushed her scalp in a rhythmic soothing motion. A sigh escaped her.

He chuckled, and just like that the spell was broken. She stiffened and he moved back to his original position. She glared at him, but he declined to look at her.

"Is that better?"

She ran a hand through her curls. "Much better. Thank you."

He cleared his throat. "Well, we had better get going."

Regret washed over her. Despite the strangeness of this place, Willan had made it quite pleasant. Or maybe it was Willan she was loathed to leave. She squashed that thought. There was no time to indulge in fantasy. She had a mission to complete.

"Yes. I guess we should." He looked quickly away, but not before she caught the look of longing in his eyes that made her heart race faster.

They helped each other back into their SCIS. Helmets in hand, they exited the Clean Room and started down the corridor. She was about to go back to the shuttle when he tugged on her arm.

"We are going this way."

"But the shuttle--"

"Will be taken care of. If we are going to sell this, I need to use an orbiter with Yorean markings."

She looked at him quizzically as another person bumped into her. He guided her closer to the wall.

"It would look really odd if I was piloting a Demeter shuttle if I'm escorting you back to Demeter."

She clamped her mouth shut. She wasn't sure how he was going to pull all of this off, but he seemed confident in his plan. She just had to be sure that she wasn't going to be detained too long.

As they turned down a branch corridor, the crowd thinned. This section was newer construction compared to the rest of the Derelict. It was mostly cobbled together from various materials. There were graphite panels similar to Demeter as well as sheets of steel, corobite, and ansem. It had an unfinished quality to it with visible rivets in much of the corridor, exposed bulkheads, and conduits left uncovered. None of this would have passed code on Demeter.

Finally, they reached the end of the corridor and doors that led out to ships docked nearby. Several of the ships were scuttles, a couple that were capable of LTO, and still others that could break atmosphere, but looked questionable. The Yorean orbiter was easy to spot. It looked shiny next to the worn and old ships.

"Orders."

Amione was startled by the guardian. He was a beefy man two heads taller than Amione with a crooked nose and beady black eyes that seemed more than a little bored.

Willan waved his wrist over the input device and it turned green.

"Don't open the door until the light turns green."

"I know the drill," Willan bristled.

The man looked indifferent.

Willan indicated that Amione put on her helmet. She clicked the latches into place and checked Willan's helmet and he did the same for her. The door opened and they walked into a depressurization chamber. The seal locked behind her and she risked a backward glance at the operator who worked the controls.

A hiss and the light clicked red. Once the process was done, it flipped to green.

"Ready?"

She gave a curt nod.

He waved a hand over the controls and the door clicked. He used the manual lever to slide the guards and opened the door. The floor of the deck was scarred with mini meteorites, wear and tear from booted feet, and the rare weather event. The mag seals were solid as she carefully made her way to the orbiter.

She tried to resist the temptation of looking at her surroundings and failed. She made the mistake of looking up and down from their position. Several meters of ships lined the side of the dock below and above giving her vertigo.

She felt Willans gentle hand on her elbow and was grateful for it. "I won't let you fall. Promise."

She had to be imagining the double meaning that seemed to be implied in his voice. She could never tell when someone was putting her on or if they were being sincere. She studied his face and hoped what she saw there was sincere.

He urged her forward as the orbiter's cockpit opened, revealing two seats, one behind the other. The entire vehicle had seen better days, but it looked far better than the other vehicles around it. Scoring, pock marks, and scuffed finishes gave it a story. She wondered what that story was and how they were able to come by this vehicle.

"Layna, is everything set up?"

"Ready to go! They won't be able to tell the difference."

"Excellent. Great work."

"Hmmph. Like I need your approval." Layna's voice grated against Amione's ear.

"Ready?" Willan didn't wait for her reply. He started up the steps and swung his leg over the edge and turned back offering a hand up.

She hesitated for a moment, then hooked her boot on the first rung and pulled herself up the ladder. She took the proffered hand and swung her legs over the cockpit.

"So, the controls are pretty standard. Just don't touch this one." He indicated the manual ejection bar.

She rolled her eyes at him. "I think I can handle it." She surveyed the controls as she strapped in. Willan settled in the seat in front and waved the cockpit closed. She could feel environmentals tap into her suit and recycle some additional air in before the engines hummed to life. They were a standard hydro drive used to escape Titian atmosphere into LTO.

Indicators blinked to life as Willan deftly powered all systems and went through his checks. She did the same.

"All systems are nominal." She called through the coms.

"We are good to go. Control, permission to undock."

"Permission granted." Layna's voice piped over the coms.

The clamps released, allowing the orbiter to shudder as it moved forward. Willan navigated their way through the mass of ships into open sky. Then he punched the engines. She was pressed into the seat and immediately a grin split her face. This never got old and Willan didn't disappoint. The orbiter spiraled down, then he rolled it and brought the nose back up. Soon they were moving swiftly toward Demeter.

Copper clouds drifted below. She looked back at the Derelict hanging right at the cloud deck and felt Willan guide the craft to a higher altitude to match Demeter. In ten minutes, she would be home, and facing a very disapproving and intimidating panel. She had gone over and over in her head what she would say, but was nervous that she would somehow say the wrong thing and end up in detention.

Shadow stirred. *I can help you.* The entity slid through her mind, making her shiver.

I don't need your help, she insisted.

You will at some point.

How do you even know that? Several images flashed through her mind. The panel with three stoic figures, the entry of guardians as they put restraints on her, and finally being in an enclosed space reserved for offenders.

What was that? She could feel her anxiety rise.

It is one possible future.

You can predict the future?

Only for the one I'm bonded to. It is not perfect. Variables change constantly based on what you decide to do next. The further into the future I see, the less accurate things are.

Amione was still trying to assimilate the fact that predicting the future was even possible much less the implications it meant for her. She swallowed hard.

What do I need to do to ensure that I don't meet that fate?

When the woman in the middle asks you, 'We talked to one of the attendants' she will be lying. Ignore it and focus on the fact that they have not arrested you.

I'm confused. Why would that matter?

What does knowing why accomplish? If you respond the way I tell you to, it will keep you out of detention. If you don't, then the likelihood that you will end up in detention increases dramatically.

But how do you know all of this?

I just know.

That is not a sufficient answer. She growled.

It will have to be. That's all I can offer you.

How do I know it will work?

I am motivated to find the seedling. That means you are the only one who can accomplish that. It is in my interest to ensure that you complete the task.

She mulled over its answer for a few moments. The logic was sound, but why did she have a nagging feeling that it wasn't telling her everything?

"We are making the final approach." Willan interrupted her thoughts. "Are you ready?"

She grimaced. "I guess I'm as ready as I will ever be.

Chapter 20

Humans

"Monsters, I understand they're bad. But, Humans? They're Scary."
Tigress

As time passed on the moon, Oal spent most of it exploring the caverns, venturing occasionally to the surface. The Sadool was his constant companion in all things. Their bond grew stronger with time, and with it, additional abilities emerged. One such ability was foresight.

The Tromfeld have never possessed such an ability which is why they didn't believe in prophecy. Neither did the Sadool. It seemed to be a unique trait that only presented itself with their particular bonding. Very little changed as time passed.

That is until they saw something new.

A small vessel approached from one of the inner planets in the system. It wasn't organic, but something that was constructed. It orbited the ringed planet in a blink, then maneuvered its way out of the system.

"What does it mean?" Oal pondered the vision.

"I do not know." The Sadool shifted restlessly in the cavern.

"Have you considered that there are other sentient species living in the universe? Perhaps there is a reason why we were led here."

"You assume there is a higher power at work," the entity stated laconically.

"Don't you?" Oal curled his body around a source of heat in the center of the caven.

"No." The Sadool's voice was flat.

"No? Just...no?" Oal inquired incredulously.

"Not in the way that you believe. Yes, there are forces greater than us, but you are implying a specific being that has created all things." The Sadool faded into a non-corporeal state as it slowly revolved around Oal.

"It was no accident that we found each other, and now we are seeing things that defy conventional explanation." The image of the strange device flashed in his mind once again. They had not seen it yet, but if their theory held true, it would arrive much sooner than anticipated.

"I will grant you that. It is not explainable, but that does not mean there isn't an explanation that won't be revealed in time," the entity was quick to remind Oal.

Oal considered Sadool's words and replayed the images in his mind. The vessel was definitely constructed, which would require a keen mind though it was a crude and inefficient device.

He had to consider that other life might not evolve as they did. Where Tromfelds used organic chemistry to create the vessels in which they traveled, it would seem these beings used inorganic materials to do the same. The entire idea of meeting life, however backward, fascinated Oal, but there could be another possibility.

"Do you think it is a warning?" Oal mused.

"Warning?"

"Do you think whatever sent that device will be detrimental to us?" Oals head plates wobbled in anxiety.

"It is far too soon to speculate. Besides, I would consume anything that could be conceived as a threat." The entity's supreme confidence bled through their connection.

Oal gave a gasp of disbelief. "That's your solution to everything."

"It's been quite effective." The entity reminded him.

"Let's see what they are before we make any hasty decisions like consuming our enemies that might not be enemies."

Silence stretched between them. "Fine." The Sadool's reluctance washed over Oal. "But if they try to harm us, I will consume them."

"That's all I ask."

"You ask much," the Sadool grumbled.

Oal was amused. It was always the same argument. Somehow, they had managed to create a relationship that was mutually beneficial. Oal had even come to respect the Sadool over the years.

The images niggled at his mind again. Perhaps the Sadool's impatience was wearing off on him. He never used to feel anxious, but then there is nothing in his parentage's history to show him otherwise. Finding a sentient being like the Sadool had been a slim possibility, and yet here it is. What were the chances that there were more, many more such species in their part of the universe?

Chapter 21

Kuramato Model

"Life is but a daily oscillation between revolt and submission."
Henri Fredric Amiel

Amione watched as her home came into view. Instead of docking in the old bay, they used the newer, sleeker, more secure one which opened on the north side of the city. Several craft were docked and one in particular caught her eye. It was crafted with the latest materials in a dark graphite exterior. Running lights and several windows dotted the sides of the vehicle, which easily dwarfed the shuttles, orbiters and other craft normally docked on Demeter.

The Caiphus logo was emblazoned on the nose of the craft, a bright red against the black. Unmistakable. It was definitely the Head Magistrate's ship. Her heart pounded harder. She had a sinking feeling she was the reason Dodd was on Demeter.

"Are you ok back there?" Willan worked the controls as he approached the north bays.

"F-fine." She struggled to keep her voice even.

"You aren't fine. I can hear your breathing. It's erratic. Take deep breaths. We will get through this," he assured her.

She breathed through her nose and out through her mouth in an effort to quell the rising panic. How was she going to get through this? A tingling spread from her fingertips and up her arms as her heart pounded impossibly hard against her chest.

Shadow stirred. *I'm going to help you.*

She couldn't answer. The panic kept growing as her mind raced to the worst possible scenario. Then a sense of relief washed over her. Her heart slowed and it became easier to breathe. The tingling in her hands subsided and warmth returned. If she wasn't strapped into a suit, she would have wiped a ridge of sweat from her upper lip.

Thank you. She conveyed the thought as heartily as she could. There was no way she could have gotten out of that on her own. She had been reluctant to bond with the entity, but it had proven itself a worthy companion.

Humans are delicate. I did not expect to so easily manipulate your systems.

And it's gone. She rolled her eyes. She didn't know why she was expecting a human response from something that was not human.

What's gone?

I was feeling all warm and fuzzy about you, then you ruined it.

Well, you are delicate and easy to manipulate, the Sadool reiterated.

She wasn't sure if she should feel grateful or angry. *We are well aware of our shortcomings. We don't need to be reminded. Besides, we have done quite well on our own for millions of years.* She crossed her arms in indignation.

A mere drop in the grand scale of time. Our species has existed for hundreds of billions of your years. Older than this star system, it lectured.

You are that old? She couldn't fathom a billion years, much less hundreds of billions.

No. I'm one of the younger ones at 5 billion.

Oh, well then, you're just a kid.

Kid? What is kid? Confusion seeped through their connection.

It's what humans call their seedlings.

Then all of you are kids.

No. We mature at about my age, nineteen. Our lifespan ends at about two hundred years.

That is such a short time.

It used to be shorter; thirty-four to forty years. She thought about it for a moment. *Ok. Maybe I can understand your perspective a little bit. I can't imagine only living forty years and then dying. That seems extremely short.*

Her Da's face flashed in her mind. He was only 47 when he died. Sadness washed over her.

It explains much. Why your species is so driven to accomplish so much in such a short time.

We don't have time to waste like your species. She grinned slightly.

We don't waste time. The entity's confusion dripped from its words.

Amione smiled when she heard the Sadool's tone of indignation. She hit a sore spot. *What would you call it?*

Being deliberate.

Let's make sure we are being deliberate while we are on Demeter.

Agreed.

A tone sounded from Willan's console.

"Orbitor 487 Charlie November, you are cleared to dock."

"Thank you, Control. Docking commencing."

"Your voice sounds like an announcer." Amione giggled.

He scoffed. "It's expected. You know that. Gotta have that pilot voice. That's how they know you are legit."

Legit. It was another odd phrase from Willan. She had never heard someone talk like him before. "I thought it had more to do with the flying."

"Well, that too, but the voice ties it all together. You don't think we would be docking if I used my Derelict voice, do you?"

She had to admit Control would probably think twice about letting someone dock if they didn't have the proper voice modulation. So weird.

Willan expertly maneuvered the orbiter into the bay. The ship shuddered when the landing struts touched down, echoing hollowly through the cockpit. Unlike the bay she and Curphay used yesterday, this one was in excellent shape. Everything was clean, painted with clear designations, and efficiently serviced by a cadre of robots that cleaned the ship, refueled and checked for any damage.

"Ready?"

Her stomach jumped. She wasn't ready at all. Curphay's face popped into her mind and her resolve asserted itself.

"I will have to be," she replied, with a grim set of her mouth.

He powered down the rest of the systems and she did the same with her console. The cockpit opened. Willan got out first and scaled the ladder. Amione took a deep breath and swung her leg over the side to follow. Her foot slipped on the last rung and she fell backwards. Willan caught her with ease.

"Watch your step. I won't be with you for a while."

Panic must have flitted across her face.

"But I won't be far. I promise," he hastily added.

"How…"

He shook his head. "It's best you don't know." He gently pushed her upright and kept a steadying hand on her elbow as they wove their way through the bay. Sparks cascaded over the walkway as one robot made repairs on a shuttle. Off in the distance beyond the force fields, she could see the Head Magistrate's ship docked on one of the larger rings. She tried to reason away why he would be there that didn't have anything to do with her, but a nagging feeling persisted.

As they neared the city's entry point from the bay, she could see several figures shadowed beyond the glass. As she drew closer, faces became more distinct. Four guardians, all of whom she had known since childhood, were standing grimly watching her approach. Energy weapons were drawn and ready. The blue of their uniforms contrasted starkly against the more conservative attire of the city elders.

Elijah Sevenday fussed with the cuff of his jacket as he absently examined a button there. His severe gray hair was brushed back from his face revealing pale blue eyes that under certain light, didn't seem to be any color at all. His cheekbones were prominent only to be outdone by his hooked nose.

Standing next to Elijah was Corsair Jones, who was a short round man with deep brown skin and light amber eyes that seemed to glow within his dark face. Usually he smiled easily, but today his face held an uncharacteristic frown.

Last, but certainly not forgettable, was Torrence Dawn. She was an exceptionally tall woman with red hair peppered with strands of white. She grew up as a Belter and came to Demeter when she married her husband, Mikah Dawn. Her ambition allowed her climb the ranks of leadership in Demeter in no time at all.

Willan squeezed her elbow in reassurance, reminding her that she was not in this alone. Shadow stirred as well. She was definitely not alone. She was also definitely in trouble.

The doors slid open and closed behind them as the pressurization process began. All she could do was stare at the officials on the other side. Her mind raced to what she needed to say when the doors opened. How would she defend herself?

The light switched to green and the moment she had been dreading was here. The doors slid open and she and Willan stepped into the entry of Demeter. Navy blue graphene tiles glistened in the low light. She concentrated on the lines between and declined to look at the elders lined up before her.

"You may leave, Guardian." Torrence's steely voice washed over Amione.

Willan gave her a reassuring smile before exiting the platform into Demeter proper. She felt abandoned, but there was no way she could justify his presence.

"Would you like to freshen up before we begin?" Torrence's gray eyes bore into her.

Amione swallowed hard and shook her head. The sooner this was done, the sooner she could go back for Curphay.

"Very well."

Torrence turned on her heel with the other two elders falling in line behind her. Her pace was slower. As much as she wanted to get this over with, her body was filled with dread.

Amione had never been in trouble before. There were things she did unintentionally that warranted a reprimand. Climbing the Arboretum walls was one of those times. But she had never really done anything to get into any real trouble. She hoped that worked in her favor, but one could never tell with Demeter.

They walked through several corridors until they reached the detention section. There were all of two cells, which were rarely in use. An occasional passenger would get out of hand or end up somewhere they weren't supposed to be, but life on Demeter was relatively untouched by crime.

They walked through the modestly appointed lobby of Detention. The robot behind the front desk sprang to life, but was quick to ascertained that it wasn't needed. One of the Guardian's unlocked the secure door and held it open for the group.

The main room had six stations set up on the sides. Two were occupied by enforcers, who gave her a jaundiced look as she passed. There were two other doors to the side which opened to who knew where. One was probably to the cells. The third door was their goal. It opened to a narrow hallway where she was escorted into a windowless room with high ceilings.

Three chairs faced a table with a stool centered against the opposite wall. The elders each took a chair and scrutinized Amione as she sat gingerly on the stool. She stared back at each one of them, and realized that this was going to be far from easy.

The guardians positioned themselves at the door.

"You may go." Torrence dismissed them with a wave.

The guardians exited the room and Amione watched the door close with a hushed whisper. She turned back to the elders and waited. The silence seemed to stretch on forever.

Amione felt the urge to bounce her knee, but restrained herself with great effort. She had to look confident or at the very least unconcerned. Fidgeting would undermine that impression.

"Do you know why you are here?"

Step one: Play dumb. She heard Willan's voice in her head.

Amione shook her head.

The frown deepened on the older woman's face. "You are accused of stealing a shuttle, going down to Hesper Mines, and seriously injuring one of the workers there." Torrence's voice went up a couple notes.

Amione declined to say anything.

"Young lady," Elijah spoke through pursed lips. "These are very serious accusations."

Amione remained silent as she gazed from one elder to the next and back again. Her back ached from sitting on the stool. It was intentional, of course. She felt the hard cold surface beneath her buttocks. She concentrated on the texture beneath her fingertips as her hands curled around the edge of the stool. It kept the anxiety at bay, but not enough to calm her racing heart.

"I'm sure you didn't mean any harm. Grief will make anyone do things that are out of character. Why don't you tell us your version?" Corsair smiled encouragingly, but Amione noticed it didn't reach his eyes.

"Am I being arrested?" Amione asked flatly.

Corsair exchanged a look with the other two. "No... but--"

"Then I would like to leave." Amione stood.

"Sit down." Torrence glared her into submission.

Amione slowly lowered herself onto the god-awful stool. She could feel an ache build between her shoulder blades.

"You may not be under arrest, but you are compelled to answer our questions. It is law that you must comply with the leadership. Do you want to be on the wrong side of the law...Amione?"

"Of course not." She gripped the stool tighter.

"Good. Now answer Mr. Jones' question. What is your version of the story?" Torrence pinned her with a stare.

"I did not know there was more than one version." She kept her voice even, suppressing the urge to laugh.

Torrence pinched the bridge of her nose before lifting her head with a stiff smile. "Fine. Did you steal a shuttle?"

"No."

"No, what?"

"No, I did not." Technically true.

"But we had a report of an unauthorized launch during a lock-down." She frowned bringing up her wrist wave and examining her notes.

"Mmm. No. I was able to fly out with no issues." She feigned nonchalance.

Torrence's face darkened. "Ms. Dhau, it would be wise not to play games with me. We have already talked with the attendant at the time."

It was the phrase Shadow had told her about. All her anxiety gave way to certainty. She would be able to avoid detention.

Amione raised a supercilious brow. "I wanted to see where my Da died. I had to see it. Don't you understand?"

Torrence's resolve flickered. The seed of doubt was planted. Amione didn't need Torrence's permission to get out of this. She just had to convince Elijah and Corsair that her trip was an act of grief.

Corsair cleared his throat. "Maybe we should consider--"

Torrence glared at him.

She flipped her red hair back from her face. "We will leave you here to contemplate your story."

"But I'm not under arrest." Amione pinned her with a look.

"Of course not." Elijah assured her. "Torrence there is no harm in letting her go to her quarters. I think this was all a big misunderstanding."

Torrence fumed at Elijah, giving him a look of death which he matched. She turned back to Amione. "We will still have questions. You are to stay confined to your quarters until this matter is settled."

"Deal." Amione jumped to her feet before they could change their minds and exited the detention. She didn't look back, just made her way to the exit with as much haste as she dared. She felt like tearing into a run, but that would just add to their suspicions.

There were some things that troubled her. Why didn't they ask her about the weapon's fire? Why haven't they asked her about Curphay? Or ask more questions about the injured guardian she left behind? Or the two men that were killed in the blast when she and Willan escaped? They were solely focused on her unauthorized launch of the shuttle. Something was not right.

Maybe they didn't know. She wasn't sure what the company shared and what they withheld. The strange circumstances surrounding the maiming of a guardian was definitely noteworthy. Yet, they barely mentioned the man.

She was far from getting out of this mess, but at least she was free for the moment and that meant she could get to the seedling.

Shadow, what do you think? She pressed her way through the trade area, past medical and into the residential corridors. She breathed a sigh of relief when the door to her Da's apartments came into view.

They are hiding something. I don't know what it is, but I would use extreme caution.

Amione felt its wariness through their connection. In this matter, they were in consensus. This whole thing seemed like a set up. Then there was the matter of Dodd. What was his role in all of this?

I will protect you.

Until when? Until the seedling is delivered safely back to your friend? Then I will be left vulnerable again.

I give you my promise, that until I know you are out of danger, I won't leave.

That gave Amione pause. *Why would you do that?*

Because you have risked your existence to right a wrong. The least I can do is to ensure that existence remains.

Even if my existence is short compared to your own? Amusement colored her voice.

I wasn't going to say it, but yes. It would be a short commitment.

I feel like I should be offended, but you are far too amusing for that.

Besides, I can't pass up an opportunity to get a close-up view of your species. You are quite fascinating despite your shortcomings.

Careful, Shadow, that almost sounds like admiration.

It sounds like admiration, because it is. Amione had a moment of pleasure before the entity dispelled it. *And at the same time disgust.*

Disgust?!

The amount of avarice and short-sighted view of your species is hard to ignore. Everywhere you go on Titan, you leave a mess.

Amione thought about that for a moment. It wasn't wrong. Waste was littered everywhere. It was a habit that was developed on Old Earth with dire consequences in the end. *I think that is a failing of our species.*

Because we live such a short time, it is hard for us to fathom how our actions affect future generations and other lifeforms.

Arrogance. But you are not like that, the Shadow mused.

Amione walked up to the door and hesitated before walking in. *I'm not so sure sometimes.*

She walked into the apartment and stopped short. Items were strewn everywhere, and poor little Dino was doing his best to clean it up. Tea bags were torn open and spilled across the counter. Tears of anger sprang to her eyes.

"Who would do this?" Her voice wavered in anger.

Her heart jumped when she realized whoever *they* were might have found the seedling. She ran as fast as she could over the rubble and into her room which had also been ransacked. Her bedding was pushed up into the corner, all her pictures had been torn down, and items were either on the floor or out of place. She opened the secret compartment under her desk and breathed a sigh of relief when she saw the seedling was still where she had left it.

She palmed it into her hand and held it to her chest. Relief poured out of her, but was short lived when she saw the carved bird her Da gave her laying in two pieces amidst the rubble.

Carefully, she extricated the two pieces amidst the shambles. The delicate whorls and flowers were interrupted by the terrible break in the wood. She broke down sobbing as she tried in vain to get the two pieces back together. It would never be the same. Just as her life was broken and would never be the same.

She saw a shadow loom over her, quickly turned, and flipped the intruder who slammed into the wall next to her bed.

"Umph!" The intruder cried out.

She blinked. The Yorean uniform was crumpled in a heap and a groan issued from a brown-haired man.

"Willan!"

He chuckled and winced in pain as he unfolded himself from the heap. "I wasn't expecting that." He rubbed the back of his head.

"How did you get in here?" She held out a hand.

"I used the door."

She frowned at his glib remark. "Only I can open it."

"Obviously not." He gave her a lopsided grin and gestured to the room around them. He absently checked the rest of his body for injury.

"Are you hurt?"

"Only my pride." He looked at her properly. "Hey, have you been crying?" He reached out a hand to wipe a tear from her cheek. She gripped his hand and twisted it behind him. "Ow! Ok. I won't touch you; I swear."

She released him and watched as he rubbed the pain from his wrist and hand. He was looking at her speculatively and she decided she didn't like it at all. She wiped the tears from her cheek, then pushed her curls behind her ears before folding her arms across her chest.

"What are you doing here?"

"I followed you as soon as you left Detention. I wanted to see how it went." He surveyed the wreckage.

"They haven't charged me with anything."

"That's a start, but I imagine they will eventually. Do you have an advocate you can contact?"

She raised her brows. "That will take more time than I have."

Shadow shifted restlessly in the back of her mind, reminding her that time was short.

"Well, it's obvious that someone was looking for something that you have." He nudged a picture over with his toe. "They have gone to a lot of trouble."

"Who are *they*?" Amione could feel a cold anxiety pool in her stomach.

"*They* are the real power of Titan. The ones who keep the Derelict in disrepair, scare you lot into conformity, and pissed off whatever that was down there."

She wanted to tell him that the shadow on the video wasn't the same one that was inhabiting her mind now. She wanted to tell him about the seedling, and everything she had learned. Shadow gave her warning. Willan had his own agenda, and it was likely in conflict with hers.

She clamped her mouth shut and turned away from him and back to the front room. The bedroom was far too cramped with the bulk of his body taking up nearly all the space.

She gave Dino a caress as she walked gingerly through the debris to the window. Saturn was still in shadow giving the landscape an eerie quality. She had never fully appreciated her home's beauty until now. It was wild, ageless, and spectacular.

She heard Willan carefully navigate the rumble to stand beside her. She felt his gaze on her face, but refused to give in to the urge to look at him. She imagined his hazel eyes were filled with questions; his brows quirked in a quizzical manner as he contemplated what he was going to say next. Her familiarity with his expressions alarmed her.

She was never one to study a stranger. She knew her Da's face well. Curphay's too. Even her mother, but she had never taken the time to actually look at people. Eye contact was too intimate to share with just anyone. Unless she was angry or unless she knew a person well, she never met their eyes instead she would cheat and look at their eyebrows. That seemed to satisfy most people, and kept her from experiencing the pain that came with something so direct.

"Did they find what you were hiding?" he asked softly.

She contemplated denial, but ruled it out. He wouldn't believe her anyway. "No."

His shoulders relaxed. "Good."

She finally turned towards him. His forehead was pressed to the glass and he looked weary.

"You don't even know what it is." Her eyes raked over his profile, trying to read his intentions.

"I don't have to. All I need to know is that it is important to you." His hazel eyes met hers.

She quickly looked away.

"So, what next?" He pushed away from the wall and walked back to the kitchen.

"I need to get back to the surface."

"How do you want to do that?"

She loved how he phrased the question. Not why, just how. Like he understood how important this was for her. "A Yorean orbitor shouldn't draw much attention, right?"

"You know orbiters don't normally go to the surface when a shuttle will do. It would never work. We need to find another way. Preferably one that won't arouse any more suspicion." He scooped the ruined tea into the recycler and moved the unbroken dishes into the cleaner.

The door chimed.

They both looked at each other in alarm.

"Expecting someone?" He nudged his head toward the door.

She shook her head.

The door chimed a second time.

He placed a finger over his lips and silently stepped over the rubble into her room and shut the door.

She squeezed her hands together rubbing her thumb across the back of her hand in a self-soothing motion. She waved over the panel to get a visual. It was her mother. After she had left, Amione made sure she couldn't come and go into the apartment without Amione's permission. At least she was able to keep one person out, but not for long knowing her mother.

She opened the door.

Jheslae Dhau looked severe in her taupe jacket with matching pants. The silver pin on her lapel winked in the low light.

Amione didn't say anything. She turned on her heel and sat on the couch and waited.

Jheslae entered the apartment and the door hissed closed behind her. Her dark eyes took in the chaos with sharp notice before landing on Amione. "Did they find what they were looking for?"

Amione's brow raised. "What could they be possibly looking for?" Suspicion caused the hair on the back of her neck to raise. Shadow took notice.

"The seedling your father took."

Amione tried to play dumb. "Seedling?"

"The one in your pocket." Jheslae nodded at her coveralls.

Amione knew that her mouth had to be hanging open. "How could you possibly know that?" Her eyes narrowed.

"You don't know what you have become involved with yet." She relaxed her stance and placed her hands behind her back.

"Then tell me." She leaned forward on the couch.

Jheslae contemplated, then shook her head. "No. You are going to be interrogated again, and it's better if you don't know anything."

Amione growled.

"Not yet," Jheslae amended. "I need the seed so I can protect you."

Shadow flared to life flooding her with defiance. "No."

Jheslae took a step back, then paced to the side and into the kitchen still keeping her eyes on Amione. Amione could feel her mother examine and evaluate and she hated her for it.

"They will find it."

"I need it. I..." She was about to let on what her real plans were, but Shadow reminded her of the mission. She clamped her mouth shut.

"I can't help you if you don't tell me the truth."

A humorless laugh escaped. "Just like you did just now? The need-to-know speech'? Forget it. I've been fine on my own for a long time. I don't need you to protect me." She hit her chest for emphasis.

Jheslae folded her hands behind her back. "For what is coming next, daughter, you will need my protection." She reached a hand in her pocket and pulled out a small device and placed it on the counter. "When you need me, activate this. I will find you."

"And do what?" Amione sneered.

Jheslae walked to the door and paused looking Amione in the eye. "Whatever is necessary." The door hissed open and she exited.

Amione stared at the closed door she didn't know how long. What was this threat she was hinting at? Who was coming to interrogate her? How was she going to get back to Curphay?

She could feel her anxiety rising as thought after thought pummeled her mind sending her into a downward spiral. All the fight she had exhibited towards her mother left her, deflating her confidence to a new low. She couldn't do this. She contemplated running after her mother. Then felt disgust for even thinking that was an option.

You aren't alone, Shadow whispered. *I am here.* She felt a sense of calm wash over her. Whatever Shadow was, he was definitely a source of strength. The symbiosis was startling. Unexpected.

"Amione?"

She looked up abruptly. She had completely forgotten that Willan was there. He stood in the door of her bedroom, holding something in his hands.

"Come in. She's gone." She leaned her head back against the headrest and pulled her knees up to her chest.

Dino had cleaned up most of the debris in that short time, and worked on the corner behind the couch. Willan walked silently through the living area and sat on the table facing her.

"Here. I tried my best to fix it."

Willan handed her the bird her Da had carved. She carefully plucked it from Willan's outstretched hand and examined his handiwork. There was a fine line where the break happened, but otherwise the bird was almost back to its original form. She ran her thumbs over the carvings finding comfort in the grooves and ridges.

Her voice came out husky. "It's a bird." She answered his unspoken question.

"A bird?"

"It's a creature from Old Earth. It used to fly in the sky and live in trees."

"I know what a bird is. Why do you have a carving of one?" Willan looked at the small carving.

She looked at him with greater interest. How did he know what a bird was?

She mentally shrugged. The same way she learned of them, through a book. "My Da made it for me. In fact, it was the last thing he gave to me before he…"

Willan's beefy hand awkwardly patted her knee. "I can understand why it is valuable to you."

A long silence extended between them as she continued to gaze at the carving. Images of her Da laughing and smiling, filtered unbidden into her mind. She shook the images away and focused on the earnest young man before her, who was looking at her with such kind hazel eyes. "Thank you."

A crooked smile tilted his mouth. "Anytime."

She unfolded her legs and started pacing. "What is the plan now? How do I get back to the surface?"

"Undetected?"

"Preferably."

"We don't."

She stopped and placed her hands on her hips. "That's not much of a plan, Willan."

He laughed. "No, but it is what we have."

"Explain."

"We don't have time to be stealthy, but we do have time to be sneaky."

"What's the difference?"

"Have you ever heard of the Stellan Technique?"

"The what?" She resumed pacing.

"The Stellan Technique."

She gave him a sidelong glance. "What is it?"

He leaned back with his hands bracing him on the table's surface. "My friend Stellan and I used to get into a lot of trouble growing up."

She placed her hands on her cheeks. "No way! You get in trouble?"

He raised a brow. "You get a little sarcastic when you are stressed, do you know that?"

She rolled her eyes.

"Any way... Stellan and I used to take things from time to time. Nothing big. Food mostly. After a while the vendors caught on to us, and took extra measures to make sure we didn't take anything. One time a vendor added a dye pack to one of the food rations and when we got out of the arcade it went off. We were dyed blue for the next month, and..." He cleared his throat when he noticed Amione wasn't laughing. "Anyway... Stellan and I devised a technique where we would find a patsy and make the vendors think it was the other person who was doing the stealing. We were able to find the dye packs and slip it into their pocket or somewhere on their person. The Vendor was so focused on dealing with the *thief* they didn't notice that we slipped in and took whatever we wanted."

Amione looked at him askance. "What has this got to do with our situation?"

"We need to give them a *thief* so you can slip by and go to the surface."

She leaned against the wall and looked at him thoughtfully. "How do we do that? I already admitted I took the shuttle."

He sighed and leaned forward with his head in his hands. "My dear woman, you are incredibly literal when it comes to things like this. Don't get me wrong, it's endearing, but endearing isn't going to get you back to your friend."

She pursed her lips. Being called literal made her bristle, but he was right. Doing the right thing wasn't going to get her out of this mess, and more importantly, it wasn't going to get her back to Curphay. "Who would we get as a...patsy? And what will happen to them?"

"Leave that to me. We only need them long enough for you and I to escape." Willan's eyes glinted with mischief.

Amione felt uneasy, but what alternative did she have? Doing the right thing was going to get her locked up. Going to her mother was definitely not an option.

What do you think, Shadow? She gnawed on her lip.

It's an intriguing idea. Whatever it takes to get back to the surface with the seedling. Of course, I could always--

Absolutely not! She closed her mind abruptly to the entity. She would not bring attention to herself by using the unusual abilities the Shadow had given her.

She looked down on Willan with a frown. "Say this works, what is the plan?"

"When the leadership is distracted by a new suspect, we sneak on to a shuttle and go to the surface."

"We?"

"Well, now, there will still be guardians crawling over the site, won't there?"

She didn't like that he was tagging along.

He will only slow us down. Shadow whispered in her ear.

That, and if she had to use these abilities again, she didn't want an audience. She didn't completely trust Willan. Especially since the Magistrate from Cadence wanted him to lift seeds from the Arboretum. It seemed she was making deals with the devil all over the place.

What is the devil? Shadow queried.

Hush! She forcefully pushed the entity back. She felt its surprise before turning her attention back to Willan. "I'm perfectly capable of getting down there safely."

"Of that I have no doubt, but I can make things easier."

"Why?"

He seemed taken aback by her abrupt question. "Why?"

"You could easily get the seeds for your Magistrate and go back to the Derelict. Our agreement would be fulfilled. Why would you take more risks and help me?"

He folded his hands and leaned his elbows on his knees. His hazel eyes pinned her in place. "Because, Amione Dhau, you have been the most exciting thing to happen to me in a long time."

Chapter 22

Incursion

"Full circle from the tomb of the womb to the womb of the tomb we come, an ambiguous, enigmatical incursion into a world of solid matter that is soon to melt from us like the substance of a dream."
Joseph Campbell

Another mechanical entity entered Saturn's orbit. This time the probe circled the moon and dropped something through the atmosphere. It was small, hardly anything at all, but it was enough to pique Oal's interest.

"We need to see what it is," Oal insisted.

"It is nothing. Why should we trouble ourselves?" The Sadool languidly circled the cavern ceiling.

"It was sent by intelligent beings. Perhaps they would want to communicate with us." Oal flexed his limbs in excitement.

"Is there something wrong with my company that you are so eager to be rid of it?" The entity drifted down to revolve around Oal's sprawling form.

Oal wasn't sure what to make of the Sadools jealousy. "Of course not, but this is an amazing opportunity. Probably the last before I have to take root."

A long pause. What would his parentage think of his impatience? Tromfeld's never jumped so eagerly at something like this. It was always wait and see, then wait and see some more. Could he be considered a Tromfeld if he was so impatient?

"Very well," it conceded reluctantly. "But we go when the moon transits behind Saturn. It will be a long journey. Are you sure you are ready for this?"

Oal flexed his curled leaves, admiring the rose quartz hue in the hazy light. "I am ready. I want to see this new thing with my own eyes, and then I will be content to take root."

The moon slipped behind Titan and full night filled the sky with darkness. Only the brightest stars penetrated the hazy atmosphere. Saturn was in silhouette against the sun. Its rings backlit creating bands of gold. The weather was dry with no danger of ethane storms passing between them and the object.

Even with the Sadool's help, it took over a day to get to the object. Oal had spent too much time in the caves with its soft hydrocarbon sludge. It had made his fore leaves tender. The rocky terrain rubbed them raw and caused much pain.

"Are you sure you wish to continue?" Concern colored the Sadool's voice. It hovered and orbited Oal as he plodded forward.

"It will be fine. Just my fore leaves preparing to take root. Tenderness is to be expected." The lie slipped easily from his thoughts.

Oal could feel the Sadool's doubt and disapproval. "You are a stubborn creature."

"Likewise, my friend."

The Sadool paused its revolution. "I suppose I am as well."

"I think that is why both of our species persist. We are too stubborn to let ourselves die out." Oal drew in a sharp breath when his forelimb slipped on another stone.

"You may be right. I wonder how many species have come and gone in the time we have existed?" The Sadool paused before resuming its revolution.

"More than we will ever know."

Oal caught sight of the mysterious object in the distance. Its electromagnetic resonance showed up as a brilliant blue among the darkness of Titan's surface.

"If it is a vehicle from an intelligent species, it would stand to reason that they would have something that would observe its surroundings." The Sadool pointed out.

"That is true." Oal shifted impatiently, eager to see the device up close.

"I'm not ready to reveal myself to them. Are you?"

Oal thought for a moment. "No. No, I'm not ready."

Disappointment washed over him. They had traveled so far, and now he may never know what these beings were like.

"I may have a solution." The Sadool stopped its revolutions and settled in front of Oal.

Hope flared anew. "What is it?"

"I have been playing with the idea of concealment. If I tweak our electromagnetic fields, we should be able to evade detection."

"That sounds promising. What must I do?" His limbs twitched in anticipation.

"Stay still." The Sadool drew closer and wrapped its amorphous form around Oal.

At first Oal didn't feel anything. Then he felt a tingling sensation at the base of his neck that spread down his spine, over his shoulders and down each leaf.

"That should be enough. Proceed."

Oal was nervous about the Sadool in such close contact, considering that it consumed things on a regular basis. However, if there were any ill effects, they were not immediately apparent. At this point, Oal didn't care even if there were drawbacks. Not if it meant seeing this new thing first hand.

As they approached the object, whatever its purpose, it was now inactive. The shell was metallic and smooth. It was slightly rounded on top with a flatter bottom. All manners of instruments were contained within its shell.

"Curious beings," Oal remarked as he paced to the side.

"It is definitely constructed." The Sadool's voice echoed hollowly in Oal's head.

"It seems odd that they would send a constructed object to explore this place," Oal mused, as he carefully circumnavigated the object.

"Perhaps this environment is hostile to their species like the dwarf planet was hostile to you."

"Perhaps you are right." Oal bent to take a closer look. "There are markings all over the shell."

"Do you think they mean anything?"

"They are too uniform to be random. They were definitely made with purpose." Oal was tempted to touch the metallic casing.

"Shall we move it?" The Sadool voice reverberated through his body.

"Absolutely not! What if they return for it? That would pique their curiosity. I think that is something to be avoided with this species if we want to remain hidden."

"I think we have learned as much as we can from it." The Sadool ignored his tirade.

"You are so contrary sometimes," Oal groused.

"And you worry far too much. Judging from their tech, I don't think we have anything to worry about."

"When we came here there was no sentient life in this system, and now we have proof that there is. If they have been able to advance that quickly what makes you think that they won't be here within a century?"

"We will deal with that if it comes." The Sadool was unconcerned.

"When. Sadool. When they come."

Chapter 23

Occam's Beard

"You know how I feel about Occam's Razor. The simplest answer isn't usually the right one. Devious and unlikely is everywhere. You ought to launch your own theory: Occam's beard, you could call it."
Sophie Hannah

A mione still didn't believe Willan was for real. There had to be a catch to his offer. There had to be. Didn't there?

Shadow, what do you think? She fidgeted with the cuff of her sleeve.

I have limited experience with your kind. What you say is often very different from what you think.

That is true. But not always. Sometimes the inner voice matches the outer one. I've never been good at determining if that is the case with people. At least, not right away. She pushed the curls back from her face impatiently.

Then you have the advantage. But if he can help you to return the seedling, then I would accept what he is offering.

She grimaced. She hated how logical Shadow could be, but it was the same conclusion that she had come to already.

"Amione?" Willan's earnest eyes expected an answer.

Why did he have to be so damn attractive? It was distracting. Willan wasn't beautiful, but there was something magnetic about him. His aura was like the sun, orange and curling about his form like it was its own living creature.

"Fine. But I did warn you." She looked at him from the corner of her eye.

He smiled widely. "You did."

"Whatever I tell you to do, you do." She pointed a finger at him.

"I will...try." His smile turned lopsided, making her heart skip.

She frowned. "I guess that will have to do. So, I need a way down."

He clapped his hands together. "I have just the thing." He opened the Wave in front of them. "There is a prep ship going down tonight. It won't get us to the exact mine, but it will get us to one of the substations nearby."

Prep teams were used to de-ice all equipment after a Titian night ended. They used a special prepping agent to work the frozen methane and ethane off of the equipment and do a preliminary check before the miners came down to do final inspections. Usually, a few dozen made the trip and personnel switched every few days and were chosen via a lottery. It paid well and was a highly coveted position.

She had to admire his ingenious solution, but was unwilling to admit it just yet. "How do we secure spots for ourselves?"

"Already done."

She looked at him in surprise through the graphics of the Wave. "When did you do that?"

"Amione, Amione. I can't give away all my secrets," he teased.

That coaxed a reluctant smile from her before turning her attention back to the Wave. "I am fairly certain they won't call me for interrogation until first thing tomorrow. I won't be missed until then."

And then I will be on my way to Curphay.

She could feel Shadow's anticipation which so closely matched her own. They were nearly done with this whole affair.

The door chimed.

Willan and Amione stared at each other. She quickly closed the Wave.

"Expecting someone else?" He raised a brow.

"No. No one." She looked at the door dreading what may be behind it.

"It's been pretty busy around here," he observed with a grimace.

She sighed in frustration. "Maybe it's my mother again. You should hide."

"Agreed." He quickly went into her room and closed the door.

The door chimed again.

She slowly rose from the couch and tousled her hair and tried to look sufficiently sleepy. She engaged the panel to see who it was. It was definitely not her mother. Instead, there was a severe looking man flanked by two guardians.

She thought that maybe she could pretend not to be home, but if they were who she thought they were, they were the same people who ransacked the apartment. Their plans would be in ruin if she resisted. There was nothing to do, but open the door.

She waved a trembling hand over the panel, opened the door, and looked at the man expectantly.

"Amione Dhau." The man's gravelly voice sounded impatient.

"Yes?"

"We are to accompany you to interrogation."

"Who are *we*?" She folded her arms across her chest.

"This way, please." The man's face revealed nothing.

"Who are you, and why should I go with you?" She didn't like this at all.

"You are expected now." Black brows sliced over hard brown eyes.

"Let me get my--"

The guardians pushed their way in and prevented her from going back to her room.

"You won't need anything." The man's cold gaze bore into her. He nodded to the two guardians who pushed her none too gently into the corridor.

She could feel the seedling press into her thigh and was afraid that they would discover it and her ultimate purpose before she had a chance to return it.

Shadow! The Seedling!

Fear not, Amione, I will be able to conceal it from prying eyes. She could feel Shadow move from her hand down her spine and to the pocket where the Seedling lay. She felt pressure, then the Seedling was inside her thigh.

She tried her best not to show any outward reaction. In fact, her fear probably worked in her favor. It was expected, but not for the reasons the guardians suspected. An ache traveled up her spine with each step.

I'm sorry to cause you discomfort, but it is the only way. The entity apologized.

What did you do? She limped.

The Guardian pushed her and she stumbled to the floor barely catching herself before her chin hit the hard surface. No one helped her to her feet. Painfully, she pushed herself up, conscious of the men watching her. She glared at them and continued to follow the leader. Instead of turning down the corridor to detention, they turned the opposite direction.

"Where are you taking me?" She frantically looked around to see if there was anyone else in the corridor.

No one answered.

She balked, skidding to a stop. "Where are you taking me?" Her voice rose in panic.

Both Guardians grabbed one of her elbows and pushed her forward, causing her shoes to skid against the slick floor. She fought back and the man's face loomed before her.

"It is in your best interest to cooperate, Ms. Dhau." His dull brown eyes cut into her own. She could feel her fear rise, threatening to overwhelm her senses. She nodded letting him know she would not give them anymore trouble.

This went beyond the Counsel, beyond Demeter. Maybe now she would find out who was really pulling the strings and why her Da was killed.

I am here. I will help you, Shadow whispered. It wasn't enough to get her to relax completely, but it did give her courage to move forward.

His gaze flicked from one to the other Guardian, giving a silent order to release her. She felt their grasps ease. The man turned and continued down the corridor toward the diplomatic quarters.

Diplomats rarely visited Demeter once Yorea was built. Her Da always thought it was a waste of space. They should have converted it into smaller living quarters years ago. Maybe they could have taken some of the residents from the Derelict, but no one could agree. As usual, the Council chose to remain unchanged.

So, who was there now? Certainly not the Elders. They would have taken her back to detention. There was only one person it could be.

The main corridor turned into a more finely maintained one with cobalt blue graphite walls polished to a mirror finish. She could see her reflection as she passed. Copper accents punctuated the walls from time to time, framing the walkway every few meters.

They entered the open area where dignitaries congregated for the view. It was conspicuously empty. In the large window beyond, she could see the beginnings of the sunrise.

She was pulled away from the view and brought before the large doorway at the other end. It was similarly decorated with large bands of copper framing the doorway and stretching across the floor. The cobalt blue winged away from the frame and ended in control panels of the latest design.

The man paused before the door. It opened revealing a lavish office occupied by none other than the visiting Head Magistrate of Titan.

She should have been surprised, but in light of everything she had uncovered so far, she wasn't.

They walked briskly into the quarters. Dodd looked out the window at Titan still in night. Some of the clouds glowed neon blue with night shine. Stars dotted the black sky while the shifting copper atmosphere writhed below.

He was impeccably dressed in an all-white suit that fit his trim form in all the right places. He was much taller than most Titians with broad shoulders and slim hips more reminiscent of an Old Earth Warrior rather than a modern Titian human.

He turned at their approach and dismissed the Guardians. The squat man bowed and left silently through a side door. The Magistrate's blue eyes seemed to see through her as she took in his carefully coiffed copper hair and square jawline.

Shadow stirred in recognition, jolting her from her perusal. Apprehension not her own filled her, making her muscle's tense.

Dodd smiled, but it did not touch his eyes.

"It seems we have something in common." His cool baritone slipped over her like silk, making her cringe.

She whispered, "What is this Shadow?"

I need permission to protect you. The entities voice sounded urgent.

Her alarm increased. *Why?!*

Give it!

Pressure built in her mind as she gazed dully at Dodd.

"Is something wrong?" His blue eyes turned from blue to a ruby red as tentacles erupted from his arms.

Her eyes widened unsure of what she was seeing, but sensing that she was in imminent danger. *I give it!*

Her body felt impossibly tight as Shadow filled her. The fatigue, pain and weakness dissipated, replaced by a surge of strength. All her Akido lessons with her Da, moved to the forefront of her mind and Shadow drew from that knowledge and built upon it with its own abilities. She fell automatically into a *hanme* position.

Instinctively, Amione moved just before the High Magistrates tentacle shot out and hit her. She rolled back and was on her feet again before the next blow occurred. She extended her leg and Shadow's tentacle extended her reach, pushing the desk against Dodd's legs. The desk squealed against the shiny graphite floor. He deflected the substantive piece of furniture easily with one blow.

"It seems, young Amione, you have acquired a companion." His grin grew more garish as he rounded the desk and stood in front of her. "You and I could come to an arrangement."

Breathing heavily, she could feel the extra heft that Shadow gave her was wearing on her body. She glared at him. "It was you, wasn't it." Fury increased her determination.

"I don't know what you are referring to." But his eyes said otherwise.

"You killed my father!" she growled. She pushed forward with a flurry of blows which he countered easily by using his tentacles to wrap around his body, creating as an oily black armor.

He chuckled, infuriating her even more. "You are much feistier than I thought you would be."

Shadow infused a calming agent into her system. She tried to hold on to her anger, furious that Shadow interfered. *Not now!*

Anger will expend your energy faster. We need to remain calm, it reasoned.

He killed my father, she hissed.

You are dealing with far more than a man.

She paused. The entity was right, Dodd was toying with her. She eased back into a *gedan* stance and watched him carefully.

He paced around her as she kept him in front, carefully watching for any additional moves he might make.

"You are not what I expected." His ruby eyes glittered in the dim room, making him look bestial.

"What does that mean?" She avoided looking at his eyes, instead concentrated on the placement of his hands.

"Did you know that there was a prophecy about you?"

She snorted. "Prophecy? You sound like something from the Bible."

"A terribly inaccurate piece of fiction, but there were some things in it that rang true. Prophets were one such being."

"If there were ever such people, they are long dead."

"We thought so too, but then we met other species. Delectable, delicious species who had terribly interesting notions about the creation of the universe." His eyes grew brighter and more feverish.

She shivered recalling the reports of how entire ships seemed to be consumed.

"And what does this Prophecy say?" She hoped Willan was looking for her. She needed to give him time to find help. That's if he knew where they had taken her.

"It says that you and I are going to be great friends," he purred.

Fury and disgust rose up from within again. "I gotta say. Forcing me into a meeting and attacking me, isn't winning me over."

He laughed. "From what I have observed, it was the only way to get you here."

"You killed my father. Why would I ever agree to work with you."

"Would you believe that killing your father was an accident?" His smile belied the words.

She lashed out with her arm and Shadow complied by launching a tentacle at the Magistrate who countered with his own and wrapped Shadow in a twist before both entities phased back into non-corporeal form.

"I guess not." He raised an amused brow. "There is much I could teach you if you are willing."

"We are not." She ground out.

The smile dropped from his face as he leveled his ruby stare on her. "That is unfortunate, but not unexpected. We will just keep you confined until I figure out what to do with you."

Panic enveloped her. She couldn't allow that to happen. She needed to get back to Curphay.

A bang sounded on the outer door. Amione quickly looked at the cobalt blue entry behind the Magistrate and back at the man in front of her. The shadow melted back into Dodd's form and his eyes returned to icy blue. He folded his hands behind his back and fixed a smile on his face.

"It seems we will have to delay our tete a tete for later."

A flick of his finger and Guardians spilled in from the side door, taking defensive stances in front of the entryway. Amione wasn't sure if she should keep her eye on Dodd or what was coming through the door.

The door opened with a squealing hiss. Amione's eyes widened in surprise when she saw her mother standing in the doorway surrounded by six guardians weapons drawn. The three elders cowered behind them, looking like they wanted to be anywhere but there.

Amione recognized Willan beneath one of the helmets. She squelched her expression, hoping Dodd did not notice her interest. One look and she knew she had failed.

Like the force of nature she was, Jheslae Dhau entered the room walking up to the Head Magistrate and giving him a withering look. An amused smile teased his lips as he gave the wordless command to stand down, allowing Jheslae to approach Amione.

She gave her a subtle questioning look, and Amione responded with a slight nod and relaxed her posture. It was the first time, as far as Amione knew, that Jheslae had come to her defense. A part of her wondered if there was a hidden agenda. The other part, the one that hoped for some sort of connection with her mother, hoped that she was there to defend her against this...monster.

The Guardians filed in behind Jheslae. Amione avoided looking at Willan and turned her focus on her mother and Dodd as they squared off.

"Why have you detained my daughter?" Jheslae stood ramrod straight and gave no ground. She was the supreme authority in this situation, and she was going to use it.

Dodd returned to his desk and leaned casually against it. "We were just having a discussion."

Jheslae's sharp eyes took in the position of the desk, the skid marks on the tile, and the disheveled appearance of Amione. "Unlikely."

An over-bright smile appeared on Dodd's face. "What do you think happened here?"

"You are walking a fine line, Head Magistrate." Jheslae's eyes narrowed. "You may have jurisdiction over Titan, but the Alliance can easily get involved if something untoward is occurring."

"A warning, then."

"A reminder."

He nodded acquiescing. "A reminder."

Jheslae gave him one last penetrating gaze, then moved to the door.

Amione followed her mother, looking back at Dodd before the door closed obscuring him from view. Whatever had happened in this room wasn't over. Not by a long shot. She had questions, lots of questions. For now, she would get away from whatever that was standing in that room.

Once away from the Diplomatic Sector, Jheslae dismissed all the Guardians except for Willan.

Jheslae turned to the elders. "Remember what you have witnessed today."

Torrence gave Amione a wary glare. "We will remember."

"If there are any more difficulties, contact the Alliance." Jheslae brought up her wave display on her wrist with her contact info attached. Torrence held up her wrist display to receive the information.

"I doubt we will have any more trouble." Torrence looked pointedly at Amione. "As long as you fulfill your end."

"It will be done."

The elders scurried to the city center at a brisk walk not daring to look back.

"What agreement?" Amione fisted her hands at her side.

"That you will go to the ARC Project and never return to Demeter." Jheslae's black eyes landed on her.

"Never return?" She could feel her ire rise in her chest.

"You stole a shuttle," she stated bluntly.

Shame burned Amione's cheeks. "With good reason."

"Regardless, you broke the laws here. The sentence would have included detention without my interference."

Amione's fury replaced her shame. "Why are you getting involved now?"

She stood squarely in front of Amione and looked her in the eye. "There are things at work that you are ignorant of. Your father and I decided that you should be kept away from it until you were old enough to make your own decisions. I had hoped that none of this would find you until after you graduated, but as so often happens, life will give you a twist. When that happens, we must adapt."

"You and Da..."

"I will explain, Amione. But right now, you need to complete your mission."

"How do you know about that?"

"I don't know the details, but I do know you are the only one who can complete it. And this young man," she turned to Willan. "Has agreed to help you."

Willan stepped forward. "We don't have much time. The Prep team is leaving in a few minutes, and I don't think the Head Magistrate is going to be placated by a few Alliance promises."

Amione stared at them both as if they had lost their senses. She felt Shadow stir.

Go, Amione. We are running out of time. Shadow sounded weak and unfocused, which scared her.

She nodded to her mother. "Ok. But I will hold you to that promise."

A slight smile curved her lips and warmed her eyes. "I look forward to it."

Chapter 24

The Root of All Things

"We breath, we live, we die, but through it all we have a choice to affect the universe in a positive or a negative way. This is the root of all things."
Ca'mi Nao, The Book of Knowledge

Oal dug his roots deep into the Titian soil, reaching for the energies stored beneath the surface. This was what he was built for, to tap into the very soul of the planet, and find the pathways to his parentage. It would be many millennia before he heard a response. The unseen network governed everything that they were, and this place was no different.

His once flexible limbs became rigid, meant to expand incrementally as time passed on. He was pale with rose quartz tips similar to his coloring from before. His branches curled into spirals and new appendages grew as he grew. One day he would create seedlings of his own and watch them as they took off to other places or stayed on planet to populate it.

He differed from his ancestors in one distinct way, he was friends with a Sadool. The Sadool had assigned itself as Oal's protector, and took the work seriously.

More constructed crafts filled the skies. A single craft multiplied into two, then four, then eight. They doubled quickly populating the surface as well as the sky.

"What have you seen on the surface?" Oal asked anxiously. "Are they friend or enemy?"

"Neither, I think."

"How can they be neither?"

"They are completely unaware of our existence and I have taken great pains to keep it that way."

"So more of these non-organic beings have arrived?"

"That is the curious thing about them. The non-organics open and smaller organic beings emerge wearing thin barriers."

"Perhaps this environment is inhospitable for their kind."

"But why come here if that is the case?"

"Maybe they are curious. After all, we were curious about many things including the rogue planet."

"The one where you couldn't go, but you didn't force yourself to endure such an environment."

"No. But maybe these non-organic constructions allow them to adapt."

"Adapt?" The Sadool was entirely unfamiliar with the word.

"To take a situation and to find a way to overcome the challenge."

The Sadool paused to mull over Oal's words. "To adapt... Such a strange concept. It either is or isn't."

"You have seen how I adapt. My form is constantly changing."

"That is true."

"It is likely that these beings are the same. Constantly changing. You must get a closer look."

"I loathe to leave you so vulnerable."

"We have the mind link. You can communicate with me that way, and I will be able to sense what you sense as if I was there. You must, MUST get a closer look. We should know as much as possible about these beings. One day we might meet one."

"Fine." The Sadool acquiesced reluctantly. "But I will stay in my non-corporeal state."

"I insist on it. We have no idea how they would react if they saw your form. We must know as much as possible before we contact them."

"IF we contact them."

"And no consuming them," Oal hastily added.

The Sadool paused. "Just a taste?"

"Absolutely not!"

"Fine."

"Go. I'm anxious to learn more."

The Sadool exited the cavern and drifted over the surface toward the vehicles parked near a hillside. The vast plains that abutted the methane lake posed no obstacle to the Sadool as it approached stealthily from the east. Two of the beings were holding inorganic items that scanning their surroundings.

The Sadool sidled up to the vehicle that had brought them to the surface, and examined its composition. It was smooth with small pock marks marring the surface near the nose. Transparent sheets allowed it to look inside where all types of shapes and surfaces covered the interior. The small lights were the most interesting. It reminded the Sadool of stars dotting a night sky. Except these were most definitely not stars. After further study, it determined the panels were electrically based. It noticed the lights flashed in a specific pattern, but had no idea what that pattern indicated.

The Sadool easily slipped through the material, allowing it to explore the inside. Strange markings marred the surface and backlit squares of light had unusual markings as well. What their purpose was, it could not fathom. It curled around the interior from the ceiling to the floor, back to front before exiting into the light once again.

It approached the beings cautiously. In its non-corporeal state, it should remain hidden, but it didn't know what kind of senses these beings possessed. So, it kept to the shadows, only moving when it was sure it wasn't being observed. It stopped several meters from the nearest being and watched.

It was covered with a cobalt blue material that had four appendages. Two were firmly pressed into the ground. The other two were on either side of the central mass and seemed to articulate with only limited movement either to gesture to the horizon, or to work the item it held. The top protrusion swiveled back and forth, down and up. Like the vehicle, it also had a transparent piece of material.

What was inside intrigued the Sadool the most. They were organic, and they were ugly. Two evenly spaced orbs moved constantly. Maybe some form of visual sensor. The hole in the middle of its face was filled with bony protrusions which they displayed with regularity. An annoying noise was emanating from the orifice. Why Oal thought these beings would ever be enlightened, he wasn't sure.

Why encase their bodies with inorganic material? The Sadool had never understood these corporeal beings. There was very little that kept the Sadool at bay. It could go most anywhere without issue. But these beings of matter and energy were limited and these beings in particular seemed very limited.

It slunk down as one of the beings turned its way. Then they both returned to their vehicle, closed the hatch, and took off. The Sadool watched as the vehicle rose higher into the sky until it couldn't sense it any longer.

It returned to the cavern more perplexed than ever.

"Did you see?" The Sadool asked.

"Yes. They are interesting beings. Very different from you and I."

"Closer to you than to I." The Sadool sniffed.

"Yes. But I have never seen inorganic materials used to encase an organic being before."

"It is hard to ascertain their intentions."

"I think that much is clear."

"Tell me."

"They are curious," Oal stated simply.

"In that they are very like us," The Sadool conceded.

"I agree."

"Will they return?"

"Of that, I have no doubt," Oal assured it.

Chapter 25

The Gaia Hypothesis

"The most powerful weapon in [the universe] is the human soul on fire."
Ferdinand Foch

Amione tried to rouse Shadow several times, but no answer. She still felt its presence. As long as she could feel that, she kept her anxiety at bay, barely.

The Seedling, however, reminded her of its presence with each step. She gritted her teeth and bore through the pain as they ran to the bay where the Prep Team was leaving.

"I know you haven't told me everything." Willan interrupted her thoughts through the helmet communications. "I respect that, but I wish you would tell me where we are going and what we are about to face."

She glanced at Willan's hulking form and debated on how much to give away. Did she tell him about Shadow, the Seedling, where Curphay has been all this time? How much did she say?

"We are going to the new mining tunnel."

"I have sussed out that much, but what is so damnably important about that tunnel? What's down there?"

"Something that doesn't wish to be found. I have to return something that had been taken and then I can get Curphay back."

"What is it?"

She sighed.

"Amione, I think we have been through enough together that you can let me in on this much. After all, I am risking my life," he reasoned.

She stopped abruptly. "I'm not asking you to do that."

212

He looked back at her. "You don't have to. But if I'm going to be helpful, I need to know the why."

She frowned at him, then started walking. They pushed past several residents before she found her voice again. "It is a seedling."

"A seedling?" Surprise registered in his voice. "What kind of seedling could be found on Titan?"

"I am still not entirely sure of that," she replied honestly. "All I know is that it was taken from a cavern near the new mine, and it must be returned at all cost."

"What does it grow into?"

"I think it would be better for you to see it yourself."

"Then it is a plant."

"Not exactly."

They turned the corner into the launch bay, which was crowded with workers going down with the Prep Teams. Each team was color coded, corresponding to the shuttles they were assigned to. They had cobalt stripes on their suits which would lead them to the Prep area closest to the new mine.

"What else aren't you telling me?"

"What makes you think I haven't told you everything?"

"Your jaw locks and your mouth does this twitchy thing."

"It does not!" She looked at him aghast.

"It's true. It's kind of cute actually."

Now she would have to check her face whenever she decided to lie. She thought she was better at covering her expressions.

"What else do I need to know?" Willan persisted.

He always had a way of making her feel exposed. Normally, she hated that feeling, but with Willan, it felt exciting and new.

"Nothing," she said to quickly.

"Amione..." His tone was a warning.

"For now. Nothing for now."

He growled in frustration. "Fine. But the minute I need to know it, you better tell me."

"I will."

"Promise me."

"Promise?"

"Give me your word that you will," he insisted.

"I said I would." She threw her hands up in the air. She wasn't frustrated with Willan. He had a right to ask. She was frustrated with being in this situation.

He fell silent again as they lined up in front of their shuttle with twenty others. It would be a tight fit, but greater numbers meant they would be less likely to be missed.

"Do you think the Dodd will follow us?" She asked as they found the furthest corner and strapped in.

"Definitely. I'm hoping your mother will be able to distract him long enough so we can get down there and do whatever it is you need to do."

Her heart jumped. She wasn't sure if she could manage another confrontation with whatever Dodd was. She had so many questions, but Shadow was still slumbering, recuperating, or healing. She didn't know which, but she needed answers.

Shadow? She reached out tentatively with her mind. *Are you still there?*

Shadow moved within her mind. He felt...thin. She didn't know any other way to describe it. After feeling its presence fill her only hours ago, this minimal presence was frightening.

I am present, Shadow wearily replied.

We are heading to the surface. But Dodd will follow. What should I do?

We must protect the Seedlings. Shadows voice vibrated before thinning out.

What would he do if he knew?

Destroy them all, or worse, exploit them for his benefit.

She remembered how the tree had communicated with her. The imagery of other star systems, other places, and the presence that encroached from Darkness.

She resented the position she had been put in and the danger Curphay was still in, but she also felt purpose. She had been meant to find these beings.

What that meant in the long run, she didn't know, but the knowledge that she belonged burned deep in her soul.

Was the entity inside of him... It... it seemed like it was very similar to you.

Because it is. We are Sadool.

Would he also possess the power of foresight?

We all have that capability. Yes.

They knew they couldn't get to you directly.

With the protections I put up, yes. It would have prevented another Sadool from coming into the cavern.

So, all of this was manipulated.

Manipulated?

Don't you see? My Da finding a seedling. The opening of a new mine without specs being done. My Da's death. Even me.

For what end?

I don't know, but it has to do with the Seedlings.

A chill ran down her spine. The Sadool had been waging a war with the outer edges of their galaxy, destroying ships and even a planet. Stories about entire beings being consumed by darkness filtered to the colonies daily.

We are missing something. Why did you and Oal come to Titan?

Oal was drawn to this system. I found Oal, and we realized that there was a connection we could not explain.

Like our connection?

Very much like our connection.

And what would happen if all three of us were together?

I don't know.

She absently noted that the shuttle had left the bay and descended to the surface. Chatter from the other team members diminished to minimal levels. She dared to glance at Willan who was watching the scenery pass outside the main window.

So, a Sadool has connected with the Head Magistrate.

Yes. It would appear so.

But you aren't on the same side.

That is also true.

She felt satisfied with the answer. *And in order for one of you to assume corporeal form, you need to bond with a willing host.*

Yes, one who is aligned with our beliefs is ideal.

What does this Sadool and the Magistrate share?

Ambition for power.

How do you know that?

I could read it from its presence. That and a hate for anything corporeal. Although there is an obvious conflict occurring within it. Shadow sounded perplexed.

What is that?

It likes being in a corporeal state. It has deviated from the original mission. Which makes it dangerous and unpredictable. That's why the Seedling needs to be returned to the cavern. It is the only place I can protect it.

Her leg started bouncing in agitation. *Then how do we stop them?*

I have an idea, but you won't like it.

She placed her hands beneath her legs to keep them still. *I have liked very little of this since it all began.*

You will have to kill Dodd and hopefully in turn we can trap the Sadool within the dying body.

Killing?

Amione had never hurt another soul. She remembered a phrase from Old Earth, *An eye for an eye.* She wasn't sure how she felt about that. Deep within her she felt a rage building against the man who had killed her Da and Leto so brutally. If she had the chance, would she do it? Could she do it?

Will that work?

It is a theory.

That is not comforting at all, Shadow. If it doesn't work...

It is the best I can offer.

She leaned her helmet back against the uncomfortable headrest, and felt the pull of gravity as they descended beneath the canopy and to their destination near the new mine. She heard the retro rockets fire as they slowed their descent in anticipation of landing. The rest of the crew shifted restlessly, eager to get to work so they could return to the city and enjoy the fruits of their monetary windfall.

She felt Willan's gloved hand wrap around her own and she returned the gesture. She met his questioning gaze with a determined one of her own. He smiled his endearing lopsided grin and felt the corners of her lips quirk up in response.

"Are you ready?"

"No, but I'm determined to bring this to an end, and to bring my Da's killer to justice."

"What kind of justice?"

She raised a questioning brow.

"Are we taking him to the authorities or are we going to implement our own brand of justice?"

She looked away and withdrew her hand. "I don't know," she replied honestly.

Willan nodded.

She felt the pull of the straps as the craft finally landed. She waited until the green light was given, then unstrapped from her seat stretching her thigh out. The Seedling wasn't hampering her movement much, but the pain was becoming a persistent ache that radiated up to her hip and down through her ankle.

They waited for the other members of the team to disembark before trailing behind, then slipping away to a deserted part of the facility. The new mine was only two kilometers to the west. It would be dark, but the indicators in their helmets should keep their path true.

The backlit Saturn on the Southern horizon was always a marvelous sight. It wasn't as clear as it was above the canopy. She could barely make out the outline of the giant planet, but the immensity of the celestial body wasn't lost on her. She hadn't had time to really take it in when she came down with Curphay. That was only four days ago.

It didn't seem like it should have been that long, but evidence that Titan was emerging from behind Saturn was everywhere. Already the methane and ethane were starting to sublimate as the sun emerged from behind Saturn.

"Come on. If we get moving, we should be there before the sun rises," Willan urged.

"Technically it is an eclipse, a very long eclipse." She looked at him curiously. Another tell that he wasn't born on Titan. Every school aged child knew that, and yet, Willan was completely ignorant.

"Oh, yeah. Right. It's an eclipse." He kept his eyes focused on the path before them.

They checked to be sure every last person was in the facility, then headed out the bay doors and towards the new mine. Equipment was neatly lined up giving them some cover from the building as well as the sublimating methane from the warming atmosphere. They shouldn't be missed for several minutes yet.

The ground was hard, crusted with ruts and bulbous masses that made navigation more than a little treacherous. Even that was preferable to a thick sludge which is what they would be mired in if they didn't pick up the pace. She watched Willan's broad back as he easily navigated the surface.

"We need to be careful. We have a head start on Dodd, but that won't last long. How much time do you need to do what you need to do?" Willan said.

"It took us an hour to get to the cavern. I'm not sure what kind of condition Curphay will be in." Amione said.

"Forgive me for saying this, but are you sure he is still alive after all this time?"

Her mouth was set in a grim line. "I'm sure of it."

"I believe you." But she could hear the doubt in his voice. Not that she could blame him. Until Shadow, she had believed in the hard science that a pressure suit could only sustain a human for a day max. Four days seemed impossible.

Are you there, Shadow?

I am.

If Dodd comes...

I am ready for when he comes. I will do whatever is necessary to keep you and the Seedling safe. She was relieved to hear its voice was stronger.

She stumbled.

"Are you alright?" Willan was at her elbow steadying her.

"I'm fine. Keep going." She had to concentrate on her leg to keep it moving. *Can you do anything about the seedling, Shadow?*

It must remain where it is. That is the safest place until we reach the cavern.

She gritted her teeth. *Then can you do something about the pain?*

She felt a warming sensation in her thigh which eased the cramping, but didn't take the pain completely away.

Thank you.

Anytime.

After several minutes traversing across the rolling hills, she finally saw a familiar ridge darken the western horizon through the mist. She allowed herself a smile. Her task was nearly finished. She could get Curphay and go home.

A pair of headlights appeared from the south.

"Fuck," Willan grumbled. "I think they are here already."

"It's too soon! They will see us if we try to go through the mine entrance."

"What now?" Willan crouched behind a laser drill and watched as three vehicles pulled into the clearing in front of the mine entrance. The doors opened revealing a dozen guardians with phase rifles and one very pissed Head Magistrate.

Shadow pressed inside her mind and started to fill her with its presence. *Not yet, Shadow.*

There are far more people than I anticipated.

Willan and I will even the odds for you. Her resolve was grim, but there was little else they could do. They were the only thing standing between Dodd and the biggest secret of their lifetime.

"What's the plan, Amione?" Willan asked as he scanned the opposition, spreading out from the clearing.

"We take them out one by one. How are your hand-to-hand combat skills?"

He glanced at her with a mischievous glint. "So-so."

"I'll take that as adequate."

"More than adequate for this situation," he confirmed.

Two guardians approached with rifles in hand.

"I'll go left and you go right," she instructed.

Another amused look, a mock salute and Willan disappeared around the edge of the machine. She wasted no time moving the other way, pausing long enough to gauge where the guardian was. The nose of his rifle poked out beyond the machine. She grabbed, twisted, and landed a kick in the stomach of the guardian. Then she shot him with his own rifle, stunning him.

She scanned the area for the next target. Willan threw the other guardian against the tire of the machine near her. She turned to aim the weapon, but found Willan had everything well in hand. She admired how easily he was able to lift the man over his shoulder, fling him to the ground, then stunned him with the guardian's weapon.

Their eyes met briefly. She could feel a fission of attraction before continuing towards the next two targets. "Two down, eleven to go." Willan counted off.

They quickly moved between the equipment, sighting another pair of guardians. They were nullified before they could even lift their weapons. Four down, nine to go. Amione thought in her head.

The next pair should have been around the next machine. Amione grunted as the weapon grazed her shoulder pushing her against one of the machines with more force than she anticipated. She dropped to the ground and rolled beneath the machine.

"Are you alright?" Willan's voice was strained.

"Yes." She groaned. At least it was her left arm and not her right. Her shoulder ached as her arm hung limply at her side, completely useless.

"You don't sound all right." His voice took on a dubious tone.

"My left arm is numb."

"I'll try to get to you."

Amione frantically tried to locate the other two guardians. Several rocks rolled down one of the rises. Her eyes narrowed as she tried to ascertain where they might be. She couldn't remain where she was.

I can help.

She could feel Shadow expanding within her and one of its tentacles ran down her left arm just beneath the skin. She could see the electro-magnetic signature from the entity flare briefly with her enhanced sight before disappearing beneath her suit. Gradually the feeling returned to her left arm and she pushed herself into a crouch and kept herself hidden behind one of the tires. If she could just locate those guardians before they found her. She wanted to avoid an all-out fight. They were still terribly outnumbered.

Suddenly a body slid down the rise and bounced into the air before settling on the ground. The Guardian sat up awkwardly shaking his head. He started to raise his weapon toward whoever had thrown him. Amione shifted and shot him in the back.

"Was that you?" She called out.

"It was," Willan whispered.

He must be on to the second one. She risked moving out from beneath the equipment in time to see Willan dispatching of the other guardian. He saw her and motioned for her to follow him at the base of the ridge. She carefully bounced across the ground avoiding the worst of the boulders and kept a low profile.

"Is your arm better?"

"It is."

"That was quick."

"It wasn't that bad," she hastily explained.

"There. Up ahead. Two more." He pointed to two more guardians who were scanning the terrain.

They silently made their way and quickly dispensed of them as well. Eight down and five more to go. They turned toward the mine entrance in time to see the remaining four guardians and Dodd scramble into defensive positions at the entrance.

"I guess they figured out we are here." Willan slid carefully down the rise.

"Our luck couldn't last forever, I suppose." Amione met him at the back of an abandoned CAT. "Now what?"

"I'm not sure we have much of a choice. We have to go through there to get to your friend."

"Curphay."

"Hmm?"

"That's his name, Curphay."

"Ok. Curphay. That's the only way to get to Curphay," he corrected.

Amione concentrated on the form of the Head Magistrate. She could sense him even from this distance. If she could sense him, he could most certainly sense her. *He knows I'm here, Shadow.*

And we know he is there. In that we are even.

How are we supposed to get past him?

A sacrifice needs to be made.

The image of Willan taking a hit entered her mind. She blanched. *I can't do that.*

Then we won't get through.

No. There has got to be another way. I won't sacrifice Willan.

Then Curphay will die.

Her heart pounded harder. She had come so far. She couldn't let something like this stop her. Frantically, her mind worked the problem. "There has to be another way," she mumbled.

"What has to be another way?"

She started when she realized Willan had heard her.

"I can't see a way to get through. We go straight in, we will be killed or captured. There is no way around without being detected. Even with us both, we won't be able to take out enough of them to make it through."

"I could distract them. Draw them away from the entrance."

"It wouldn't work."

Willan turned toward her. "Why wouldn't it work?"

"He would know."

"Dodd?" Willan's voice was filled with confusion.

"Yes."

There was a long pause. "Is this one of those things you should probably tell me about now?"

It was Amione's turn to pause. *I need to tell him Shadow.*

It would not be advisable.

Damn your logic. If you want to sacrifice him, he should at least know why.

She shuttered her mind to Shadow and felt its surprise. Apparently, that was something he had not expected her to be able to do.

She was furious. She was furious because she had been put into this situation, furious because her Da was dead because of these entities, and now it was asking her to sacrifice either Willan or Curphay.

She rubbed at the ache in her thigh. She hoped this little seedling was worth all the trouble.

Chapter 26

Jus in Bello

*"The greatest enemies of **ants** are other **ants**, just as the greatest enemies of men are other men."*

Auguste Forel

The Sadool watched with interest as these beings used their inorganic devices to dig into Titan's crust. It had learned a lot by being around them. The devices were an extension of their limited abilities. They were highly adaptable, making them interesting to watch. They regularly extricated materials from the crust to be used to make more devices. Some of these ended up in the sky.

Back and forth they would travel. Once the Sadool had followed one until they breached the canopy. High in orbit, there was another construction floating above the thick atmosphere.

Devices came and went over and over. The habitats started out small and gradually grew larger as time passed. Then something even more astonishing occurred.

One group of organics faced off against another, and began destroying each other with devices designed to damage, maim, and render useless.

The Sadool floated down to report the strange behavior.

"They are destroying each other. Why would they do that?"

"You don't have war where you are from?" Oal asked in astonishment.?

"What is war?"

Oal contemplated the answer before he spoke. "It's not something we dwell on. But my kind did war with each other when our species was young and lacked wisdom."

"But what is it?"

"In a word, conflict."

"How does conflict lead to destroying things? They spent so much time and energy constructing their marvelous machines, and now they are destroying them."

"I guess that would seem like a strange thing to Sadools." Oal flexed his curled limbs in deep thought. "I think the closest thing to your understanding is one party has something, or someplace the other desires."

"Shouldn't they just discuss it?"

"Well, yes, and sometimes successfully. But when talk fails, then war becomes inevitable."

The Sadool considered this for a while. "How did your species overcome war?"

"We started living longer. When that happens, you realize that you aren't in a hurry to engage in war. Talking takes so much time, that the emotions that drove that initial urge no longer matter."

"This species lives a short time."

"Then the lessons of peace haven't yet ingrained themselves into their culture. They flare like a star, burning brightly before being snuffed out."

"It makes no sense. They engage in this behavior that is sure to shorten their lives. How will they ever get to a point of enlightenment?"

"It will happen. Look how far they have come in such a short period of time. And what a terrifying thought it is if they ever do figure out that peace. These beings would be a great force that would take over the entire galaxy in a few short millennia."

"Then they are to be feared."

"We will watch them further and see how they progress. I am optimistic that there are at least a few beings who can grow into something more."

"I will set traps and diversions to keep them unaware of us. And I will continue to observe them."

"I think that is wise, my friend. Hopefully, that will allay your fears."

"Doubtful, but there is always a chance. I think the reason why Sadool have never encountered this is that we have always been. We are so long lived, perhaps we have forgotten wars. But maybe, just maybe we never had them in the first place."

"An interesting if overly optimistic thought."

"You doubt that is true."

"I have no frame of reference for comparison. Your species and this one is all I have known. Perhaps it is true that your people have never had war. But I think maybe they have; it has just been forgotten."

"We are without substance. What would we go to war over?"

"I will think about this more when you return to the surface. I feel the pull to procreate."

"Then I will return immediately. I would like to see if their devices are still intact."

Chapter 27

Hooke's Law

"It takes twice as much force to stretch a spring twice as far."
Robert Hooke

"The sun will emerge soon," Amione commented.

"And?" Willan's voice was tense.

"And it will cause the methane and ethane to sublimate faster, giving us cover to do whatever we are about to do next." She could feel the ground soften beneath her feet.

"Ok. We can work with that. I will draw their fire and you can work your way around to the entrance from the opposite direction." He gestured.

"But what about you?" She turned toward him.

"I have more than a few tricks, and a lot more practice than you with these kinds of situations. I will be all right," he assured her.

She frowned. "I don't like that at all. Do something else."

"There is no other option." He laughed, shaking his head in incredulity. "You know that. If you are going to get to Curphay in time, we need to do this." He captured her gaze, making sure she understood.

She searched for another way, and could only come up with one small addition. "We can use one of the CATs as an additional distraction."

"How?"

"They have an auto drive system that can be activated. I can get into one and reprogram it to move away from the mine. It would at least divide the numbers and give you an advantage." She was surprised at how much he had grown on her. She was as almost as fond of Willan as she was of Curphay.

He smiled, warming his hazel eyes. "Why Amione Dhau, I think you are sweet on me."

"What? No!" Her cheeks ignited in embarrassment. "What does that mean exactly?"

Willan laughed harder. "I think the lady doth protest too much." She frowned even harder. What was that from? She remembered reading something with a similar vernacular. "We don't have time for this," she hissed.

"We make the time for things that are important to us." His gaze was suddenly solemn with emotion she didn't dare identify.

She didn't know why he was getting philosophical on her, but she had no intention of giving up on either Willan or Curphay.

Willan grabbed her gloved hand and squeezed, making a point to meet her gaze. "It has been a pleasure getting to know you, Amione."

"You sound like you are saying good bye." A knot formed in her stomach.

"No. I just wanted you to know that I truly appreciate you." He cleared his throat, then released her hand.

She nodded, unsure how to respond to his emotional revelation. She raised her hand to touch his shoulder and then let it awkwardly drop to her side. "It has been... good." Stupid. She always sounded so inadequate when conveying strong emotions to others. "I expect to see you again," she insisted.

He nodded, accepting her awkward response with a faint smile of amusement. Though she could not fathom what he found so amusing about her.

"I'll wait until I see the CAT moving and then I'll strike," he confirmed. "Good luck!"

She watched as his large form disappeared into the mist. She glanced around the machine to be sure another guardian wasn't lurking in the shadows. The CAT was a vague form the mist. Already, the sun was lightening the sky. She had to hurry. This would only work while Titan was still behind Saturn. After that, even she wouldn't be able to see in the increasing mist.

She clambered up the ladder and opened the doors dropping expertly inside with a crouch. She took a quick look around to make sure she was alone, then went to the console near the back of the pilot compartment.

Breaking into the machine was relatively easy. The software hadn't been updated in the last ten years. Her eight-year-old self would have been able to crack the code. Lucky for her, she hadn't forgotten the lessons given by her Da.

The console chirped to life and she quickly programmed it to start in five minutes. Hopefully, it would draw at least two guards away from the entrance. Willan would be able to draw the other two. That left Dodd.

Are you ready, Shadow? She continued to move code on the CAT's wave. It didn't have to be perfect, just convincing enough to draw away the enemy.

We will have to be.

What do I have to do? She closed out the Wave and pushed her way back to the exit.

I have been studying your mind, and replaying our last encounter with Dodd. I think if we use your Akido skills we will be able to gain an advantage.

We also have one of the guardian's guns. She patted the firearm on her thigh.

Those will be useless.

What if he tries to shoot me? She peaked out the door to make sure no one was around before swinging her leg onto the ladder.

It will be useless against you too.

Really? It wasn't earlier. She grunted when she dropped the rest of the way to the ground.

It was also the first test of our union. It expends a lot of energy.

She thought back to the fight on Demeter. "*So we can make an armor like the one Dodd used?*

Our unique bond makes it possible.

229

Amione leaned against one of the machines trying to keep her balance. *What else do these mergings bring out?*

Almost anything you can imagine.

I can imagine a lot.

Then I would put that to good use. Whatever you think, I can make it a reality.

Amione didn't have time to think because she heard the CATs engines switch on and move away from the clearing. As predicted, two of the guardians followed, intent on catching "her" before she reached the substation.

She counted to ten, then heard weapons fire from her left. Willan was right on schedule, engaging the remaining two guardians in a cat and mouse game.

That only left the Dodd.

She pushed away from the machine, drawing in a deep breath and setting her resolve. Dodd was in her way, and she was determined to move him in whatever way possible.

She rounded the machine and carefully stepped forward. Sunlight increased causing the sublimation to accelerate, and obscured her view of Dodd. However, she knew exactly where he was, and she was sure he knew where she was.

Two red pinpoints flared to life. In response her visor registered two violet pinpoints of light.

"Where is that coming from?" she mused aloud.

You, Amione.

What?!

Just as the Magistrates eyes glow red, yours glow violet.

Why? How? Just when she thought things could not get weirder.

It has something to do with our connection.

When this is all over, we need to sit down and work out any other surprises you may have forgotten to mention, she grumbled.

Were these abilities always present in her genetics, or did they cause a mutation? Definitely something to examine when things calmed down.

Let's just deal with this first, Shadow hedged.

Amione continued to draw closer to Dodd until the gaping maw of the new mine loomed behind his still form. She stopped several meters from his position and waited.

Her external com chirped to life. "You know, you and I could make an interesting pair." The hollow sounding baritone caused her to shiver.

"I don't think so," she clipped.

"Surely you know by now that this...symbiosis is unique." His head tilted to one side while the rest of his form remained unnaturally still.

"Not as unique as you thought before you met me, I'm sure."

He chuckled. "That is true. I was the only one, but now that I know what is possible, I could raise an army and you could be a commander at my side."

"For what purpose?"

"To rule Titan, to rule our system, to rule it all." The last was said in a silky-smooth tone.

Oh yeah, this guy has to be stopped. Amione stated bluntly to Shadow.

She could feel shadow expand into the rest of her form, lending her additional strength, stamina, and whatever else she could think of.

"Mmm, no. I think I like things as they are." She took a stance placing her booted feet shoulder width apart. Her fingers toyed with the strap over the gun.

"You can't be serious. You would leave the Derelict as is?" His tone was incredulous.

She hesitated before reaffirming her resolve. "Of course not, but I don't think world domination is the way to go."

"Says the naive young woman," he scoffed.

"Says the even more naive old man."

His eyes flared a brighter red in response.

"I guess I hit a nerve." She chuckled.

"It's a shame. I'm going to have to destroy you now. I can't have you challenging me." He paced to the right. His gaze traveled to her thigh. His smile broadened. "And you have something I want."

Her first instinct was to shield her thigh. "What is that?"

"Whatever it is that you have buried in your thigh. You didn't think I wouldn't notice, did you?" He continued pacing to her right and she matched by skirting the uneven terrain.

Light filled the sky, turning it from black to gray and finally to copper and gold. The light had returned, burning away the darkness once again. The sublimating ethane shimmered through the air making him seem to tremble in her eyes. He stopped and faced her.

The entrance to the mine was to her left. All she had to do was sprint for it and she would be in the cavern in moments, but he would be right behind her. She had to stop him here and now.

"And you have something I need." She toed the ground, making sure she had solid footing.

"What is that?"

"Freedom."

"Freedom? That is an Old Earth myth. I guess we are at an impasse."

"I guess so."

Several long moments passed. She wondered if he was going to make the first move when a tentacle shot out from his arm and threw her to the ground. Shadow encased her with armor and rendered the assault inert before retaliating with its own barb at the legs, knocking Dodd back a couple of paces.

He grinned through his visor and ran toward her. She pushed off from the ground and Shadow gave her an extra boost as she flipped over Dodd's head and landed lightly on her feet behind him.

He whirled around aiming for her helmet to disable her life support. She countered each thrust with a defensive shield that materialized and phased away with each countered blow.

She feinted toward his exposed lower half, then followed with a roundhouse kick to the head made more forceful in the low gravity with the help of Shadow. He was taken by surprise and forced to the ground, skittering across several smooth rocks and sliding through the melting methane.

He pushed himself away from her, floating backwards until he landed on his feet and faced her again. This time several tentacles flashed from his arms and waist. She managed to dodge a few, but was soon overwhelmed by several blows to her head and back.

"Warning. Suit is compromised. You have ten minutes to get to a secure location." The mechanical voice sounded from her display.

Amione gasped for breath and closed the distance between her and Dodd. He stopped her mid jump and used his tentacle to close around her fist and force her to her knees.

"There is still time to change your mind." His ruby eyes bore into her, supremely confident that he had won.

"Never." She gasped as pain radiated down her arm into her shoulder.

She twisted away from him, wrenching her hand from his grasp and returning with a blow of her own that caused him to stagger back.

He lashed out with another blow with both tentacles. She manifested a shield and blocked the blow, causing his tentacles to fade out of existence. She still held the shield and waited for his next move.

"Warning. Suit is compromised. You have five minutes to get to a secure location."

A slow smile spread across his face. "I have all the time in the world, Amione Dhau. You, however, have less than five minutes."

Her violet eyes flared brighter. "Why did you kill my father?"

"That's what you want to talk about?" He shook his head in disappointment. "Very well. You know why. He had the seedling. I needed it. He refused to tell me where he had taken it. I thought it would be on him. I was wrong." He shrugged.

Her hatred grew with each insipid word. "What is so important about this seedling?" She could feel herself grow lightheaded.

He snorted. "Like I would tell you."

"I'm dying anyway."

He laughed. "So, I spill my plans to you and then you miraculously survive and then you use the information against me? Amione... Do you think I'm that gullible?"

She saw a flicker of movement behind Dodd. It took her a moment to realize it was Willan trying to sneak up behind him. She wanted to shout out a warning, but lightning quick, Dodd turned on Willan. A tentacle shot out wrapped around Willan's midsection and threw him against a machine with a sickening *thwack.*

She cried out and ran to his side. Fine cracks spiderwebbed across his visor. She wasn't sure if his suit was compromised or not. Willan lay far too still for her liking, but she could tell he still breathed.

"Warning. Suit is compromised. You have thirty seconds to get to a secure location."

She impatiently turned off the alarm. If she was going to die today, she didn't need to be reminded. The rage she felt was white hot. She could feel her chaos fight for release, instead of suppressing it as she always had, she allowed it free reign within her.

She could feel Shadow expand inside of her and through her fingers. The seedling in her thigh throbbed and seemed to expand and curl around her. She could feel herself rise higher into the sky until she was looking down on an astonished Dodd.

The air around her shimmered with shadow and light as she felt power build up inside of her with her roiling emotions. She allowed her fury to fuel the fire welling up within her, burning away her suit and exposing her to Titan.

She should have been dead, but whatever symbiosis occurred between her, Shadow, and the Seedling, protected her. Her suit split and cracked falling away from her in shreds as she continued to expand.

In a futile display of courage, he put up a shield of shadow. She released her chaos, preventing the entity inside of Dodd from phasing out of its corporeal form. Instead of stopping, she continued to allow both darkness and light to consume him. She barely registered the frightful screaming as his flesh charred from the inside out melting off his bones. Once her fury was spent, all she heard was a gurgling sound as what was left of the Head Magistrate liquified.

He dropped to his knees. His eyes no longer glowed red because there were no more eyes in his ruined face. He fell to the side in a smoldering heap.

She gently floated back to the ground and felt the shadow and light shrink back to her form. She was bare to the elements, but none of it seemed to affect her. Her breath tore at her chest not from lack of oxygen but from the dawning realization that she had just killed a man.

"What have I done?" She tried to still her trembling hands.

She felt Shadow wrap comfortingly around her shoulders. "You defended us. You defended your friends. He would have killed them and you," it reasoned.

She turned toward Willan still prone on the ground completely oblivious to what occurred moments ago.

"I need to get him in the CAT before his air runs out."

She felt Shadow fill her limbs with strength which allowed her to lift Willan's large body into the CAT and hook him into the atmo. A spare pressure suit hung in the back. She put it on, covering the tattered remains of her clothing.

"How am I still breathing? How am I alive?"

"You protect us, and we protected you."

"We?"

"The seedling and I."

"Is that why the Magistrate wanted the seedling? Did he know it would do this?" She was still shaking as she rummaged in a compartment for sealant. She shook her hands out before carefully applying sealant to Willan's fractured visor.

"I don't know. He might have known enough to try and find out."

"Will there be more?" Satisfied Willan was out of immediate danger, she turned on the tracking within the CAT. She couldn't tell if the blips heading her way were friend or foe. She was wise enough to know that her display of energy would be noticed.

"I don't know that either. I have been away from the Sadool for a very long time. Things have changed."

"That's an understatement." She looked at Willan's unconscious form. She wanted to check his pulse. "Do you think he is ok?"

"He is stable."

She pushed the door to the CAT open and slid down the ladder and faced the mine entrance. She needed to find and bring Curphay out before the calvary came in. She tried ignoring the corpse, but it was a garish reminder that she was no longer the simple awkward, Amione Dhau. She was something more.

Chapter 28

Procreation

"The practice of love is the procreation of hope."
Bryant McGill

O al started the painful process of creating seedlings. Waves of energy radiated from his form buffeting the Sadool. Oal's roots had dug deep into the surface of Titan. He was able to draw from the moon's energy. Soon the beginnings of new life formed on the curling limbs, and the waves of energy ceased, allowing the Sadool to resume his non-corporeal state. The seeds were small at first, but grew larger as time passed.

Wars came and went above the clouds. At the moment, it was a time of peace. When peace happened, more things were built. Another city emerged in the clouds to go with the first. The Sadool went to investigate this new structure. It's smooth construction also housed an oxygen/nitrogen rich atmosphere and something else.

At first, the Sadool thought they were creatures like the others, but they were stationary like Oal. They inhabited a central cavernous space at the center of the city. They grew incrementally and smaller creatures lived among their leaves and branches. The most exceptional thing about them is that they consumed light.

The Sadool went up to a particularly tall plant. "Who are you? What are you?"

It remained silent, not because it refused to answer, but because there was no sentience to be had. It grew, it flowered, and it reproduced seeds. The residents of the city would harvest the seeds and eat them, which it found familiar and relatable. It felt conflicted. It understood the need to consume, but at the same time, the entity did not want these creatures to consume Oal's seedlings.

It returned to the cavern to let Oal know what it had discovered.

"They eat the seeds!" It cried out without preamble.

"What are you talking about?" Most of Oal's energy was focused on producing the seedlings. Any conversation was difficult until the task was done.

"They have living things similar to you, but different. They consume light."

"That is interesting. Are they sentient?"

"No. They are not sentient in the slightest. At least not yet."

"Sentience is not a guarantee," Oal reminded it.

"Yes, but they could be. But the creatures! The creatures were eating their seedlings!"

Oal was perplexed. "Eating them? That is also interesting."

"Perhaps to maintain their corporeal existence as I do."

"These creatures are not like you, but I imagine it is how they have evolved. They must consume these living things and somehow convert that into what they are. It would be an interesting study."

"Study, he says," the Sadool muttered. "You do not see the threat yet."

"What threat?"

"If they consume those seedlings, what do you think they will do if they found yours?"

Oal paused and then mentally shook in denial. "That will not happen."

"It might. These creatures are voracious when it comes to acquiring materials. They consume the soil here, why wouldn't they consume one of your seedlings?"

"Because I have faith that it won't come to that," Oal said simply.

"Faith..."

"There is far more in this universe that is unknown than known. I think these creatures will prove to be an asset down the road."

"How do you know?"

"I just know."

It made a sound of disgust. "You just know. I know what I saw. This will be a danger to you and the precious lives you are creating."

"Then it is fortunate that I have you."

With that Oal conserved his energy and went back to his seedlings.

Chapter 29

Science and Faith

"If you study science deep enough and long enough, it will force you to believe in God."
Lord William Thompson Kelvin

Amione walked into the entrance of the mine, careful to disable the lighting system. She didn't want to draw unwanted attention. Not when she was this close to getting Curphay back home.

She hesitated at the entrance to the cavern. Was Demeter home anymore? She didn't know. Without her Da and Leto there, it wouldn't be the same. Regardless, Demeter didn't want her. The only thing to do was to move forward.

She wandered through the lattice work of beings that glowed brilliantly beneath her enhanced eyesight. Who knew that life had been here all this time? Maybe it hadn't wanted to be found. Collective consciousness was a possibility.

She remembered the last time she had been here, taken hostage by Shadow. Well, that wasn't entirely true. She had been given a choice. She resented it at the time, and now? Now, she wasn't sure if she could live without the dark entity.

The cavern opened before her and she carefully walked in the area that she and Curphay had traveled. Oal came into view, glowing a glorious luminescent white in the dim cave. The seedlings had also started to turn color from a low frequency infrared to a soft blue white glow as if they were preparing for something big.

Amione only had eyes for Curphay who lay in repose next to the Oal.

She hurried as quickly as she could to his side, hoping that he was alright. The inside of his helmet fogged, and she sighed in relief.

"I have returned with your Seedling." Amione looked up anxiously at Oal.

Oal expressed his gratitude in her mind.

"Let me assist you." Shadow nudged her.

She nodded, stretching her right leg out and sitting next to Curphay. She wasn't going to let him out of her sight any time soon. Not until this was done and she was sure he was ok.

She felt Shadow stretch down her left leg and surround the seedling, gently extricating it. She gasped in pain, then felt a release as the pressure within her muscles decreased and returned to normal again. She rubbed her thigh vigorously, grateful that it was once again only her.

The Seedling had grown. It's rose-colored flaps expanding and separating ever so slightly since she had seen it two days ago. It too glowed an ambient blue in her enhanced sight.

Shadow extended its tentacle and the Seedling floated towards Oal and drifted to the base of the tree.

"Now you fulfill your end of the bargain," Amione insisted, placing a protective hand over Curphay's gently rising and falling chest.

"I will, but first we need to discuss some things."

"But Curphay—"

"Will be fine. We have him in stasis. What we have to say must stay between us."

Amione searched Oal for a face, but all she could see was the gently pulsing light that ran the length of its trunk and down the curling branches.

"Fine." She clenched her right fist on her knee and waited.

"We knew there was a unique connection between myself and the entity."

"Shadow. She calls me Shadow," Shadow corrected.

"Very well...Shadow," Oal acknowledged. "We also knew there was potential, limited as it may be, for Shadow to connect with your species."

"There have been others?"

"There have been attempts in which we learned things," Oal hedged.

Amione frowned. "What does that mean?"

"I had attempted to bond with others of your species with varied success. It is how I know a host must be willing."

"Did you kill someone?"

"Once." Shadow's voice was filled with regret.

Amione tried to process that information and failed. "Why did you take the risk with me?"

She could feel Oal's approval. "You are asking the right questions. The simple answer is faith."

She had not expected that answer. "Faith? That sounds spiritual. We abandoned those concepts long ago."

"Not so long ago when compared to our existence. Only a hundred of your years."

"Which is half a lifetime ago and certainly before my existence."

"Your species is so short lived; you still haven't acquired the ability to see beyond that."

"We have done much to add to our knowledge," Amione said. "We crawled up from the mud, built great things, and looked to the stars. And here we are, exactly where we were never meant to be."

"Forgive me, Amione. I forget how passionate your species is. Another byproduct of your short lives, I imagine," Oal mused.

"Why do I feel as if you are insulting us at every turn?"

"We mean no offense," Shadow assured her. "We find you very alien to ourselves. It took many millennia for Oal and I to understand our differences. You are quite unlike us. It will take a while for us to understand your species."

"No offense, but you are both very strange. We have encountered other species, but you are by far the most unusual."

"Thank you," they said unanimously.

"Not sure that was a compliment," Amione mumbled.

"There is more," Oal hesitated.

Amione shifted nervously, making sure to keep her hand on Curphay's slowing rising and falling chest. "What else could there be?"

"Not the Prophecy..." Shadow sighed dramatically.

"I know you don't agree, but it must be said. She should know." The rhythm of Oal's luminescence changed with increased anxiety.

"Prophecy?" A feeling of anticipation made her extremities tingle. Once was a novelty, hardly worth noting, but a second mention?

"It is not a popular idea on Trom. Our people seek knowledge and believe in the Continuum of Knowledge that is passed on from adult to seedling. Generation after generation our experiences are embedded in the very fiber of our being."

Amione put it into a context she could understand. "Like our DNA and epigenetics."

Oal sent a questioning image wanting her to show him what she meant. Communicating this way was still uncomfortable, but she saw value in its efficiency. She concentrated on her current research into paleogenetics.

"Ah, yes, precisely! It is buried in our genetics. Even this idea of Prophecy is written there, although many generations have rejected it since then."

"Why don't you reject it?"

"I have long since learned that I am unusual among my people. Far too curious for my own good. I believe that there are some truths that withstand the test of time, faith, love, and hope. That is what a prophecy represents after all. Believing in something you cannot see, hoping that the outcome will be positive and using love to see it all through."

Amione recalled her reading on the subject. It was a mixed bag, and most times it was self-fulfilling and self-serving. And yet, she had to admit there were times when Prophecy defied explanation. Her people had long since rejected such simple ideals.

"I can feel your doubt, Amione Dhau, but I have been waiting for someone like you for a very long time." Oal infused their connection with hope and gratitude.

"Someone like me? Why?" She blinked back sudden tears. She felt so out of place everywhere she went. Right now, she felt like she belonged with these two outliers. They felt different from their own people. They found each other and now they found her.

"This prophecy talks about a joining between three entities. One of darkness, one of light, and one of chaos."

She felt her heart jerk in her chest. "One of chaos?"

"Yes, the energy that propels the universe forward," Oal said.

"Chaos is to be feared."

"Not feared. Embraced."

Amione felt like pacing, but she remained at Curphay's side, gripping his suit. "And you believe I am part of this?"

"Shadow is darkness. My kind is light. That means you are chaos."

"Why me? There are millions of humans to choose from."

"You could have taken your father's death at face value, but you didn't. You chose to learn more."

"And almost got Curphay killed in the process."

"He was never in any danger. You required motivation, and have delivered far more than we had anticipated."

"I still don't understand."

"Neither do I," Shadow said. "I agree she is chaos, but Oal, my friend, the Prophecy?"

"I know you don't believe, my friend, but have I steered you wrong in all this time?"

"No. I trust you."

Oal turned his attention back to Amione. "There is war coming. The first in billions of years. The order has been disturbed and there are many who will not embrace it. But your species is unique. It seems to thrive off of chaos and adversity. So much so that you build devices, machines, and change raw materials into something more. It is unique."

"But the Nouri do the same thing. They create ships and other materials just as we do," Amione said.

"But they did it over the course of millions of years. Your species has accomplished the same thing in a fraction of that time."

"There is so much that we have to learn. My species can't even agree to help each other. How is it that I am supposed to help the universe?"

She sent images of the four cities and how they could not agree on a way to help the least fortunate.

Oal shifted in color from bright white to blue. "It is meant to happen, and you are the one who has catalyzed it."

The entire cavern shook. She looked up in alarm. "What was that?"

"I will see." The Sadool floated to the ceiling and disappeared.

A stalagmite fell with a deafening crack over Curphay and Amione. She shielded Curphay as small rocks pelted her back. Shadow returned and filled her. She created a barrier. A large stalagmite broke across the invisible field and fell to the cavern floor with a thud.

"Is it a quake?" She yelled over the din.

"No. Someone is shooting at the ridge with energy weapons." Shadow expanded itself further. "I can't protect you and Oal at the same time.

"It's ok, my friend. Take Amione and as many Seedlings as you can. I will wake Curphay."

"What about you?" Shadows voice was strained.

"This is what is supposed to happen." Oal sent peaceful images along their links.

"You will die!" Shadow grew more agitated floating in increasingly faster revolutions around Oal.

"I know. Which is why you must get everyone out of here before the entire cavern collapses."

Curphay stirred groggily, looking around at the chaos surrounding them, "Amione?"

"No time to explain, Curph. Pick up as many Seedlings as you can. We are getting out of here."

"What?"

"Do it!" She demonstrated by collecting as many as she could, stuffing them into every available pocket and loop and cradling still more in her arms.

We need to go. I cannot hold it all, Shadow said.

Another deafening crack sounded. She shoved Curphay down the rise and slid headfirst to the bottom looking back in time to see a large rock cleave Oal in two.

Shadow's agony filled every fiber of her as his grief poured unchecked. The curling white branches flickered, then went dark, leaving only the Seedlings giving off their faint electromagnetic glow.

Amione could not move. Her sorrow joined Shadows. *Oh Shadow.*

Oal. Another wave of sorrow washed through her.

She looked at the seedlings in her hands. This was what was left of Oal's legacy. The importance of getting the seedlings out of the cavern increased exponentially.

The cavern popped and cracked let them know they weren't out of danger yet. Another impact shook the ground. She scrambled to her feet in the hydrocarbon slurry. Fortunately, the Seedlings floated, and she quickly gathered them into her arms.

"You still with me, Curphay?"

He groaned. "Nice way to wake up from a long nap."

"We aren't out of it yet. Grab the rest of the Seedlings and let's get out of here!"

She grabbed the last one and waded as fast as she could, avoiding falling rocks whenever she could, and listening to the rest ping off of her helmet and against her shoulders and back. She glanced back at Curphay, making sure he was close behind. They finally reached the exit when the entire structure collapsed, throwing them forward into the honeycomb maze.

The Seedlings scattered everywhere, her ears rang, and her head pounded from the force of the shockwave. The entire mountain shivered beneath the massive aftermath of the rockfall.

She pushed herself to her hands and knees and groaned. This was definitely going to hurt in the morning. A couple of weeks ago, she was mourning the loss of her father, today, she was mourning the death of a being she had met only days ago. She was convinced she would never meet another being like him. She would honor Oal's last wish and make sure the Seedlings were safe.

Shadow, are you ok?

She didn't hear an answer. She didn't feel his presence either.

Shadow? She could feel panic rising. He was non-corporeal, but that didn't mean he was invincible. What if he perished with Oal?

A slight flicker told her otherwise.

I am... here.

I'm so sorry, Shadow. Its loss was now her loss.

Its only response was to shrink further from her mind, still present, but grieving.

Curphay grunted through her com. "Remind me never to go on another trip with you." His cheek and forehead were scraped and his nose bled into his scraggly beard.

"You look like shit."

He rolled his eyes. "You don't look much better."

She could feel blood dribble from the corner of her mouth and over her chin. There was nothing she could do about it until she reached breathable air. She had to figure out how to get all of these Seedlings out of here before the rest of the mine collapsed.

"Here, we need to get the Seedlings and go." She bent over and gathered the scattered Seedlings. They seemed to vibrate in time with the strange honeycomb creatures that lived here. She noticed one that was different from the others. It was her Seedling. The one who had been placed in her leg and who had saved her from Dodd. She carefully cupped it into her hand and placed it in her breast pocket and secured it before moving on to the others.

Curphy gathered the last one and moved toward the mining tunnel.

"Careful. We don't know who is out there." She tried to hunt beyond the lip of the entrance, but all she could see was darkness.

"Are we still being chased?" Curphay looked her way his brows raised.

"Likely. Considering I killed the Head Magistrate." She switched her viewer to infrared. The tunnels were definitely empty.

Curphay's eyes grew wide, "The Head Magistrate? I go to sleep for a day and you kill a guy?!" He stepped up behind her. "I can't see a thing."

"Switch to infrared. It was more than a day, and yes. I promise to tell you the sordid details." She stepped cautiously into the tunnel.

"It's like I don't know you," he said almost to himself.

After a pause she replied, "I don't really know myself."

Curphay joined her in the tunnel and walked as quickly as possible to the entrance. Lights flashed ahead and she pressed herself against the side of the tunnel and Curphay followed suit. She peered around the edge and saw several figures hovering over the mass that had been the Head Magistrate. Several more surrounded the CAT she had put Willan into.

She could see Willan sitting on the ground, head in his hands.

"Amione."

She jerked at the softly spoken voice and quickly tried to locate the source. "Mother?"

"Did you complete your mission?" she answered in her usual clipped manner.

"Where are you?" She continued to search the crowd of people.

"I'm with Willan by the CAT. We are assessing his condition now."

Amione watched as one of the figures from the CAT separated from the rest.

"Is he ok?" She tried to keep the concern out of her voice and failed.

"We think so, but we will take him up to Demeter to be sure."

Amione bowed her head in relief. She hadn't realized how worried she was for him.

"Amione, where are you?" There was an unfamiliar note of urgency in her voice.

She debated replying, then realized she was going to need her help to get the Seedlings out. "I'm close. The cavern collapsed behind us. What's going on?"

"Caiphus launched weapons."

"Why?!"

"The Head Magistrate failed in his mission. They decided if they couldn't have what was in that cavern, then no one would. They are telling the rest of the colony that it was a planned demolition in response to the deaths."

"They failed again. We have seedlings." She looked down at the precious cargo she was carrying.

There was a sigh that sounded strangely like relief. "Good. Very good. Then there is still hope."

"Hope for what? I still don't understand what your role is in all of this."

A long pause. "You know I am part of the ARK Project."

"Yes."

"What you don't know is the ARK's real purpose."

Amione waited for her to go on. Her mother folded her hands behind her back and paced further from the group and out of her line of sight. Whatever needed to be said, she didn't want to be overheard. Amione kept her eyes glued to Willan as the other figures lifted him to his feet and helped him to the waiting JUTE at the other end of the yard.

"It's not just a venue for scientific research for the Alliance. It's part of a grand experiment and something more," she paused.

"Leave it to you to explain something without actually explaining anything at all," Amione stated wryly.

"It's best if I show you. That's why I want you to come to the ARK. You are trained as a paleogeneticist, but your connection to... others is what will set you apart." She came back into view of the tunnel.

Could she trust her mother? She had a visceral reaction that wanted her to say no, but her rational mind demanded that she listen. She looked at the Seedlings in her arms. There was no way she could hide them all without being noticed. She would need help getting them out of there.

"You asked me about my mission. A mission implies that I was assigned to something. Who assigned me?"

"I did."

"Why?" Cold washed over her limbs as anxiety began to pool in her stomach.

Another long pause. "Because, daughter, you are entropy. One who not only embraces chaos, but is chaos."

She scoffed, "Entropy can't be a person."

"Can't it? You have spent your whole life fighting your chaos, being told it was something to be feared, disciplined to death, and discouraged." Her voice took on a fervency.

"What do you know of my life?" Amione challenged.

"More than you believe. Your father and I spoke regularly."

She didn't know what to say to that revelation. "Why wouldn't he tell me?"

"We decided a long time ago that the best way to nurture you was if I wasn't there. Surely you have noticed I am not a warm person."

Amione almost missed it, but a note of humor hung in her earpiece for just a moment before it was gone.

"I was already gone a lot, building the project which was light years from here. The time dilation alone made things difficult. What was days for me, was weeks for you and your father. Eventually, the difference expanded." Regret tinged her voice.

"Which is why you look almost unchanged." Amione watched the JUTE with Willan in it take off and head toward Demeter.

"Precisely."

"I need to know I can trust you." Amione didn't take her eyes off of the JUTE until it was too small to track.

"You can."

Amione wrestled with her doubts a moment more and then her chin set in a stiff line.

"I know that look." Curphay's voice rumbled in her ear. "You have decided something."

Amione looked over at her dear friend. "I'm about to trust my mother."

Curphay's mouth dropped open and quickly snapped shut. He nodded, nudging her with an elbow to show his support.

She turned back to the mine's entrance, watching as they lifted Dodd's limp body onto a stretcher and walk carefully to another JUTE.

A chunk of flesh fell off and one poor man had to pick it up and place it back on the stretcher. Her stomach turned. She had done that. She was terrified with what else she could do with this bonding.

She knew her mother was holding back. She just wasn't sure of her intentions. "Fine. We don't have a way of getting the seedlings off of Titan without someone noticing."

"Let me send off the rest of this group. I have a shuttle at the other station. We can take the CAT there and then leave."

Her mother crossed in front of the mine's opening to the JUTE powering up. Soon the vibration caused by the JUTE's engines could be felt through her feet as it lifted off from the surface and headed to Demeter. She watched as it ascended and disappeared quickly into the mists.

She carefully edged her way to the opening of the mine and looked out. She quickly spotted her mother walking toward her. Her impassive face was lit by the interior of her suit. Amione acknowledged her with a nod.

"Hi Mrs. D." Curphay's voice was sugary sweet.

A small quirk of her mother's lip was the only indication that she was amused. She didn't reply and walked steadily toward the CAT expecting them to follow.

"Do you think she likes me?" Curphay asked in a stage whisper.

"She kinda smiled. So, I'm going to say yes." Amione still wondered if she was doing the right thing.

As they approached the CAT, her mother offered a bag to her and she dumped the Seedlings into it and Curphay followed suit. Minus the Seedling she had in her pocket. She refrained from placing a comforting hand over it as its spherical shape pressed into her shoulder.

What would Oal want us to do with them? she asked Shadow.

She wondered if he was going to answer, but then she felt his presence expand in the back of her mind, sorrow dripping from the core of its being. *Help them become what they were meant to be. Allow them to roam to other worlds, and to expand their knowledge of other places and share... Share their parentages story with the Continuum.*

What about this Seedling? She had grown attached to it.

Another long pause. *This Seedling has decided to stay with you.*

Amione was pleased. After all that had occurred and the promise of everything that was about to occur, she would have been sad to see it go with the others.

It will be our little secret then. She frowned as she followed Curphay up the ladder into the CAT. *What do I call it? I don't want to keep calling it Seedling.*

Her name is Vara.

Vara. She tried the name. *I like it.*

Vara. Child of Oal. Child of Yael, Shadow corrected.

I'll stick with Vara.

"Amione, move a little faster," Curphay admonished. "I'm really really hungry. How long was I out again?"

"Four days."

"It seemed a lot less." He strapped himself into one of the seats directly behind her mother who was powering up the CAT.

"Mother, what will happen with these Seedlings?" She secured the strap over her seat.

She gave her a quick glance and returned to her checks. "The ARK will decide."

"I think we should let them go." She remembered Oal's wish.

Jheslae looked at Amione sharply. "Go where?"

"Just allow them to travel to the next system as they have always done."

"These are populated systems. What if the same fate happens to them as it did to their parent? We need to protect them."

"Oal. His name was Oal." She could feel her anger rise.

"Oal. Amione, they will be much safer with the ARK." Jheslae met her gaze.

"But--"

"Amione, haven't I earned at least a little trust after all of this?" Her mother pinned her with her black eyes.

Amione pressed her lips together and finished strapping in.

Seeing that everyone was secure, Jheslae put the CAT into drive and swung past the mine entrance and on the road east toward the nearest substation. The hum of the engines drowned out any potential conversation as the CAT traveled over the rough terrain that was quickly reshaping in the dim sunlight.

Vague shapes came into view and faded just as quickly in the copper mists. She replayed her encounter with Dodd over and over. He didn't seem surprised by her abilities. He wanted to teach her. Teach her what? What was she exactly? What did Shadow and Vara do to her body?

She would have to run some tests and find out. Deep down she felt as if something fundamental had changed within her, and that she was being herded toward something else. Something that she wasn't going to like.

She looked over at her friend. She was so relieved to see Curphay was ok. She had feared the worst, but Oal had kept his word. His hands were gripping the armrest tightly as the CAT careened down a particularly slippery slope. At least some things hadn't changed. Curphay was still her brave snowflake. She was very fortunate to have him as a friend.

Then there was Willan. She drew in a deep breath and let it out slowly. She hoped that whatever injuries he experienced were on the mend, and that Demeter was taking care of him. She wondered if she would ever see him again.

Images of his crooked smile and laughing hazel eyes flashed through her mind. Then the cords of his muscled back and his well-formed-- She shifted in her seat and flushed. The indicators in her helmet registered an increased heart rate. She glanced toward her mother hoping she didn't notice. Her mother had her full concentration on navigating the treacherous terrain.

She turned her thoughts to his bravery. He could have gotten himself killed. She would have to find a way to thank him, to at least get a message to him on the Derelict. She owed him her life.

The substation came into view with its flashing lights, indicating the top most height of the buildings. She could see a shuttle parked on the rooftop platform presumably there to take them back up to Demeter.

A flash and the shuttle broke apart hit by phase fire. Jheslae braked, throwing Amione and Curphay against their restraints.

"Hold on!" Jheslae pushed the CAT faster.

She banked quickly to the right and wove into the varied terrain that surrounded this substation like a labyrinth.

Another blast hit their left, sprinkling debris across the windshield.

"Why are they shooting at us?"

"It's the Head Magistrate's people."

"What?"

"He wasn't the only one interested in you and the Seedlings."

Another blast hit a few feet in front of them. Jheslae pushed the CAT faster and drove through the dust, slowing down only to navigate the curves.

"We won't be able to outrun them," Amione reminded her.

"No." Jheslae's brow was furrowed in concentration.

"I have an idea..." She unstrapped from her seat.

"Amione?" Curphay gripped the straps to his seat tightly while looking at her with frightened eyes.

She gave him a reassuring squeeze as she stumbled to the back cargo area. Just as she hoped the drone was still engaged. Another blast and a jerk to the left, had her falling hard against the seats. She drew a painful breath hoping that her ribs were only bruised and not broken.

She crawled to the panel that worked the drone and engaged the autopilot. She quickly typed in a destination and reworked the transponder so it emitted an electromagnetic signature similar to the Seedlings. Hopefully the sublimating methane would throw off the sensors and they would follow her decoy.

Amione's hand hovered over the controls as she looked over her shoulder to see where they were. Another blast hit to their left and Jheslae swerved to the right. Amione hit the controls releasing the drone.

"Turn left!" She yelled over the din at her mother.

Jheslae didn't hesitate, and went left. Amione watched the tracker as the drone made its way to the right. She watched as the ships latched on to the drone and followed it away from the CAT. She heaved a sigh of relief, wobbled back into her seat, and strapped in.

"I think we lost them."

"Good." Jheslae's face was a mask of concentration as they wove deeper and deeper into the labyrinth.

"Where are we going? And how will we get off the surface?"

"Not much further. I just need to get off of Hesper Corp's land and out into the unmarked lands."

"But there isn't anything out there," Amione protested.

"Isn't there?" Jheslae shot her an amused look.

"Mother, what's out there?" Amione gripped the hand rests more tightly.

A long moment passed before her mother replied. "There is a covert war happening between those who support the ARK Project and the other."

"Hesper Corp? But they just mine Titan and a couple of asteroids."

"It is a front for something bigger."

"What exactly does that mean?"

"There is a Prophecy..."

"There's that word again." How did such an archaic concept land in this age and time? First the Head Magistrate, then Shadow and Oal and now her mother.

"Is it such a stretch? Time dilation exits. It's not such a stretch to believe in time travel, is it? That's all prophecy is, knowledge of the future."

"Time travel is real?" Amione wasn't sure what to think about that revelation.

"It is the reason I stayed away for so long. I couldn't risk that they would come for you before you were ready." Jheslae increased speed.

She groped for Curphay's hand squeezing it tightly as the CAT shuddered along the uneven terrain.

Jheslae glanced over her shoulder. "I know you don't believe. Neither did I, but your father had a way of..." She looked back at the terrain turning to the left to avoid a large bolder. "He had a way of making you believe." She gave Amione another glance one that was soft and loving. She had never seen her mother look that way before. They loved each other. She had always blamed her mother for their split, but in fact, it was the biggest act of love of all. Everything she ever believed about her mother now needed to be reexamined.

The Prophecy sounded like something Amione would have read out of a story. Things like this didn't happen in real life. But then, bonding with a shadow and absorbing a mushroom into her thigh weren't on her radar either a couple of weeks ago.

"You left me on the doorstep of the enemy? Did Da know?"

"It was his idea. He said that the last place they would look for you would be right under their noses. If he worked for them, he could keep an eye on anything they might do. I was used as bait. We knew that if I gave them an enticing enough target that they would follow me thinking that I would lead them to the one who would fulfill the Prophecy."

"And you did."

"We thought that we had done enough to protect you. They must have figured out what your father was doing and killed him." Her voice caught at the last.

Amione couldn't remember the last time she had heard any significant emotion in her voice.

Everything that she had believed was a lie. Even her Da lied to her.

"When were you both going to tell me?" She felt Curphay squeeze her fingers more tightly.

"After you graduated. I'm sorry. I'm sorry your father is dead. I'm sorry you are finding out this way. I had wanted to do this together with your Da and introduce you to it all slowly, but even the best laid plans go awry." Regret weighed on her normally controlled voice.

Amione didn't know what she felt. Anger certainly, but also sadness, regret, and trepidation.

"What am I supposed to do now?"

"We will meet up with the Alliance and get you off of Titan for good."

"What about Curphay?" Amione looked over at her friend who sat silent and pale next to her watching the exchange.

"Our agreement stands. That is, if he still wants to come?"

Amione looked at Curphay, the question on her lips.

Curphay's determined brown eyes looked back at her. "Dhager and Dhau forever, remember?" His brows quirked up.

Relief flooded through her and tears threatened to spill from her eyes and obscure her vision. Gratefully the vacuum system in her helmet was working and wicked away the excess moisture. She squeezed his hand again and released it.

Jheslae nodded as if she expected that response. "Very well. We should be there in five minutes."

They exited the labyrinth and onto a plain with relatively free of large rocks obstructing their path. An alarm sounded and an energy blast cratered the ground in front of them.

"HQ this is Technocrat requesting assistance." Jheslae's voice held an edge to it.

Another blast had them fishtail before her mother could right the vehicle. It was only a matter of time before they were hit.

Do you wish our help, Amione Dhau?

She had forgotten about Shadow and Vara.

Yes. Please.

The next blast launched them into the air, flipping the CAT over its nose and crashed into the ground. The force of the crash yanked her against the restraints and she floundered helplessly like a rag doll as the CAT's momentum continued to roll and flip in the low gravity until it landed against a large boulder and finally came to rest on its side. Alarms went off and she could hear the atmo escaping through a crack in the windshield.

The pursuers flew past them at high speed and banked to make another run at them. She worked the restraints and checked on Curphay, who was unconscious, but alive. She dropped to the console and checked on her mother who was moaning softly. She could see that her mother's arm was broken.

The craft had banked and was heading toward them. *Shadow, can you help me stop them?*

We can.

She felt Shadow extend into the rest of her body. The seedling burrowed into her shoulder. She grunted, taking deep even breaths as the pain radiated from her chest over her shoulder and neck.

She hit the panel to the door and exited the CAT. She stood on the side panel and waited for the craft to make its approach.

Chapter 30

Need more Data

"Torture the data and it will confess to anything."
Ronald Coase

Oal watched the progress of the creatures through the mental connection he had with the Sadool. The creatures called themselves *humans*, small brown and beige people who were curious and avaricious at the same time. Oal found the dichotomy interesting.

The Sadool was able to touch their minds from time to time. Just enough to know that what they did not match their inner thoughts. How any species could survive with such duplicity, Oal could not fathom, and yet, in spite of these failings, humans had a remarkable ability to cooperate towards larger goals and do it at a frightening pace.

"I have learned all I can through observation. I think we should go further." The Sadool commented one day after a rather lengthy trip to the newest city in the sky. He began revolving around Oal in a self-soothing gesture.

"Go further? What would that entail?" Oal was unsettled by the rapid changes, and was unsure it was wise to push further.

"I think I should attempt a symbiosis." The Sadool stopped revolving around Oal.

Oal's limbs curled more tightly before releasing their tension. "Do you think that is wise?"

"I see no alternative. If we are to understand this species, we need more information." The Sadool resumed its restless revolution around Oal.

Oal didn't think this would end well, but could understand why the entity wanted to try. "We have no idea how they would respond."

"Precisely why we need to try."

"What can I do?" Oal missed his mobility especially when there was so much going on above the surface.

"Nothing other than to monitor my progress."

"Do you have someone chosen?" Oal sifted through the images the entity had sent him.

"Yes. One of the leaders of the newest city. That should provide adequate insight." The Sadool settled near the ground in front of Oal.

"Very well."

Saturn hung serenely in the sky half in light and half in shadow, watching with indifference as the Sadool ascended into the hazy copper sky. It followed a shuttle filled with individuals until it veered towards the older city. The Sadool peeled away and turned west towards the newest shining city in the sky.

It was not lost on the Sadool that each city's residents lived very different lives. Why they should be different he did not understand. Which is why, it wanted to bond with one of the leaders and ask.

The entity deftly navigated the shuttles, orbiters, and pleasure craft that flew between the cities. Finally, it lazily circled the exterior, looking for the one he had chosen.

It spotted the unsuspecting human making his way from an upper level to a lower level. He was tall and thin as most Titians were, with mid-length blond hair that was graying in spots. Small blue eyes searched the crowd as he walked but never registered anyone.

The entity shadowed the human as he pushed his way through throngs of people. These humans were always in a hurry.

If the entity had a head to shake it would have. The humans had not learned the secret of time. Hurrying as they did only made their lives shorter. They could use a perspective beyond their own. It was doing them a favor by bonding with them.

It waited until the human was in a secluded area, pausing to look at a device on his wrist. The Sadool fluttered with expectation. Other than

Oal, it had never bonded with anyone else. Things could go right as it did with Oal, or it could go very wrong. It hoped for something in between preferably closer to things going right.

He reached out tentatively, gently brushing the back of the human's neck. He raised a hand to scratch at the sensation it evoked. It entered the base of the human's skull.

There was flesh and bone which it expected. What it didn't expect was a strange pulsing rhythm from the human's life functions. That explained a lot. If humans were constantly aware of this rhythm, it was no wonder they were obsessed with time. Their own bodies counted off the seconds for as long as they lived.

It probed the mind of the human, gaging if its interference was too much or too little. At first there was nothing, but a web of neurons that seemed to fire off randomly within the structure. The longer it observed, the more it realized that there was a pattern related to the behavior of the human. It dove deeper and found a primitive telepathic organ hidden deep within the tissue. It heard internal thoughts, emotions, and visions that rode in waves through the mind. It was chaotic, terrible, and wondrous all at the same time.

The human continued walking. It tapped into the human's ocular nerves to see what he was seeing. The image looked strange and limited through his eyes. There was no electromagnetic resonance, no infrared, no ultraviolet, just middling wavelengths interpreted as color, depth, and tone. How did humans ever survive with half the visual spectrum missing?

It looked at the device in the human's hands. It wasn't sure what he did with the devices. From its observations, all humans had them. Perhaps that was how they "saw" the rest of the world through these adaptive devices.

An awful sensation passed through it, making it feel disorientated and weak. The human stopped walking and raised his appendage to his face. A long groan reverberated from his throat and echoed through his mind. The discomfort increased.

Other humans walked up to him and made sounds. Their orifices opened and closed and the human responded. His body swayed, then fell to the floor. His eyes closed, cutting the entity off from the visual world.

Something was wrong. It needed to leave. Panic set in when it realized it couldn't.

Chapter 31

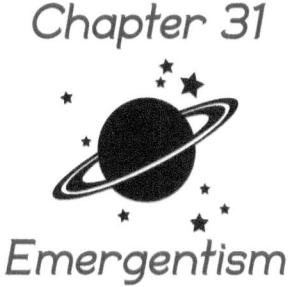

Emergentism

"Human beings, viewed as behaving systems, are quite simple. The apparent complexity of our behavior over time is largely a reflection of the complexity of the environment in which we find ourselves."
Herbert A. Simon, The Sciences of the Artificial

"I don't know how to do this." Amione placed a steadying hand on the open hatch as the fighter flew closer. "They are going to kill us."

"You can do this, Amione. We are with you. Just think about what you would like to do, and we will make it happen." Shadow tried to be reassuring, but it came across as an order.

Panic threatened to overwhelm her. "What if I get it wrong?"

"Then you won't be here to know the difference."

A rough laugh surprised her. "I suppose that is true."

There was no more time to think, the fighter was on them. Time seemed to slow as the flash from their energy canons flared, aimed directly at their vulnerable craft. If only they had a shield.

She could feel power fill her as the Seedling burned into her shoulder and Shadow expanded impossibly large within her. A large violet dome expanded outward and created a protective barrier over the CAT.

Time sped up. She flinched as phase fire crashed into the barrier and sizzled harmlessly away from them and into the ground.

"Did I?"

"Yes. You wanted a protective barrier over the CAT and we made it happen."

"It's coming back."

The fighter banked and started another pass.

Again, Amione thought about protection and the dome captured the phase fire and dissipated it harmlessly into the ground.

She felt her knee buckle. "What's happening?"

"We can only keep this up for so long. We need to take more offensive action."

"Like what?"

"We must disable their craft."

"How?"

"Think what you want, and it will happen."

Amione concentrated. She wanted the craft out of the sky, then focused on its next approach. She could feel Vara and Shadow shift within her. Her body protested under the unusual stress, but she maintained her focus. She had to protect Curphay, her mother and the Seedlings.

Time slowed again as she watched the craft approach. Tentacles of light and darkness emerged from her chest. She screamed under the strain. Time sped up and the tentacles expanded impossibly far from her body, ramming into the craft before it could release it could fire.

The craft stalled in the air, then broke apart as the tentacles crushed the metal skin of the fighter, crumpling as easily as a sheaf of paper. She wanted to stop, but the power that she released was out of control. The fighter dropped debris across the plains until it crashed into the ground. She already knew the pilot was dead before they hit.

The power continued to build until she thought she would burst from the pressure. She screamed as it built to the crescendo, then she released it, a kinetic wave spread out from her in all directions as if a bomb went off.

Once the wave was released, she felt drained and dropped to her hands and knees.

"Amione, you must rise. There will be more to follow."

Shadows' voice sounded faint as if it was far away. All she wanted to do was sleep. The ache in her shoulder intensified, dispelling any hope of that.

"You must get the Seedlings, Curphay, and your mother out of the CAT."

She shook her head and focused on what it was saying. She had come too far to let Curphay die. Whatever animosity she had toward her mother could wait. She still didn't understand everything, but the only way she would get more answers was to make sure her mother was alive to give them. Then there were the Seedlings.

The pain in her shoulder reminded her that these little seeds had the potential to create great power in the right circumstances. In the wrong hands, the Seedlings could be used in a massively destructive way.

She crawled to the open hatch and peered inside. The glow from the indicators was the only significant light. Dust coated the windshield obscuring any natural light the sun offered. A groan issued from her mother.

Amione dropped back into the CAT careful not to slip off the seat and onto Curphay who hung from his seat belt. She located the Seedlings toward the back of the CAT glowing a soft shade of blue. They were intact, tough little things.

She pushed toward her mother. "Are you alright?" She examined her suit to see if it was compromised.

"I'll manage." She grabbed a hold of the bar on the roof and braced her feet on the console as she unbuckled with her uninjured hand. She slipped and steadied herself, her left arm hung uselessly at her side. "How is Curphay?"

She pulled a first aid kit out of a nearby locker. "He is alive, but still unconscious." She dropped to the side of the CAT now against the ground. She examined Curphay and saw that he looked unhurt. She banged on his helmet. "Curph. Wake up."

He mumbled something and twitched.

"Curphay. We need to get out of here." She examined his oxygen gauge. "Shit. He has a leak somewhere. There is only an hour of oxygen left. What does yours say?"

"Seven hours."

"Mine has five. We need to find the leak, seal it, and share our air with him."

"Agreed. First let's get out of this place." The entire vehicle creaked and groaned as it was buffeted by the gentle wind outside.

"Amione?" Curphay's groggy voice was the best sound she had heard today.

"Welcome back. Now let's move." She unbuckled his restraints.

"What happened?" He grunted.

"Later. First, let's get out of here. Can you do that?"

"Sure." He grabbed a bar and finished unlatching the restraints. He fell heavily to the side.

Seeing he was well on his way out she pushed to the back and gathered any scattered Seedlings making sure all 30 were accounted for. She grabbed ration packs and water, just in case and followed her mother and Curphay out the hatch.

The wreckage of the fighter could be seen in the distance scarring the ground with its impact. She looked away sickened by what she had done. It was self-defense, but still, that was the second life she had taken today. She didn't like where this was heading.

"Come. More will be on the way." Jheslae urged as she tied a makeshift sling around her neck to cradle her injured arm.

"What happened? Is that a fighter?" Curphay gaped at the downed fighter.

"It crashed." Hoping that answer would be enough for now.

"It looked like it had help, but how did that--"

"Enough." Jheslae's stern voice echoed in their helmets. "First, we need to get away from the CAT and then we will speculate on the fate of that fighter. Survival first."

Jheslae exchanged a significant look with Amione. She was grateful for the reprieve, but she wondered if her mother knew or at least suspected Amione brought down that fighter.

They trudged forward. She swung the Seedlings over her shoulder and kept an eye on Curphay's suit to see if she could spot the leak. As soon as they were far enough away from the wreckage, she would patch him up and get him the oxygen he needed.

They carefully navigated the uneven terrain as quickly as they dared. There wasn't a lot of cover and distances were deceiving. They had no choice. If they stayed in one place, they would definitely die. It was up to her mother to get them to wherever this Alliance was holed up. She glanced at the hazy sky. They wouldn't have much warning if another fighter came toward them.

After only fifteen minutes, Curphay's suit pinged its first warning.

"I don't want to alarm anyone, but it says I only have fifteen minutes of air left." She could hear the edge of panic in his voice.

"Mother, we have to stop." She dropped the Seedlings gently on the ground and pulled a patch kit from one of the pockets on her thigh. "Don't worry Curph, we'll get you patched up in no time. Hold up your arms."

Curphay obeyed and Amione carefully examined his suit inch by inch until she found the leak and applied the patch.

"Amione." Her mother pointed to the south beyond the smudge of smoke to the west.

"I see them." Two more fighters had dropped from orbit and were heading to the wreck. "We need to keep going. Is it much further?"

Her mother scanned the horizon in the east. "Not much further. I've activated a beacon. Hopefully someone is coming."

"But not before those fighters get here."

Jheslae met her gaze. "No."

Amione's heart sank.

"Amione?" Curphay's face was filled with concern.

She unhooked her transfer hose and tugged on Curphay's arm.

"You are going to need that air." Curphay insisted.

"You need it more. I've got plenty." She had a feeling that if push came to shove, she would be able to survive like the last time. She hooked the hose and watched the gage move from red to yellow.

"You know that it will take every ounce of air to get to that base," Curphay protested.

"I'm not doing this without you." She gave him a warning look.

Jheslae moved to Curphay's back and hooked her transfer hose. Curphay tried to twist around to look at her, but Jheslae pushed his shoulder firmly forward.

"No one is leaving anyone behind," Jheslae stated firmly.

Amione was grateful for her mother's abrasiveness. Maybe after all this was over, they could get to know each other properly. Her mother met her gaze briefly before turning her attention back to the transfer.

Amione glanced at the fighters which were growing in size as they neared their position. She looked for some sort of cover and spotted a boulder a few meters away. "We won't out run them. Maybe we can hide before they pick up our body heat."

Her mother nodded. "Let's do it. Ready to go?" She directed the question to Curphay.

"Gladly."

They struggled together toward the boulder moving much slower than if they had the CAT. Even with the gravity belts it only gave them slightly more traction than they would normally have on Demeter.

Amione felt herself sweat with exertion. She was still exhausted from her earlier burst of power. She couldn't afford to lose water, but there was no alternative. They had to reach the boulder before those fighters came into range.

It gave her time to examine recent events. *What was that, Shadow?*

It is symbiosis. Though, I wasn't sure what to expect. She could hear the surprise in its voice.

But you suspected that something like this might happen, she probed.

After our encounter with the other entity, I knew we had the capability, but it seems that the power is growing faster than I had ever imagined.

Is this a good or bad thing?

Oal talked of the Prophecy often. I thought it was fanciful dreaming, but if there is truth in it, then there is much more at stake than I thought.

I wish Vara could talk. I wouldn't mind hearing the Prophecy again. Vara has Oal's memories, right?

That was how he explained it. There is another way.

Another way? She stumbled, quickly righting herself. Curphay stopped to help, but she waved him on.

Vara could show you the Prophecy.

Then that is what I would like.

Later. When we aren't in the middle of being shot by the enemy. Preferably some place quiet.

Why?

It will be overwhelming for you.

Amione thought back to when she touched Oal the first time and the sheer number of images that were transferred. It knocked her on her ass. *Agreed.*

Satisfied, Shadow retreated into the back of her mind.

A proximity alarm went off drawing her attention back to the fighters. "Down!"

They all ducked against a smaller boulder as the fighters screamed past them and over the wreckage. As soon as they passed, they scrambled the last few meters to the larger boulder and wedged themselves beneath the overhang. She wasn't sure if it would be enough to conceal them.

Shadow. Can I use this ability to hide us?

You are already overtaxed.

Can we do it? she insisted. *Our lives depend on it.*

Give me a moment.

All they had was a moment. The fighters were banking to make a return pass. If they were found, it would be all over. She had no idea what they would do with them. What they would do to her and the Seedlings.

She glanced over at her mother and Curphay holding their breath, waiting to be discovered. She looked out over the landscape to the east and hoped that whoever was with the Alliance was well on their way. In the meantime, she could give them every fighting chance.

She let her eyes fall close and concentrated on connecting more deeply with Shadow. Tendrils of thought twined with her own. She then reached out to Vara, searching for her bright white filaments and connecting with her. The chaos that constantly boiled just beneath the surface was carefully controlled. She couldn't allow it free reign this time. She just needed enough of her power to make the connection between light and dark.

The chaos bucked beneath her will as she concentrated on the desired result. Concealment. She wanted to be invisible. The chaos begged to be unleashed, but she forcefully bent it back to her will.

She wasn't sure if it was working or not. Her hold on the chaos was tentative. If she tried to look, she would lose control.

All sense of time was distorted as she concentrated on this one thought. Hopefully that would be all that they needed.

Shadow strained against the connection. Vara drew closer. She regulated the ebb and flow between them. Vara pulled against the tether and Shadow drew nearer; back and forth in a rhythm of their own making.

The ground rumble beneath her legs. It was imperative that she maintain her concentration. Someone grabbed her arm, but still she maintained her focus. Her breath came out ragged as the energy she exerted increased. Perspiration broke out on her forehead and on her upper lip. The tug between the two entities and the chaos burn between pushed her past her breaking point.

The vibrations faded and everything was still once again. The energy they expended decreased and she finally allowed herself to relax into a limp huddle.

"Amione?" Curphay's worried voice came over the com. He shook her shoulder. "Amione!"

She opened her eyes and stared at him.

His shoulders relaxed when he saw her acknowledge him. "You scared us. Where did you go? Did you see the fighter? It was right in front of us."

"Slow down." She croaked and swallowed painfully, trying to get moisture in her throat. "You will use up too much air."

He laughed and nodded. "I will try. I don't know how the fighter didn't see us. We were right in front of it." He went on excitedly.

Amione looked over at her mother, who watched her carefully. Her mother knew. She wasn't sure how she knew, but she did.

"We need to keep moving before the fighters come back. I don't think we will be this lucky next time." Her mother pushed herself away from the boulder to survey the sky before heading off to the east once again.

Curphay helped Amione to her feet. She almost fell forward, but Curphay was there to keep her upright. "Are you ok?"

"Just hungry and tired. I haven't slept in over 24 hours." She stifled a yawn.

A look of sympathy crossed his face. "Here I am prattling when you have done so much for me. Let me carry your burden for a bit." He took the bag of Seedlings from her. "Here we go. Now we are moving."

She allowed Curphay to lead them through the rough terrain. *Can you tell how much further we need to go, Shadow?* Shadow stirred. *I think one of the Alliance will find us before we need to go much further.*

As if on cue, she could see the dust trail behind a vehicle coming from the east. Relief poured through her. She didn't have enough strength to endure another encounter.

What life would be like now that she was a fugitive of Titan she didn't know. She wasn't sure that this was the life her Da had in mind when he last saw her. How much did he really know? A wave of grief washed over her.

"Da, why didn't you tell me?"

Chapter 32

Trapped

"I got Trust issues because people got lying issues"
Unknown

Nightmarish images invaded the Sadool's mind. Images that it didn't completely understand. There were several iterations of the humans, flashing through the human's mind, but something didn't seem right. The proportions were off, and they were destroying each other. The human felt great distress and pain. The entity felt the terror along with him.

"Oal!" It cried out, hoping its friend would be able to reach it through their link. It was afraid that Oal might not be able to help and it would be lost in the human's mind forever. Or at least until the human died. Either way, Sadool could not remain here.

The human's mind was like a universe of its own with twists and turns beyond the Sadool's imagination. What a terribly chaotic existence, one that it didn't want to be a part of.

"Oal, where are you?"

It became increasingly desperate as the disorientation increased. It was aware that human's body was moved. It could hear the sounds the humans were making, but it couldn't understand what was being communicated or why.

This was a bad idea. It should never have allowed its curiosity to get the better of it. It was the only way to learn more about these prodigious creatures who were delicate and destructive at the same time.

"I am here." Oal's voice came to the Sadool faintly.

"I can barely hear you." No matter where it turned, it was trapped, being pulled deeper and deeper into the human's mind.

"Let me try something."

The entity could feel the connection strengthen and relief flooded through it.

"Is that better?" Oal's thoughts were louder and more succinct.

"Yes. Oal, I am trapped in the human."

"What do you mean trapped?" It could feel Oal's confusion and anxiety.

"I cannot disengage from his mind. Something is wrong."

Oal gently probed their connection. "It's the chaos."

"Chaos?" The concept of chaos was foreign. Nearly as foreign as light was millions of years ago before he met Oal.

"Yes. These humans are rife with it. We wrongly assumed they were creatures of light like I am."

"What does that mean?"

"It means it will take some time to untangle you from this human, if we can."

"But what if the human ceases to exist? He is in distress now." The Sadool struggled harder against the binds and only succeeded in tangling itself further.

"I don't know. I'm not sure if my parentage had ever encountered a life form composed of chaos. I need to search for an answer."

"Hurry."

"Stay calm, my friend. Do not struggle. I will find a way."

The connection decreased in intensity, but it was still there. The Sadool clung to that connection as another wave of images washed over it. Countless images of destruction, humans against humans, humans against machine, humans against nature. How could this human have destroyed so much? Was this from his past?

The Sadool tried to extricate himself from the human again and the web pulled tighter. The human opened his eyes. They were in a sterile room with masked humans peering down. Bright light flashed over his eyes, causing the entity to flinch in pain.

The sensation of touch, sound, and sight were too much. It yearned for its non-corporeal state. If humans lived with these sensations all the time, it was no wonder they were chaotic. How did they exist without tearing themselves apart?

Pain ripped through the human's arm and into the entity. If it could have screamed, it would have. The humans were inserting instruments into the human's arm with fluids dripping into his veins.

"Oal," it moaned.

It felt the connection strengthen. "I am here. Get ready. I will try to sever the connection."

It could feel a tug from the outside of the human and reached out for that connection. Oal gripped it tightly, then worked to free the entity from the human's mind. One connection was severed and another rose up. It was tedious and the Sadool could feel time grow short. The humans were growing more frantic as the man slipped further into oblivion.

Oal continued to saw at the binding and finally the Sadool felt something give. It pulled on the binds and finally it was free. It hovered over the prone form of the human, watching as the other humans delivered electrical pulses into the body. Three times they shocked the human and three times they failed. All life that had been in that form was gone.

One thing was clear, the human would still be alive if the entity had not entered his mind.

"Come back." Oal's voice sounded tired over their connection.

The entity took one last look at the human, then left the city in the sky for the safety of their home below.

Now that the pain had ceased, it had a chance to examine the experience. What had gone wrong? It didn't believe that a connection wasn't possible. Perhaps it needed to find a different human. However, it would take additional precautions. It didn't want to be trapped in a corporeal body ever again.

The haze parted in its wake and it enjoyed drifting through the rain clouds and over the rocky tops of the terrain. Humans did not know this kind of freedom.

It entered the cave and was relieved to feel Oal's steady presence.

"I'm glad you made it back safely," Oal greeted.

"I'm not sure what went wrong."

"We will need to examine the experience. But not today. I need rest. I wasn't sure if I would be able to free you."

"These humans…"

"Yes?"

"I'm not sure what to make of them. The images I saw were confusing. I could not determine if it was real or not."

Oal's surprise filtered through their connection. "What do you mean?"

The Sadool sent a few of the images through their link.

Appalled, Oal withdrew from the link. "How do they function with any order?"

"I don't know. I'd have to try again to find out."

"We will need to take additional precautions."

"Agreed. I have no desire to end my existence in one of these humans."

"The risk is high, but not understanding these beings is a much higher risk."

"Let's rest."

Chapter 33

Potential Energy

"The greater the contrast, the greater the potential. Great energy only comes from a correspondingly great tension of opposites."
Carl Jung

Amione was carried from the rescue vehicle. She was far too tired to do anything else. She remembered Curphay's concerned face and Jheslae's hawkish one. Her eyes drifted closed, releasing her into blissful oblivion.

She woke to the buzz of Treto lighting which cast a ghostly white glow in the room. Her eyes wandered over the domed ceiling which was covered in mesh and the yellowish amalgamation of Titanian soil carefully 3-d printed. It was an older construction using techniques since outdated. Which meant wherever she was, the structure was well over 200 years old.

She raised a hand to her forehead and groaned. Even that small movement caused pain to radiate everywhere. Even the air hurt. She licked her cracked lips. A cursory glance around the pallet she was on, showed a water bottle standing next to her. She reached for it, and succeeded in tipping it on to its side. She watched as it rolled away from her.

She cursed, swallowing with a very dry throat. Her eyes felt gritty. Well, she couldn't lay here forever. She was going to have to move. She just needed to rest a bit before she tried.

"Shadow. Are you there?" Her heart thudded when it didn't respond right away.

"I'm here." It sounded subdued.

"What's wrong?"

"You have been damaged."

"I'm sure I will get better." She groaned again. "Although, I do feel as if death won over."

"You nearly died."

"I'm sorry. I'll try not to do that again."

"We need to be careful next time. You are fragile."

"Compared to you, I suppose I am." A panicked thought raced through her. "Vara?"

"Is resting. She is still there."

She gently felt the place on her chest where Vara resided and sighed in relief when she felt a little flutter in response. She let her breath out slowly.

"Good. How long have I been here?"

"Three of your days."

"Three?!" No wonder she felt like crap. "What's been happening?"

"Several ships have attacked the area, but they don't seem to be able to find the alliance base. It is only a matter of time before they do."

"What does that mean?"

"Since the base has been exposed, the Alliance is planning on leaving."

"To go where?"

"To the ARK."

Her heart jumped with excitement. She had not imagined her arrival at the ARK like this, but to go to the very place she dreamed of?

A Nouri walked into the room. "I see you are finally awake. I'm Na'Ta,Tien." She knelt at her side and laid a hand on Amione's forehead and checked her eyes. "How do you feel?"

Amione studied the Nouri. She had seen several over the years since they were an ally to the Sol System. This one seemed quite typical of their species with small features, copper eyes, and fur that looked like a mohawk. Her lavender skin was flawless, enhanced by the lighting.

Amione swallowed painfully. "Thirsty," she croaked.

Na'Ta,Tien located the bottle nearby and scooped it into her hands and gently lifted Amione's head so she could drink.

Amione pulled water from the bottle like a suckling baby.

"Not too much. You are still quite weak."

Now that she had some moisture back, she could finally speak. "Curphay? My Mother?"

"Are anxiously waiting to see you."

"How bad am I?"

"We think you are just exhausted. Another day of rest will do you good."

Amione was surprised that Na'Ta,tien was able to answer her questions so quickly. Amione decided to see if she could stump her. "When will the Alliance be moving out of this place?"

Amione felt satisfaction when Na'Ta,tien didn't have a ready answer for her. The expression on the Nouri didn't change, but her eyes seemed to glow brighter in the strange light.

"How do you know about that?" Her tone was cold.

"So, you are planning to leave?"

"Yes."

"When?"

"Soon. Which is about how long you have to get on your feet."

Amione nodded.

"Is there anything else?" Na'Ta,tien's warm demeanor had turned icy quickly. Amione wasn't sure what to make of the mercurial change.

Amione shook her head slowly.

"I have other patients to attend to." She rose and went to the door.

"Thank you."

The Nouri looked back at her as if quietly contemplating something, then nodded before exiting.

She laid back and stared at the ceiling. She tried lifting her right leg and couldn't get it off the pallet. Burning pain raced up her thigh into her hips, bringing tears to her eyes. The only solace for the pain was that eventually it would abate.

"Shadow."

"Yes, Amione."

"The Nouri didn't like that I knew about the exodus."

"There was no way you could know information like that since you have been bed bound. You need to be more cautious."

"I needed to see how she would react. There is something going on that I want to know more about. If I'm to put my fate in these people's hands, I need to know that I'm not being jerked around."

"Jerked around?"

"That they are being truthful and not just telling me what I want to hear."

"Do you want me to listen in on them?"

"Yes," she stated emphatically. "I need to know so I can protect myself and Curphay."

"What about your mother?"

What about her mother? She had shown herself to be truthful. Even with recent events, there was a decade of hurt to mend. That didn't go away overnight. She wanted to trust Jheslae, but she couldn't do that just yet.

"Very well." She could hear how unhappy the entity was. It separated itself from her and she could feel a lessening of pressure in her head. It remained tethered presumably so it could return quickly if needed. She had not realized how full she felt when the Sadool was in her. Now she felt empty. Had she always felt this empty or was she just now noticing it with the entity's absence?

She was hardly alone. She could feel the gentle pulse of the Seedling nestled against her shoulder. She did not mind Vara's presence. There was a lightness to it, an innocence Amione found intoxicating.

Maybe Vara was exerting some sort of influence on her. Certain animals on Old Earth were known to influence their prey so that they could be consumed. She shuddered. That was not the case here, but perhaps Vara was stimulating her endorphins so the pain of her presence didn't overwhelm Amione. She wished she could communicate her gratitude somehow to her.

Now that she had water in her system, she decided to try getting up again from the pallet. Slowly she rolled to her side and pushed herself onto an elbow. Even that small movement sent the room spinning. She resolutely stayed in place praying that it would pass. She could have waited for Curphay, but that could be hours. She needed to know that he was ok and to find out what was really going on here.

A boom shuddered through the room, shaking the ceiling. Dust sifted over her. She sneezed and cursed the pain that shot through her head. She hoped Shadow was finding out more information because she wasn't going to be moving very fast as it was.

Another vibration shuddered through the structure. She reached for the water bottle and chugged the last of the liquid. Hopefully that would perk her up a bit. Her stomach growled, reminding her that she had not eaten much since this all started. What she would give to be back in the comfy quarters she shared with her Da.

A pang of sadness threatened to overwhelm her. Not only had she lost her Da, but everything he ever owned. Everything she had ever held dear.

She patted the pocket of her vest.

Not everything. She still had his unopened letter in her pocket. She carefully fished it out and stared at his scrawl on the envelope. She ran her fingers along the edges and debated if she should open this very ordinary letter.

She had nearly died a couple of times in the last couple of days. She had found his killer and brought him to justice. She had met Willan who helped her for reasons she still did not understand. She had saved her friend. She was bonded to a non-corporeal entity and a mushroom, and she had taken down a fighter.

Ordinary sounded really good at the moment. She flipped over the envelope, paused briefly before sliding her nail beneath the seal. Crisply, the glue released its hold and the contents were exposed. Her Da's tight script was on the folded pages and the edges of an illustration. She slipped it out of the envelope and listened to the satisfying crumpling sound it made as she unfolded it.

Dear Amione,

By now you know I didn't make it.

Amione stifled a sob. He knew he was about to die. She had assumed he didn't know, but this indicated that he knew something more. What the hell was this?

She wiped away her tears and pressed a hand over her mouth to keep her sobs from escaping.

I wish we had told you much sooner about your place in all this.

What is *this*?

Your Mother and I decided when you were born that you were to be protected at all costs. Your mother was sent away so that we could do that. She is a high-profile figure in the Alliance and a magnet for the enemy. Loving you from afar was the only thing she could do. I regret that you didn't know her love. I know she is a hard woman to know, but it is worth it, Amione. She is someone you can trust.

There is something bigger happening on Titan. It has to do with the Seedling. Maybe you will figure out how it all connects together. In the meantime, I'm going to protect you one last time. I am returning to the mine, to the cavern. They will try to get the information from me or kill me while trying. I wish there was another way, but this is too important. You are too important.

My biggest regret is that we didn't prepare you for any of this. I'm afraid for you. I'm afraid of what will happen to you. Know that above all else that I wish I was there to help you through it all. I have left you some things that will guide you to the path you were made for. You can do this, Little Bird. I know you can. There is nothing you can't do if you decide you want it enough. I wish I could be more specific, but I'm confident you will find the answers you need exactly when you need them.

I love you.

Your Da

Amione stared at the pages, trying to decipher the hidden meanings. Would anything have changed if she had read this letter two days ago? Maybe she would have given her mother a break, but she still would have investigated her Da's death. She still would have gone to the surface for answers.

She carefully folded the pages and replaced them in the envelope and placed it inside her vest. She would reread it later. Right now, she needed something to eat and to get off this pallet and on her feet.

Another rumble shook the room. This one was stronger than the others. Something was definitely happening and since no one was coming to her, it was up to her to go find them.

She rummaged through the cabinets, finding several protein bars. She tore into the packaging, forcing herself to chew each bite slowly and carefully before swallowing.

"Shadow."

She waited as she chewed. She could feel a slight tug of acknowledgement and relaxed waiting for its return.

She felt stronger after eating and washed it down with more water. Pressing her hands onto the cool floor, she heaved herself into a sitting position. Good, no dizziness. The smell of fallen plaster tickled her nose, making her sneeze.

Next step was to get her knees under her. She heaved herself up and swayed as overwhelming fatigue washed over her. Once she was up, she was sure she would feel more like herself, not that she had a choice.

She grasped the stainless-steel medical tray and used it to pull herself to her feet. She braced her hands on either side of the tray and noted the instruments laying there on a sterile cloth. One of them was a hypersonic scalpel. She palmed it and headed to the door, leaning heavily against the counters lining the wall.

She had a feeling that whoever was causing the ceiling to vibrate was also intent on breaching this facility. She peered out the small window in the door. Several people were running up the corridor carrying weapons, boxes of data crystals, and other equipment as they evacuated.

When were they going to tell her? Where was Curphay and her mother? She went back to the pallet and grabbed the water bottle and refilled it and grabbed more protein bars and shoved them into her pocket. She grabbed a few medical supplies too and shoved them into a makeshift sling that she wrapped over her shoulder.

She pushed her way out of the room and into the melee. Insistent hands pushed her along if she hesitated. She hoped wherever they were going that Curphay and her mother were there too.

Red lights flashed on and off, bathing the crowd in red one minute and blue the next. She could feel her mind detach from the frenetic scene, concentrating only on the shifting colors and where they were taking her.

Now would be a good time to come back, Shadow.

She could feel their connection strengthen as Shadow drew near her position. It wrapped itself around the base of her skull, then was absorbed into her. She stumbled and the person behind her protested. She righted herself and slipped into an alcove to catch her breath.

A series of images flashed through her mind from Shadow; part of a structure collapsed in on itself, several bodies littering the floor, a view of the outside of the facility. Large craft hovered overhead, bombarding the structure with phase fire. Smoke smoldered in the gold atmosphere. No sooner would a craft lift off, then it was shot down by a fighter. Flashes of frightened faces and finally a glimpse of Curphay.

Where is Curphay? Where did you see him?

We are nearly there. He is looking for you too.

And my mother?

I did not see her. Its voice was filled with regret.

Her heart lurched in her chest. What if she was beneath the pile of rubble? She didn't want to think about that possibility. She was alive until she learned differently.

Another concussive blast shook the facility, throwing her against the wall along with the other frightened bodies, hurrying toward escape. The corridor opened into a hanger. People were hurrying up ramps into the vehicles. As soon as one transport was filled, it lifted off and out of the hanger into the line of fire.

She moved off to the side, scanning the crowd for her friend's lean form.

Do you know where he is, Shadow?

I'll need to separate from you again.

Do it. Her breath came out ragged.

She felt Shadow return. *We need to go this way.* It indicated a less traveled corridor.

Where does that lead?

It is a smaller hanger similar to this one. Curphay is waiting there. You must hurry.

She hesitated, looking back at all the people trying to find space on a transport. Another one lifted off, it slowly made its way toward the door and was promptly shot down. She shielded her eyes as the fire ball momentarily blinded her. The building shook as it collapsed into the floor. Twisted metal mingled with the flames as they reached for other combustible objects nearby.

She felt sick to her stomach. How many people had been on that transport? Hundreds? She turned away from the carnage and swiftly made her way down the narrow corridor. There was nothing she could do for them.

Conduits and wires hung from the ceiling as she navigated the debris piled in the corridor. She hoped where ever this hanger was, that it wasn't far from there. She was tiring again, and a persistent ringing wormed its way into her mind.

The corridor opened into a smaller hanger that had one ship in it. It looked fast in the dim light. Only a hand full of people stood at the doorway. She nearly fainted with relief when she recognized Curphay.

He hadn't seen her yet. His body language was belligerent and rigid. She had never seen him look so angry. He argued with a man in coveralls. Curphay tried to push past him and was physically pushed back.

"I'm not going without her," he insisted through gritted teeth.

"We can't wait any longer. You are going on that ship even if we have to physically pick you up to do it."

"This whole place is going to come down." The building shook emphasizing his point. "I have to find her before that happens." He pushed his way past the guardians and a scuffle ensued. The guardians wrestled him to the ground.

Amione was still too far away to call out. She walked faster, hoping her bold approach would get their attention. The largest explosion yet shook the floor and brought her to her knees. Twisting metal ominously sounded over her head. Adrenaline pumping, she pushed to her feet and ran the last few meters.

"Let him go."

"Amione!" Curphay yanked his arms out of the guardians' grasp and hugged her tightly to him.

"Let's get out of here," she said.

They scrambled up the ramp, the pilot engaged the engines as the hatch closed. Amione and Curphay hastily pulled on their suits and strapped in to the passenger seats near the rear of the orbiter. She looked around and noted how state of the art everything was. This was more than an orbiter. It looked like it was a craft they used on long haul ships.

Several other people occupied the remaining seats. She counted 12 besides the pilot and themselves. She frantically looked at each face, hoping to see her mother, but none of them was Jheslae.

Regret filled her. She had been so angry. What a waste. She could have learned more about her mother. Instead, she was so consumed with her hurt and anger that she would never have the opportunity for any of that now.

Curphay grabbed her hand as the craft rocketed out of the crumpled hanger. Fighters shot at the craft, but bounced harmlessly off of the hull. It must have advanced shielding which solidified her belief that this was part of a long-haul craft.

She looked out the window as they banked away from the hidden base. She gasped.

"What is it?"

"The Derelict. It's on fire."

She looked on in horror as fighters bombarded the dying city. It was below the canopy and collision with the ground was imminent.

As if in slow motion, she watched descend, crash into the ground, and collapse in on itself. Debris billowed out and expanded across the landscape. She remembered all of those people who lived there. There weren't enough crafts to evacuate them all and those that could, wouldn't be able to sustain anyone for long.

She looked down at the smoldering heap. There was no way that there were survivors. She thought about the Magistrate, Layla, and all of the children she saw there. Willan.

She knew Willan was going to Demeter, but what if he had been diverted to the Derelict. She had to believe he had found a way to survive.

The craft nosed through the canopy and reached the topside. Her stomach sank. Fighters surrounded Demeter and fires had already broken out in the more damaged areas of the city. Explosive decompression sent debris floating in all directions. Several bodies drifted slowly through the canopy.

She made a strangled sound in her throat as she realized everyone and everything she ever knew was now gone. Demeter's position on

Titan had always been precarious. She thought that meant they would end up like the Derelict. She didn't know how true those words were at the time.

"I'm sorry, A." Curphay squeezed her hand.

She felt numb. If Willan had been there, he probably did not make it out. It seemed impossible and she couldn't deal with the unbearable ache in her chest.

So much loss. It seemed so senseless. Even with these new found powers, there was nothing she could do to prevent it. Nothing she could do to bring those lives back.

She cried silently not caring that her tears blinded her in the low gravity. The craft swiftly ascended, leaving Titan's atmosphere behind. She turned the vacuum unit on in her helmet to remove the tears from her eyes and took one last look at the hazy globe that had been her home. She was going from beneath the copper sky and into the inky blackness of space.

Chapter 34

Individualism

"You have your way. I have my way. As for the right way, the correct way, and the only way, it does not exist."
Friedrich Nietzsche

Oal examined the images from the Sadool's foray into the human and came to a conclusion. Humans were exceptionally individualistic.

They approached this all wrong. These humans had dormant telepathic abilities, but had never developed them. Why they never used it, he wasn't sure. Perhaps they had this in their early evolution and lost the ability, or the ability was beginning to emerge.

"I know where we went wrong," Oal stated. The Seedlings were heavy on his branches. The first few had finally dropped and lay nestled in the hydrocarbon sludge.

The Sadool drifted down to Oal and connected with him as it had done so many times in the past. "What is it?"

"We assumed the humans were like us."

"We know they aren't like us."

"What I mean is, working communally comes naturally to us. It doesn't to them."

The Sadool mulled over Oal's revelation. "You may be right. They speak manually by making sounds through their mouths, but not with their minds. How they have managed to work this well together is beyond me."

"It must be isolating to never share another's thoughts," Oal mused while connecting easily with the entity and with his seedlings.

"It might account for their competitive and territorial behavior."

"Perhaps."

The Sadool thought back to its interactions. "They pride themselves on consent. Someone must ask consent even for the smallest things."

"I think you hit on it perfectly. When you tried to merge with the human, its mind rebelled. We were too foreign, and we violated the human's individuality." Oal's luminescence thrummed excitedly, giving off white and blue light.

"What do we do about it?" The Sadool expressed frustration.

Oal sat in silence for a long while, mulling over what the solution might be. There was only one.

"We ask for consent."

"As easy as that?" Doubt crept into the entity's voice.

"It is as easy and as difficult as that," Oal affirmed.

THE SADOOL WENT BACK UP to the cities in the sky in search of a human it could connect with. This time it would ask for consent. How this would be accomplished it was not certain.

It entered from below, threading its way through the mechanical workings of the city and avoiding certain materials that if it came into contact with as they could make him more substantial. It needed to be able to pass through each layer unhindered.

It emerged in the central square surrounded by organic living things and water. Lots and lots of water. Which made sense considering humans were mostly composed of water. Another weakness. Water was rare and the humans could not survive without it.

The Sadool hovered over the atrium looking at each human with intense interest. It pushed its connection with Oal. "Do you see anyone who might be a good candidate? How do we even know which one will work?"

"Not trying means we definitely won't find that answer. We keep trying until we do."

The Sadool grimaced. It didn't like the idea of attempting a bonding and failing again and again. "If I am doing this, I want to be sure we get it right." The entity searched the crowd. "They all look like the other human. We need a better way of discernment."

"I will be able to tell," Oal assured it.

"How?" The Sadool was not at all confident.

"I will know when I seem them."

"That answer is unsatisfactory," the entity groused.

"There." Oal drew the Sadool's attention to the left side of the atrium.

"Show me."

Oal pushed further into the entity's mind and focused its sight on one particular human, a female. She was dressed in tailored clothes, her black eyes were sharp and aware, loose black curls framed an angular dark face. In her capable hands she examined a tablet in a secluded corner of the atrium.

"How do you know she is the one?"

Oal superimposed his ability to view electromagnetic fields. A myriad of colors and wave formations swirled around the humans. Most were subdued blues, greens and grays. When it looked at the woman, she looked like a star, brilliant oranges, energetic reds, mellow yellows, electric blues, and crisp greens swirled around her form.

"Why does she look like that? And how could I have missed it?" The Sadool approached her cautiously.

"I'm not sure what it is, but she is the one. She will be open to possibilities and if I'm right, she will agree to the bonding." Oal's voice was excited.

"All right. I will make contact."

Oal receded from the Sadool's mind, allowing the entity to concentrate on the delicate operation of first contact.

It reached out with tentacles of its mind and tentatively touched her mind. "What is your name?" The entity whispered.

The woman stiffened at the contact. At first the entity thought she would withdraw, but her curiosity was greater than her fear. "I am Jheslae."

Chapter 35

The ARK Project

*"With faith, discipline and selfless devotion to duty, there is nothing
worthwhile that you cannot achieve."*
Muhammad Ali Jinnah

Amione walked off the transport in a daze and didn't care where she was led. Curphay didn't say anything other than to gently instruct her to turn or to stop. He helped her out of her suit like a parent would help a child. She could feel his questioning eyes on her, but she couldn't look at him. If she looked at him, the dam would burst and she wouldn't be able to hold herself up.

They were gone. All gone. Her Da was gone, Leto, her mother, Oal, and Willan. Willan. She had known him only a few days. How could her heart ache for him so unbearably? Flashes of his lopsided smile, the warmth of his hazel eyes, how his hands felt when he held her close. She flushed at the last memory. She shoved it all away. Curphay helped her to her feet.

"We are going to get something to eat. They still need to organize where everyone will sleep." He sighed when she didn't answer.

She didn't resist and allowed him to lead her back through the melee of people milling about, wondering where they should go and what they should do. She could hear guardians yelling instructions over the crowd.

People bumped into her and the air was warm with so many bodies pressed together. She clung to Curphay's hand and released her breath when they finally reached the edge. Hastily erected tables held ration packs laid out for people to take. Curphay snagged two and led her to an open space on the floor. She slid down the wall, and closed her eyes.

"Do you want something to drink?"

She shook her head and felt hot tears betray her as they crept from beneath her closed lids and slid down her cheeks.

"Ah, Amione, I'm so sorry." Curphay wrapped an arm around her and drew her close.

She allowed herself to lean against her friend. She couldn't allow herself to feel the full impact of her grief. Not yet. Maybe when they had someplace to sleep. Then she could cry, but not now.

It took hours, but they were led into a converted cargo bay. Makeshift pallets were laid out and Amione collapsed onto one and fell asleep. Unconsciousness was the only place she could go to escape this reality.

Amione? Shadow whispered to her.

What?

Do you want me to take the pain away?

She contemplated the offer. *No. I will endure.*

Is there anything I can do?

Can you bring back the dead?

Regret filled their connection. *I'm afraid that is beyond my power.*

Empathy filled her. *I'm sorry. You have lost a friend too.*

Oal was unique. I cherished our bond. I am glad we have Vara to carry on his legacy. Just as you carry on your parentage's legacy.

Her heart felt empty as she thought about its words. She was all that was left of her parents. What would she do now? She placed a hand over the letter in her vest pocket. It was too raw. She would have to think about what was next later.

She searched for her connection to Vara and found the light she exuded soothing. It didn't take away her pain, but it made things manageable. Amione hoped Vara understood how sorry she was that her parent was gone.

"Amione Dhau?"

She looked up at a fierce looking guardian in full gear. Her mind jumped to various possibilities. Was he here to arrest her? No. She would be restrained by now.

"Yes?" She cleared her voice.

"Come with me." The guardian stepped to the side, indicating that she go to the far exit where two more guardians were waiting.

"Why?"

"The Captain would like to speak with you." Amione searched the quiet gray eyes for any indication of what that might be, but the guardian revealed nothing.

She rose and indicated that Curphay come with her.

"Alone."

She raised her brows. "Alone?"

"Why does he want to see her alone?" Curphay bristled.

"I don't ask, I just do as I'm told." The guardian shrugged. He thumbed the clasp of his weapon, the only indication he was impatient.

"Of course, you do," Amione growled.

He held out his hand again, indicating that she should go forward.

Curphay grasped her arm. "Amione..."

"It's ok. I'll be fine." And she would be. She could already feel Shadow and Vara stir.

He reluctantly withdrew his hand and sank down on the pallet.

"I'll be back before you know it." She smiled encouragingly.

She walked past the guardian to the exit of the cargo bay. Once outside the guardian was joined by another comrade who led the way through the ship to the bridge of this massive carrier.

Since coming on board, she had scarcely acknowledged her new surroundings. Everything was dimly lit with copper thread lights clearly marking the way. The floors of the corridors were immaculately maintained. She could see engineers repairing conduits and relays, damage left over from their encounter with Titanian corporate mercenaries.

She noted the location of the mess hall which had an extensive line running the length of that corridor. The med bay was equally crowded with injured refugees. She found herself searching faces, then shook herself. Her mother nor Willan were there.

They entered a lift. She couldn't keep track of how many levels they travelled. By her estimation it was ten. The lift stopped at the top and the doors opened into an impressive bridge.

They could have taken her to the brig if she was in any real trouble. Instead, she was summoned here. Why?

Several of the crew watched as she was led to the Captain's Ready Room. The eerie glow from their wave displays cast a sinister light over their features. From the viewer up front she could see several angles from outside the ship, including the aft view which showed Titan and Saturn receding. A wave of sorrow washed over her as she realized she would never go home again.

The guardian stopped her in front of the door and waved over the panel. A chirp and the indicator went from red to green. The doors slid silently open and she was coaxed into the room.

The feeling of being trapped intensified as the door closed behind her. She wanted to turn around and run back to Curphay and the relative anonymity of the cargo hold. Instead, she stood uncertainly in a small monastic room that held a wave and little else.

The Captain had her back to Amione. She was looking out the viewport at several ships traveling in conjunction with this one. Their running lights could be seen just beyond the window.

She was tall with curly black hair tightly confined to a bun. Her dark skin contrasted starkly with the stiff white collar. Large amber eyes took in everything, but revealed little to the observer.

Amione shifted uncomfortably from one foot to another, waiting. She had no idea why she was in here. Several possibilities raced through her mind, but none of them prepared her for what the Captain said next.

She turned those too knowing amber eyes on her, making her feel exposed. "Amione Dhau." Her voice was course and loud. Definitely someone who was used to being obeyed at a moment's notice."I'm Captain Arlith Tanz."

"Yes, Ma'am." She saluted halfheartedly, uncertain how to respond in this situation.

The Captain noted the attempt with a frown before continuing. "I have received instructions regarding your first assignment."

"Assignment? What assignment?"

The captain's left brow quirked. "Your assignment with the ARK Project. I was told you had recently joined."

Amione's mind raced back to her mother's correspondence. She hadn't wasted time getting her assigned to the Project.

"I must have missed that communique." This was her opportunity to change her mind. She had lost her home, her family, her... "Ma'am, I'm not sure I want to be part of the Project any more in light of what happened on Titan."

"Indeed. Regardless, I am to give you instructions. What you do from there is on you." The Captain paced behind her desk and placed her hands on the back of her chair.

Amione cleared her throat. "What is the assignment?"

"You are to go to Old Earth. They found something that needs to be examined by a paleogeneticist. You are a paleogeneticist?" Her tone suggested that she had doubts.

"Yes, of course."

"Very well. You will be transferred to Nightshine. We will rendezvous with them in two days. I'll put you in contact with my quartermaster to make sure you are kitted up. Dismissed."

"Wait! What about my friend, Curphay?"

A look of annoyance crossed her face. "What about him?"

"He is also part of the ARK Project."

"I don't know anything about that."

"But--"

"You have your instructions. Dismissed." The Captain opened a wave screen.

Amione started to say something else.

"Dismissed." The Captain stated with finality, her eyes warned her not to press any further.

Amione clamped her mouth shut. The Captain wasn't the one she needed to talk to anyway. She would have to find a com and figure things out for herself. She turned and left before her emotions could betray her further. The guardians escorted her back to the cargo bay.

"Where did they take you?" Curphay crushed her against his chest obvious relief could be felt in every muscle.

"To the Captain."

"I know that. Why?" He drew her down next to him on their makeshift pallet.

"I got my first assignment from the ARK Project."

His face lit up. "That's great!"

She shook her head, tears filling her eyes. "It's an assignment just for me. They need a paleogeneticist."

He squeezed her shoulders and gave her a smile he reserved when she was being unrealistic. "Amione, you didn't think we would be assigned to the same things, did you?"

"I thought maybe a little." She wrang her hands in her lap.

"I'll be fine. This is exactly what you wanted. I know the timing isn't the best, but it will be just the thing you need. Work is good for the soul."

She nodded, not completely convinced.

"Where are you going?"

"Earth."

He let out a low whistle. "Definitely, what you have always wanted. When do you go?"

"We will rendezvous with another ship in two days," she replied miserably.

"Then we had better make the most of it, hadn't we?" Curphay's mocha-colored eyes were encouraging.

"I guess so." She pulled her knees up to her chest and wrapped her arms around her legs.

"Besides, we will find a way to connect no matter what." He gently shoved her knee.

"I hope so."

"Dhager and Dhau forever?" She could never resist that brilliant smile.

"Dhager and Dhau forever," she confirmed.

Epilogue

Willan

"I love you because the entire universe conspired to help me find you."
Paulo Coelho, The Alchemist

Willan watched Amione from across the cargo bay. She looked so vulnerable and grief stricken. She had lost her home and everything she had held dear. He knew what that was like. He wanted to go to her, wrap his arms around her, and let her know that it would get better eventually.

He had walked into the cargo bay with the intention of returning the little carved bird her Da made her. He pulled it out of his pocket and ran his thumb over the delicate carving and along the seam where he had repaired it.

He wanted to see her face when he gave it to her. Instead, he selfishly held on to it. Once he gave it back, he would have nothing of her, and he so wanted to have a piece of her.

His next mission would be dangerous. More dangerous than this one. It was best if she continued to believe he perished on Demeter. He pushed his bulk away from the wall, exited the cargo bay and made his way down a couple of corridors and up two levels, and entered the quarters he had been assigned.

He tucked the little bird into the sling that cradled his arm against his chest. It was just a severe sprain. That creature was much stronger than Jheslae had described. He had underestimated it. That wouldn't happen again.

They had just finished examining him when the first fighters hit the Derelict. He wasn't sure if Layla or the Magistrate had escaped or not. He knew thousands had perished; many were children. He knew it was going to happen, but it still was a shock to see it firsthand. Demeter was next. He was lucky to get out of there before the fighters hit. Again, just as predicted.

He pulled out a small hand-held device and activated it. An image of whorls and swirls blossomed into a three-dimensional rendering of the time continuum and the threads that bound the very essence of existence as they knew it.

He pulled apart several whorls to find what he was looking for. In the original timeline Amione Dhau died on Titan. He was sent to prevent that. He could see minute changes in the present timeline that grew more divergent as time wore on.

Time. He laughed to himself. Such a limited concept. It was only one aspect of the greater whole and not a very prominent one. There was so much more to existence. He couldn't wrap his head around any of it. He just did as he was told.

Flashes of his old life invaded his present. When Jheslae had found him, he had just been orphaned by the first Covid Pandemic. At 18, he was on his own in a world that was simultaneously cruel and wondrous. If people had known what was coming, maybe they would have made different decisions, but the scary thing was, he didn't believe most of them were capable of making any meaningful change even when the truth was staring them in the face.

Jheslae plucked him and a few others from that timeline and brought them to a very different future to a time and place where they could make a difference. Earth was on a path of destruction regardless of anything they could do. But in this time? They could do a lot.

What he had not anticipated was falling in love with Amione. He had only known her a few days, but he felt as if he knew her for much much longer. If Jheslae knew, she never let on.

Jheslae.

He had not heard from her. He couldn't tell if the continuum was affected or not. He only had access to his assigned part, and that did not include Jheslae Dhau.

The device chirped. A new packet of information arrived. It was from the ARK.

He opened it. The old information was wiped from his device and a new map replaced it. He examined the new threads.

He was returning to Earth. Another event was building and they needed to prevent it. These Sadool were pernicious. They had sent ripples through the universe unlike anything seen before.

He turned off the device, leaving the room in darkness. Since he had to save the universe once again, he might as well get some sleep.